T0129211

In battle-torn Scotland, a castle's mistress awaits her groom, a warrior she has never met...

Lady Gwendolyn Murphy's fiancé has finally arrived at Latharn Castle, but she expects no joy in their introduction. Gwendolyn is well aware of Bróccín MacRaith's cold reputation. Yet from first glance, she is drawn to the intimidating stranger. Impossible! How could she be dazzled by such a callous man?

Little does she know, Bróccín is dead. The man Gwendolyn believes to be her intended is actually Sir Aiden MacConnell, a member of the Knights Templar and her enemy, masquerading as the earl to gain access to the castle. His soul is dedicated to God and war; he has no time for luxuries of the flesh. But Gwendolyn's intoxicating beauty, intellect, and fortitude lures him to want the forbidden.

With the wedding date quickly approaching and the future of Scotland at stake, Aiden gathers critical intelligence and steels himself for his departure, vowing to avoid an illicit liaison. But a twist of fate forces him to choose—move forward with a life built on a lie, or risk everything for the heart of one woman?

Visit us at www.kensingtonbooks.com

Books by Diana Cosby

The Forbidden Series
Forbidden Knight
Forbidden Legacy
Forbidden Vow

The Oath Trilogy
An Oath Sworn
An Oath Broken
An Oath Taken

MacGruder Brothers Series
His Enchantment
His Seduction
His Destiny
His Conquest
His Woman
His Captive

Published by Kensington Publishing Corporation

Forbidden Vow

The Forbidden

Diana Cosby

LYRICAL PRESS
Kensington Publishing Corp.
www.kensingtonbooks.com

First Electronic Edition: May 2018
eISBN-13: 978-1-60183-756-1
eISBN-10: 1-60183-756-9

First Print Edition: May 2018
ISBN-13: 978-1-60183-757-8
ISBN-10: 1-60183-757-7

Printed in the United States of America

While living in Spain, I was blessed to meet Sonia Fernandez, an incredible woman who became more than a friend, but a part of my family. Sonia, you're truly a blessing in my life! *Hugs*

Chapter 1

Scotland, August 1308

A hawk screeched overhead as Sir Aiden MacConnell strode past several large oaks. He wiped the sweat from his brow, noted his men's positions, and then scoured the uneven ground thick with summer dried grass, clumps of brush, and rocks that littered the forest's edge.

Still no sign of the enemy who'd ridden into view moments before. Considering how the warrior's eyes had widened and the way he'd whirled his mount and fled, Aiden was sure he'd identified him and his men as a threat.

Aiden cursed. All his bloody fault. Before he had waved his men into the clearing, he had double checked their surroundings and had seen naught to alert him that the enemy lurked nearby.

They must stop the bastard before he could warn Lord Comyn of their presence. Their mission, to evaluate Latharn Castle's weaknesses, discover the number of knights in residence, and uncover potential points of entry, was paramount. Given the stronghold's treacherous cliffside location, the information he and his men provided to Robert Bruce would play a crucial role in the king's upcoming attack.

A cool breeze rich with the scent of rain buffeted him. He glanced north, grimaced at the darkening clouds. Blast it, they had to find the lone rider before a downpour washed away his tracks.

Nor was the knight in full health. As the man had galloped away, Aiden had noted the blood-smeared armor, the way his body wove in the saddle, and the panic in the warrior's eyes. He grimaced. No, the man hadn't traveled far.

He scoured the rough slide of land for further signs of the enemy. With Scotland at war, only a lackwit rode without an escort.

At no sign of danger, he continued on. As he stepped past a clump of trees, his gaze narrowed on several large boulders. Red stained the jagged edge of the closest rock.

Blood.

Aiden waved his two friends over, pointed to where the land cut away. "He must be hiding down the brae," he whispered. "Rónán, circle around to the right. Cailin, you come in from the left. Once in place, await my command."

His men nodded and then slipped into the dense foliage.

Dagger in hand, Aiden crept through the brush. Below, between a break in the rocks, a bay munched on sun-bleached grass, his reins dragging on the ground.

A moan sounded farther down the embankment.

Aiden motioned for his warriors to hold. Weapon readied, he edged around the shield of stone. As the bank began a steep decline, he squatted, his gaze centering on the prone form.

Through the summer-burned shafts swaying in the breeze, the armored knight gasped for air. Blood smeared his mail, and one of his legs lay twisted in an awkward position.

Aiden caught a glimpse of his face. High browed, with blond hair now sticky with blood, and his lips thinned by pain. Nor did he miss that the bastard wore Comyn's colors.

After another meticulous scan of the clearing, confident the warrior rode alone, Aiden stood. He frowned. The dying man looked familiar. A foolish thought. Too many years had passed since he'd lived in the Highlands for him to recognize anyone now.

Eyes dark with pain focused on him, grew wary. "To whom do you swear your loyalty?" the man rasped.

"Lord Comyn," Aiden replied, his gut tightening around the lie. With the injured man wearing the noble's colors, he'd be a fool to state otherwise.

"Thank God. W-when I saw you, I thought you were with the Bruce." The stranger gave a rough cough and then sagged back. "Early this morning, my c-contingent was attacked by his forces."

"God's sword, are they near?" Aiden spat, needing the man to believe him not a threat.

"I think I lost them, but I canna be sure." Wracking coughs again shook his body, and a drizzle of blood slid from his mouth.

Aiden knelt beside him, took in the deep sword slashes along his neck. 'Twas incredible he still lived.

Face ashen, the stranger grabbed Aiden's arm. "Y-you must swear to help me."

Help him? With the knight's allegiance to Comyn, he would rather drive a dirk into his heart and end his miserable life. Aiden took in his finely crafted armor, stilled. Few could afford mail of such quality. Whoever this man was, he wasn't a simple knight. Mayhap the warrior held sensitive information valuable to King Robert?

"Of course I will assist you," Aiden replied. "How?"

Fingers trembling, the man withdrew a sealed writ, handed it to Aiden. "D-deliver this to Lady Gwendolyn Murphy of Latharn Castle. 'Tis a decree from Lord Comyn, commanding us to marry. Warn her that the enemy is near." Grief-stricken eyes held his. "Let her know I regret having failed her."

Aiden's throat tightened as he glanced at the rolled parchment, the importance of the man's disclosure pounding in his chest. He refocused on the wounded knight. "I would need your name to tell your betrothed."

"B-Bróccín MacRaith, Earl of Balfour."

Aiden stared at him in disbelief. "Of Gilcrest Castle?" His question sliced out between tensed lips.

"Aye."

Memories from his youth rolled through Aiden: how he and Bróccín had sparred, hunted, the first time they'd tasted mead. A friendship of long ago.

No longer was he an innocent lad with dreams of war and victory in his head. Over the years, with his service to the Knights Templar, he'd seen enough bloodshed, and had witnessed the deaths of too many of his friends.

"I will have your name," Bróccín forced out.

"Aiden MacConnell, Earl of Lenox." He swallowed hard. That he'd long lost his title mattered little now.

Recognition flared in the nobleman's eyes, replaced by a fleeting sadness. "After the death of your family, I-I never thought to see you again."

Ice slid through Aiden's veins at the mention of his horrific loss. He shoved aside the painful memories that however much he tried haunted him still. Neither could he forget how the English had seized his legacy. "Nor I you." He nodded to the writ. "I give my word I will deliver your missive to Lady Gwendolyn."

"I thank you. 'Twas a b-blessing that 'twas you who found me." A shudder raked his body. "After all these years, I canna believe we meet again. W-we had so many dreams, didna we?"

He forced a smile. "Aye, foolish ones."

"They were." Bróccín coughed. His face twisted in pain, he settled back.

"I will tend to you as best—"

"'Tis too late; my fate is sealed."

However much he wished to assure the man otherwise, he wouldn't lie. Aiden offered him a sip of water from his pouch. "Take a drink, 'twill cool your throat."

"My comfort matters little now." A wry smile touched Bróccín's mouth. "In truth," he rasped, "I have never met my betrothed, but 'tis rumored the lass is a beauty. With the stories I have heard—" Pain dredged his face, and for a moment he closed his eyes. On a rough exhale, he lifted his lids. "I was anxious to bed her."

Coldness seeped through Aiden at the thought of any woman weakening him to where he'd think of little else. His life was dedicated to God and war, not the luxuries of the flesh. He rested his hand on the earl's shoulder. "I will tell her that you were a fine man."

"I thank you." More blood oozed from Bróccín's mouth. The noble shuddered and then gasped. His eyes grew fixed.

With the images of his youth fading, Aiden stood, waited as his men approached.

"Is he dead?" Cailin asked.

Aiden nodded. "His name is Bróccín MacRaith, Earl of Balfour. Incredibly, we were friends in my youth. Except, 'twould seem now, unknown to him, we are mortal enemies."

"A Comyn supporter," Rónán said with a grimace, "a bloody shame."

"'Tis the way of war." Aiden shoved his sadness behind his carefully built wall of indifference, having lost too many friends through the years to allow the hurt to burrow deeper. "Yet he has presented us with an unexpected opportunity." He lifted the writ. "'Twould seem by Comyn's dictate, the earl was betrothed to Lady Gwendolyn Murphy. He was on his way to marry her."

Cailin arched a doubtful brow. "What does a wedding have to do with our gaining information for the Bruce's upcoming attack on Latharn Castle?"

"The lady in question," Aiden replied, "is the stronghold's mistress."

Rónán frowned. "'Tis a surprising coincidence, but knowing the woman's name or Lord Balfour's reason for riding to the castle far from aids us."

"It wouldna," Aiden agreed, "except before Lord Balfour died, he admitted he had never met the lass."

Cailin's eyes widened. "God's blade, you are not thinking of taking his place?"

The thrill of the unknown filled Aiden, and he clung to the thoughts of danger, to a way of life on which he thrived. "I am. I swore to deliver this decree, a promise I shall keep. 'Twill be a simple enough task to play the part of her suitor for a day or two. Once we have the information we need, we shall slip away and report to the Bruce all that we have learned."

"We?" Rónán asked.

"Aye," Aiden said with a flourish, enjoying crafting the story. "The Earl of Balfour and two of his stalwart knights escaped the ruthless attack of King Robert's men."

A frown deepened on Rónán's brow. "A brilliant plan, but your memories of the earl were those of a lad. Nor do you know if his intended was accepting of the betrothal, not to mention that someone in the castle might know him."

"I have heard the earl was a warrior to fear, a strict leader, and a man who refused to compromise, knowledge that will suffice for the meager time we remain within the stronghold." Aiden shrugged. "Weighed against the vital details we shall learn, any other concerns are insignificant.

"What of the lass?" Cailin asked. "Even if she is in agreement, with her anticipating marriage, however brief, she will expect a courtship."

"A minor distraction," Aiden said. "Before Bróccín died, he confessed she was fair to look upon."

Rónán chuckled. "Wooing her might be a pleasant diversion, more so taking her to your bed."

Far from amused by the jest, Aiden stowed the writ. "My intent is to gain information for our king, naught more. Though the Knights Templar are secretly dissolved, my allegiance remains with the Brotherhood."

The humor in his men's eyes fled. "Never will I forgive King Philip's treachery," Cailin hissed.

"Nor I," Rónán spat.

France's sovereign had betrayed the Brotherhood, knights who had guarded him over the years, loyalty the bastard had rewarded with deceit. Almost a year had passed since Aiden and the other Templars had sailed from the port of La Rochelle. Yet, each time he thought of the French king's treachery, fury blackened his soul.

He glanced at the fierce warriors at his side, Knights he'd fought alongside in many a battle, men he would give his life to protect. "We will map the castle grounds, take stock of its stores, the number of guards, and note any other details we decide are imperative for King Robert to plan a successful attack."

"Mayhap," Cailin said, "we will discover a secret entry."

"Given the stronghold's location," Aiden said, "I suspect a hidden tunnel runs beneath, a passageway nay doubt Lady Gwendolyn is aware of. The question is whether, during our brief stay, we will have time to ascertain where it is."

"What will happen to the lass once King Robert seizes her castle?" Rónán asked.

Aiden shrugged. "If she is as beautiful as Bróccín claimed, 'twill be a simple task for the Bruce to find a nobleman to wed her."

"Mayhap the woman will have an admirable spirit that will catch the king's notice," Cailin said with a smile, "and, like Stephan and Thomas, our sovereign will guide you down a wedded path."

"With the demands on the king's time," Aiden said, his voice cool, "I doubt he will meet Lady Gwendolyn much longer than to learn her name and decide upon an appropriate match." Refusing to entertain the topic further, he glanced at the dead earl. "We bury Bróccín, then ride to Latharn Castle."

* * * *

Wind raw with the scent of the sea whipped against Lady Gwendolyn Murphy as she aimed her dagger, threw.

Thunk.

A deep chuckle sounded to her right. "I dinna think your betrothed would be praising your skill, my lady."

"As if I care what the Earl of Balfour thinks." She turned toward the well-armed knight leaning against a nearby rock. At the humor in her friend's eyes, she glanced at the rough charcoal outline of a man on the nearby sun-bleached limb, her *sgian dubh* lodged in the center of the crudely shaded heart.

"I know you are upset with Lord Comyn's dictate to marry," Sir Pieres continued, "but with Lord Balfour occupied with the upkeep of his numerous holdings, along with engaging in combat for your liege lord, 'tis rumored he is often gone."

Scowling, Gwendolyn walked over to jerk her blade free. "As far as I am concerned, he could stay away. In truth, if I did not need Comyn's guard, I would keep the gates barred and deny the earl entry."

"If you wish, that could be arranged."

The lazy teasing in her friend's voice prodded a smile. "You would do that for me, would you not?"

Pieres's expression grew serious. "My lady, for you I would give my life."

Humbled, she shook her head. "Never would I ask such."

Eyes dark with concern, he walked to her. "'Tis said your betrothed is a hard man, one feared by many, but those beneath his command give him their respect."

She smothered the slide of nerves. "And you tell me this because...?"

"You need truth, not wisps of fancy. That the earl earns respect from his men reveals that however strict, his dictates are given with reason. His success in battle, along with the praise earned from your liege lord, reflect his cunning as a warrior."

She gave a curt nod.

"My lady, Lord Balfour is a man of war and willna tolerate defiance on any level." Expression grim, he paused. "With your headstrong ways, I beseech you to tread with care. You could do far worse."

"A warning?" Furious he'd feel the situation warranted his caution, or that the time had come in her life when she'd need such, she stalked to where she'd drawn a line in the sand, turned, threw. A chunk of the charcoal-stained heart broke free as the dagger sank deep. "I am not a fool."

"Nay," he said, his voice softening. "You are a woman whom any man would be blessed to have as his wife. Sadly, many nobles dinna want a lass beyond that of bearing their heir."

She jerked her weapon free. "I willna be cast aside in my own castle, treated as if I were naught but a scullery maid fit only for the bedding. I need nay husband."

Sir Pieres remained silent, the worry in his gaze easy to read.

Frustrated, she sheathed her dagger, faced the waves sliding up the shore tossing about stones and shells within the tangled rush. Bedamned this entire situation! "If only I could convince Lord Comyn that I dinna need to wed."

Firm steps crunched on the sand. Pieres paused at her side. "'Tis too late; his decision has been made."

The exasperation in his voice matched her own. "I know." She wanted to scream at the injustice of losing her home to a stranger. In the weeks since the writ had arrived announcing her betrothal, she had tried to think of a way, often with Pieres's aid, of negating the union and, at every turn, had failed.

On a hard swallow, Gwendolyn picked up a fragment of an abandoned shell. She cupped the fragile piece in her hand as the damnable frustrations weighed heavy in her chest. "Over the years my father would bring me here and tell me of his dreams, or talk about mine. He never laughed at what I shared, but encouraged me to achieve any goal that I could envision."

"He was an extraordinary man."

"Aye, he was." Emotion welled in her throat, and she swallowed the rush of grief. "W-when my mother died during my youth, 'twas here my father consoled me, and years later, where he asked me to marry Lord Purcell to strengthen our bond with our neighboring clan."

Pieres's mouth tightened. "Your father was wrong to have forced you into a marriage, more so to a man who couldna see what an incredible woman you are."

The soft fury in his voice left her humbled. Her fingers curled against the memories of how she'd pushed away Pieres's subtle advances since their childhood. However much she'd wished otherwise, never had she felt more than friendship, nor would she dishonor him by offering false hope. She prayed one day he would find a woman who could give him the love he deserved.

"And 'twas on this stretch of sand," Pieres continued, drawing her from her musings, "that you learned of your husband's death but a month after you had wed."

She grimaced. "With my father's blessing, I was foolish enough to believe that never again would I have to marry for duty, that I could live the life I chose." Anger twisted inside. "Yet with my father's death, I have become little more than chattel."

"I am sorry."

Mouth tight, Gwendolyn cast the fragment into the incoming wave. The battered, sun-bleached shell that once had held life tumbled beneath the current and was swept out to sea. Like her life, she was naught but a pawn to those in power.

"I will do my duty and wed Lord Balfour," she stated, "for my people's protection and for that of my home, but I willna tolerate being treated like a fool." She started toward the castle. "'Tis time I checked on Kellan."

"With her girth," Pieres said as he fell in alongside, "I thought your prized mare would have foaled by now."

"As did I. This morning I found her pacing in her stall. I expect her foal will come this day, and I want to be with her when 'tis born."

Warmth touched her as she started toward the cave. She remembered when the coal black mare was born, how her father had gifted her with the filly. Emotion stormed through her. Now Kellan would have a babe of her own.

"I wish my father was alive. I—" She stumbled, and Pieres caught her, turned her toward him.

"I am here," he said, his voice solemn.

"I know," she whispered, thankful for his friendship. "'Tis just that even though half a year has passed, I still struggle with his death."

"'Twas a horrible loss," he said, his voice somber, "but he died a warrior's death, fighting for—"

A horse's neigh sounded in the distance.

The slide of steel upon leather hissed as Pieres withdrew his sword. "Hurry inside the secret tunnel."

Gwendolyn unsheathed her dagger. "If there was danger, we would have heard warning shouts from the castle guards and the ringing of the church bell." She scanned the lull of land and rock above that led to the castle entrance.

Three knights came into view.

Relief flooded Gwendolyn. A larger force would ride beneath the Earl of Balfour's standard.

The trio of men halted before the gate.

Even from this distance, she noted the lead warrior. Broad shoulders. His stance confident. A shiver of unease rippled through her.

"Do you think 'tis your betrothed?"

She shook her head. "The writ stated the earl would arrive with a sizable contingent. I suspect 'tis but knights traveling through."

A faint echo of a man's deep voice reached her.

A guard's voice rang out. A clank sounded, then the slow rattle of the portcullis.

Gwendolyn relaxed. Whatever the travelers had told her guard, they were not a threat.

A frown thinned her mouth as she entered the secret tunnel. With King Robert determined to unite Scotland, how many years would pass before their country found peace? She damned the war, the struggle for power that had claimed too many innocent lives.

Inside the cave, Pieres lit a candle. Golden light cut through the blackness, the wet walls slick with moss and the sandy path scattered with wave-smooth pebbles.

She inhaled to settle her nerves, then focused on the upcoming birthing of her prize mare. "I wish the groom was here. 'Tis Kellan's first foal, and 'twould ease me to know she was in Edmund's competent hands."

Her friend raised the taper, started down the tunnel. "MacDuff has helped Edmund several times with a mare's birthing."

"He has. But a few months studying beneath Edmund's skilled guidance far from gives MacDuff the experience he needs."

The smell of hay and horse filled the air as they reached the hidden door outside the stable. With a tug of the latch, Gwendolyn pushed aside the entry, then stepped onto the soft dirt.

Pieres followed, secured the door behind them. "I will check to see who has arrived."

"I thank you." Afternoon sunlight flickered over her friend's shoulders as he entered the bailey.

A snort sounded from the corner stall.

Warmth spilled through her as she hurried over. "How fares Kellan?"

"She has begun birthing," MacDuff replied.

At the worry in the stable hand's voice, her chest tightened. She hurried inside the stall.

Heavy with foal, the mare staggered upon the bed of straw. She nickered, half-collapsed to her side, rolled, shoved back to her feet, then began to pace.

"Easy, girl," Gwendolyn soothed as she stroked her velvety muzzle. "How long has she been unsettled?"

MacDuff rubbed the back of his neck. "Since a short while after you left."

The mare tossed her head and half-reared. As her feet hit the floor, her entire body shook. On a whinny, she again dropped to her knees, fell to one side, then rolled.

"There should be some sign of the foal coming by now," MacDuff said, his voice rough with worry. "I... I fear the foal is turned the wrong way."

God, no! Dread filled Gwendolyn as she remembered horrific stories of a mare's screams as she suffered during a difficult foaling, of the loss of blood, and the trauma that could leave both the mother and foal dead.

Male voices echoed from the stable entry, but she ignored them, damning her lack of knowledge concerning the upcoming birth, a fact she would remedy after this day. "Surely Edmund has delivered such difficult births in the past?" she forced out.

A ruddy hue swept the man's face. "Aye," the stable hand replied, "but none after he began instructing me."

Furious at her helplessness, Gwendolyn knelt beside Kellan. Hand trembling, she stroked her sweat-slicked neck. *Please, God, do not let her die.*

The mare snorted, kicked.

Gwendolyn ducked beneath the slash of hooves, terrified as the horse again squealed in distress. "Fetch the healer. Delivering a foal canna be much different from a babe."

"Aye, my lady." MacDuff bolted from the stable and ran toward the keep.

On a tormented scream, the mare fought to struggle to her feet, collapsed. Froth slid down her ebony coat.

Tears burned Gwendolyn's eyes at Kellan's each snort, her every whinny of distress.

The horse again kicked out, slashed, missing her by a hand.

An ache built in her chest as she reached over to try to relax the mare. Behind her, the gate scraped open. "Get away from her," a deep voice boomed.

Stunned at the harsh command, Gwendolyn glanced up.

An enormous man with raven black hair towered a pace away. Green eyes riveted on her with unyielding authority. "Move!"

She slammed her brows together. "I willna—"

With a muttered curse, the stranger hauled her up and pushed her aside. "Aiden, Rónán, help me get the mare on her feet!"

Shaking with outrage, Gwendolyn elbowed her way past the two burly knights and glared up at the beast. "How dare you—"

"We are trying to save her life," he growled as he shifted his body against the horse's rump. "If you want to be useful, stand by her head and try to calm her while I deliver the foal."

She smothered her angry retort as the warrior and his men worked in unison to shove the horse to her feet, then moved to stroke her neck.

"Dinna let the mare move while I turn the foal." The fierce knight moved to her rear, worked without hesitation.

Impressed, Gwendolyn watched him. Whoever he was, he knew what he was about.

"I have the foal's foot," the stranger called a moment later.

Kellan screamed a strangled nicker, then shifted.

The stranger's mouth tightened. "Keep the mare still!"

Hooves scraped across the bed of straw. On a strangled whinny, Kellan started to step back.

"God's sword, hold her!" the warrior roared.

Muscles flexed as his men complied.

Distant footsteps slapped upon the dirt.

Gwendolyn glanced out the entry to see the healer and MacDuff running across the bailey.

"'Tis done," the stranger called out. "Release her."

She turned as he lay the newborn on the hay.

His men stepped away.

On a soft snort, the mare turned and nuzzled her foal. Coal black, like his mother, and the proud lines of his sire, on spindly legs, the colt shoved to his feet. The mare nickered at her son, nudged him to suckle.

Tears burned her eyes at the miracle before her, how within but moments she'd witnessed the beginning of life. Gwendolyn swallowed hard. "He shall be called Faolán," she whispered as MacDuff halted beside her.

"Wolf, aye," the stable hand said, "'tis a fine name."

Face flushed and her breath coming fast, the healer halted before the stall's entry. Her gaze landed on the foal, and aged eyes wrinkled with pleasure. "It looks like you dinna need my help after all."

Her words a stark reminder of the strangers, Gwendolen shook her head. "Nay, but I thank you for coming."

As the elder departed, Gwendolyn studied the imposing man who had dared to take charge. Under ordinary circumstance, he would receive her censure for his bold manner. But he'd saved the foal and, given Kellan's distress, the mother's life as well.

Her fingers trembled as she held out a nearby cloth. "'Twould seem I owe you my thanks."

A scowl marred the knight's handsome face as he wiped his hands. "Why was she unattended when she was clearly in distress?" he demanded.

His two knights moved to the warrior's side.

Refusing to be intimidated, to justify anything to this arrogant man, she glared at the daunting stranger. "I owe you nay explanation."

He cast the stained cloth aside. "Aye. That you can give to the mistress of the castle."

Indeed. She angled her chin at the towering dolt. "Then," she said with cold authority, more than ready to take him down a well-deserved notch, "as mistress of Latharn Castle, you may speak."

Stunned disbelief flickered in the knight's eyes before he shuttered his expression. He gave a formal bow. "'Tis my pleasure to meet you, Lady Gwendolyn."

That she doubted. "And you are...?" she prodded, ready to toss the boil-brained lout out on his ear.

His fierce gaze leveled on her. "The Earl of Balfour, your betrothed."

Chapter 2

Aiden arched a brow as Lady Gwendolyn's gray eyes widened with disbelief. 'Twould seem the lass had heard of Bróccín's temperament. As if he gave a damn of the noble's unyielding reputation. When he'd entered the stable and caught the distressed mare's hooves slashing toward the woman, he'd feared for her life.

By a sheer miracle, she'd escaped harm. A fact that far from excused her reckless behavior, especially given her responsibilities to this keep and the people beneath her care. "Why in blazes were you so close to the mare?"

The irate goddess, hair the color of sunshine tumbling in wild disarray around her shoulders, angled her chin. "I was *trying* to soothe her."

"And was almost killed."

"I was never in any danger," she scoffed.

Aiden narrowed his gaze and stepped forward, towering over her. Bedamned this daring lass. Marry her? God's teeth, he'd rather shake some sense into her thick-headed brain.

Cailin cleared his throat and stepped to Aiden's side. "My lady, we are all *thankful* you are safe."

The lass's wary gaze cut to the peacemaker, whose lips curved in an easy smile. "And you are...?"

"Sir Cailin, one of my knights," Aiden snapped.

"My lady," Cailin said with a bow.

Aiden nodded to the other man. "And Sir Rónán."

Her face softened as she glanced to each man. "I thank you both for your aid." The warmth in her expression cooled as she faced Aiden.

He drew in a steadying breath, relieved he'd be saddled with the reckless lass for days at most. Once he and his men departed, if they ever saw the other again, 'twould be after the Bruce had seized this stronghold. Then, thankfully, her fate would lie in his king's hand.

Aiden handed her the writ.

She broke open the seal. Lady Gwendolyn's fingers trembled as she scanned the words.

A dull ache pounded in his head. Bróccín said they were to marry, but the lass might not have known. "You were expecting me?" he demanded.

Face pale, she rolled the parchment. "Aye. A fortnight ago. I thought…"

A stocky, well-armed knight stepped into the stable. "Lady Gwendolyn, I regret my delay. The guard informed me that the Earl of Balfour has arrived, but when I looked, he wasna inside the keep." Shrewd eyes assessed Aiden and his men as the warrior strode to her side. "Is all well?"

Fascinated, Aiden watched her visibly push whatever emotions she was experiencing aside and become the hostess her position required.

"Aye." Cool eyes shifted to Aiden. "Sir Pieres, may I introduce to you Bróccín MacRaith, Earl of Balfour, my betrothed."

Nostril's flaring, her knight's gaze riveted on Aiden. He issued a stiff bow. "My lord."

"Lord Balfour," Lady Gwendolyn said, a swath of red sliding up her cheeks, "Sir Pieres is my personal guard."

Her protector. And a man who took his job quite seriously. Aiden nodded. "Sir Pieres."

"Sir Pieres is in charge of the defense of Latharn Castle," she said, her voice cool. "You will defer to him in any questions about the castle until we are wed."

Like Hades he would.

She cleared her throat. "Now that the earlier unpleasantness is behind us, I welcome you all to Latharn Castle."

Aiden nodded, thankful she hadn't questioned his identity. Her reluctance to their betrothal would serve him well. She wouldn't press for time together, leaving him free to gather information about the stronghold.

"A chamber has been readied for your arrival, my lord," she continued. "Your men may bed down in the guardhouse."

"My knights will stay in the keep," Aiden said. Lodged in enemy territory, if things went awry, he wanted Cailin and Rónán close in case they needed to escape.

A frown crossed her brow. "I will—"

The rush of steps had Aiden glancing toward the stable entry.

A scrawny lad ran inside, skidded to a halt before them. "My lady," he hurried out. "I was in the kitchen and—" His eyes widened on the foal with appreciation. "He has come. What a beauty!"

"He is," she replied, a breathtaking smile softening her features. "His name is Faolán."

Red swept the lad's face as his gaze darted to Aiden, then he turned to his mistress. "I have come to care for the knight's horses."

Lady Gwendolyn's smile widened even further and laughter lit her eyes.

Aiden stilled. Earlier, with her face flushed with anger, hay strewn in her hair, and mud on her cheeks, he'd thought her intriguing.

A pathetic description for the captivating woman standing before him. Alabaster skin swept across high cheekbones, framed eyes the color of warmed pewter with flecks of gold, and lush lips that would tempt a man to linger. God's sword, she was beautiful. Heat surged through him, and he smothered the unwanted desire. A lass and the complications she invited wasn't something he wished.

Furious he would notice, Aiden scowled. "My men and I will see to our own mounts. Afterward we will come to the keep."

"Dolaidh," she said, her tone with the lad devoid of the anger simmering in her eyes, "fetch the mare fresh water and an extra scoop of grain and oats."

"Aye, my lady." The lad ran from the stall.

Her gaze leveled on him. "Lord Balfour, I agreed to our impending marriage in payment for Lord Comyn's protection of Latharn Castle, but know this: Until our vows, I am its mistress, one who willna take orders, even from you."

Aiden stifled a chuckle, took a damnably slow step back, and bowed in acquiescence. Straightening, his gaze locked on hers. "May I suggest we discuss sleeping arrangements in private?"

Her hands fisted at her side. "Once you are settled, my lord, there is much we shall discuss." She scanned the stable, then hesitated. "I was informed you would arrive with a large contingent."

Bróccín's bloodstained body flashed to mind, his friend's dying words, and if only for a moment, unmarred memories of his childhood. "We were attacked by King Robert's men."

She gasped. "The rest of your warriors—"

Aiden thought of the Knights Templar betrayed, allowed his outrage for the many who'd suffered horrific torture to taint his reply. "Dead."

"Mary's will," she breathed, her gaze lowering to the smear of blood across his mail. Her face grew ashen. "'Tis not from helping the mare foal?"

"Nay." 'Twas a stroke of luck that Bróccín's mail had fit.

Her lower lip wobbled. "Forgive me, my lord, for my rude behavior. After your loss this day, you are distraught. Once you and your men finish tending to your horses, I will ensure a warm meal and readied chambers await you."

"I thank you," Aiden said.

She started to turn away and then halted, the sincerity of her expression at odds with the fierce temptress of moments before. "I am sorry. 'Tis hard to lose those you care for."

Aiden gave a curt nod, not wanting her to understand or to care. The lass represented a means to an end. When he departed, he would leave no one behind who mattered, less so a woman who'd sworn fealty to his enemy.

At his silence, she headed to the keep, Sir Pieres at her side.

Once Gwendolyn and her knight were halfway across the bailey, Rónán grunted. "King Robert would be impressed by the lass's spirit."

Far from amused by his friend's implication, Aiden led his mount to an empty stall. Their sovereign's penchant for making matches between strong-willed women and the men he favored was well-known, a fate already burdened upon his friends Stephan MacQuistan and Thomas MacKelloch. And against incredible odds, both had fallen in love with the women they'd wed.

Except the Bruce wasn't here. Nor did the king's orders extend beyond those to retrieve information to plan the upcoming attack upon Latharn Castle.

As his men led their mounts into empty stalls, Aiden dismissed the wayward thought. "Once Latharn Castle is in our sovereign's control, Banff will be the last remaining stronghold north of Mounth still held by the English. The Bruce hasna time to waste in dealing with a spirited lass. Until Scotland is united, I suspect he will leave the castle beneath the guard of one of his trusted nobles, and Lady Gwendolyn will be married to a favored noble."

"A logical move," Cailin agreed. "Once Banff is seized, his focus will be on capturing Perth, Roxburgh, and Edinburgh."

"Plans that canna move forward until this stronghold is seized," Rónán said.

Water sloshed from the edges of a bucket as Dolaidh hurried into the stable. Curious eyes flickered toward Aiden before the lad set the vessel near the mare.

As well, Gwendolyn's protectiveness toward those who lived beneath her spoke well of the lass, enemy or not. "Once you have your gear in your chamber," Aiden whispered, "meet me in the chapel."

* * * *

Eyes narrowed, Sir Pieres glanced at Gwendolyn as they crossed the bailey. "After you learned the stranger was your betrothed, what were you thinking of by challenging him? Did I not warn you that Lord Balfour was a man not to anger?"

Gwendolyn forced a smile at two women passing by, then scowled at her friend. "I did not challenge him."

"Telling your intended that you will not take orders from him until you are wed isna considered gentle conversation."

"Nor do I care. How dare he dictate anything to me when we havena said our vows? He is arrogant, aloof, and unapologetic."

"He is, and as I cautioned you earlier, a man of war. During battle, if those beneath his command dinna follow orders, men die. As well, 'tis wise to remember that if he hadna intervened, Kellan and her foal could have died."

She gave a curt nod. "I will not forget his brave act, nor that the healer arrived moments after the mare had given birth, and mayhap could have done the same."

Sir Pieres gave a frustrated sigh. "I know you dinna want to marry, but never have I seen you react so vehemently toward anyone. Regardless, Lord Balfour's actions were given to save the mare and foal's lives. If the earl had threatened you, harmed you in any manner, I assure you, 'tis my blade he would have faced."

"I am grateful for his timely intervention, but..."

"A battle-seasoned man, I know his ways are hard, but do you despise him so much?"

"I dinna despise him, 'tis that he is unlike any man I have ever met." She recalled how his green eyes held hers, unwavering, unapologetic, as if on a dare. Except she hadn't sensed malice, but a silent provocation that lured her to meet his challenge, to show him that, unlike the other women he'd met, she wasn't one who he could order about.

"Whatever happens, I will be here to protect you," Pieres said.

She rubbed the tightness in the back of her neck. "I know. 'Tis the upcoming marriage that has me on edge. Never again did I expect to marry. And I do him a disservice to ignore the fact that his contingent was attacked. Men who served him, ones no doubt he cared for, died. Yet, upon his arrival, he saved the life of a mare." She paused. "If I had known of his loss..."

"But you did not. Still, with his reputation 'tis unwise to push him."

"I did naught but state fact. The castle isna his."

"Something your marriage will erase."

A brutal truth that burned in her gut. And then what? Given his harsh manner, would he allow her to stay? *Allow?* Fury rushed through her that the option to remain in her home could be usurped. As quick, she realized the foolishness of her thought. A powerful lord wouldn't send his wife away, but keep her to give him an heir.

She refused to think of the intimacy she must endure until she bore him a son. Would one be enough?

During her first marriage, she'd been blessed by her husband's gentle manner, but she dreaded being forced into another man's bed.

"My lady, you look unwell."

At the concern in her friend's voice, she shook her head. "I am tired. It has been a long day." One that was far from over.

"Though harsh," Pieres said, "Lord Balfour seems reasonable."

She gave a wry smile. "I must have missed that quality."

Humor touched his gaze. "For a man of war."

At the keep, Gwendolyn halted. "I thank you for your gracious council. I dinna know what I would do without you."

He gave a slow nod. "I am always here for you. I regret that circumstance has led to this end, my lady, but I believe once the earl comes to know you, he will discover he is a fortunate man."

She arched a doubtful brow. "With his reputation, and after meeting him, I am not fool enough to convince myself of such. Lord Balfour sees naught but the next battle, what weapons will serve him best, not a wife's place, with the exception of a means to procure a successor."

"War is a heartless mistress and taints many a warrior's heart. The way he aided the mare this day, I believe, however deeply hidden, there is a good man inside."

Mayhap Pieres was right. In the stable, Lord Balfour hadn't touched her with intent to harm, but to move her to a safer location near Kellan.

Gwendolyn calmed a degree. She was a strong woman. The fact that the man's presence left her on edge could be dealt with.

After speaking to the servants to ensure food was prepared, she informed a maid to ready two chambers for Lord Balfour's men. Needing a reprieve before facing her betrothed during in the upcoming meal, Gwendolyn exited the keep.

Wind ripe with the scent of sea caressed her face as she crossed the bailey. She yearned to walk along the beach to mull the upcoming decisions she must make. The brief time with Sir Pieres on the rock-strewn sand this morning had been a luxury. With the unrest in the Highlands, neither was she foolish enough to return to the shore without a guard.

She despised the thought that in the future her betrothed would demand she receive his approval before she left the castle. Gwendolyn paused. Mayhap, as earlier, she was being too harsh. They'd met but once, and then in a hectic situation.

In truth, what worried her most was that she had no idea of Lord Balfour's expectations. When she'd married Luke, she'd known him for years. Though they had not been in love, he was a kind man. Now, she did not even have that.

The sound of the church bell echoed throughout the castle, announcing None.

Gwendolyn drew a deep breath to calm her nerves. For the safety of her people and castle, she must acquiesce to the marriage. Still, she found herself restless.

What was it about Lord Balfour that unsettled her, a fact that made little sense? Never before had anyone affected her so. Many times over the years she'd met with influential nobles and even kings. Neither was she ignorant of how to run the castle, innocent of the demands of marriage, or unused to dealing with powerful men.

Gwendolyn stopped, surprised. Lost in thought, she'd walked to the chapel. The scent of frankincense and myrrh filled the air as she stepped inside. She pushed the door closed, and a stifling gloom enveloped her.

Her eyes adjusted to the muted light. Overhead, swaths of stained glass of royal blue, ivory, and gold, crafting the image of the Virgin Mary glowed within the candlelight. Whirls of soft color spilled into the holy chamber to blend with the tapers seated within a gold candleholder upon the altar, ensnaring her within their somber mix.

Memories rolled through Gwendolyn of standing within these sacred walls sobbing at her father's side after the loss of her mother. Of how, years later, within this chapel, she'd pledged herself to a man she did not love. And how but months before, where she'd wept after learning of her father's tragic death.

With each event, she'd sought solace in the chapel. Yet with each desperate plea for succor, any sense of hope had evaded her.

She swallowed hard, glanced toward the baskets in the corner near the statue of Jesus, filled with bottles of oil, rosemary, and sage, which she'd placed there earlier. The sweet, succulent aromas from her youth.

To her right stood a statue of Jesus, along with a chalice and numerous other holy items the priest used during Mass. Gwendolyn focused on the crucifix mounted on the wall. Her throat tightened, and she pressed her hand to a nearby column.

Why had she come inside? Well she knew 'twas a mistake to think she'd find any comfort here; 'twas only for those who believed. After Luke's death, she'd assure herself that never again would she belong to any man. Yet here she stood days away from losing even that.

She glared at the hand-carved platform where soon she again would be forced to pledge her troth. Bedamned King Robert for shoving the Highlands into war, an act that had forced Comyn's hand and severed any hope that she could live out her days in peace.

Now she would marry.

A stranger.

A man she did not want.

Coldness wrapped around her heart. Like a fool, she stared at the cross, awaited the sensation of hope, of anything to assure her that somehow, in this mayhem she would find a sliver of peace.

The reckless wavering of the candles on the altar smeared the ceiling with broken shadows, as if mocking her dreams.

Disgusted she'd sought any optimism within these walls, allowed herself to turn to Him for hope when her prayers had gone unanswered many times in the past, she turned to leave, then paused. She glanced toward the basket near the statue of Jesus, which needed to be stowed away. A task she'd planned to tend to tomorrow, but now here, she may as well complete it.

With a tired sigh, she moved behind the ornate carving. Enveloped within the shadows, she knelt in the corner, opened the hidden door. With care, she set the oils upon the shelves.

The soft scrape of the door sounded.

Through the slight opening between the statue and wall, she glanced up, stilled.

Silhouetted in the stream of golden light stood Lord Balfour, his imposing presence seeming to fill the room.

Her heart tripped a beat. She should stand and announce her presence. Torn between finding herself alone with the daunting noble and her curiosity at why he'd come to the chapel when he must be exhausted, she remained silent.

Tense seconds passed.

She waited for him to leave.

After a moment, he walked to the front pew, knelt, made the sign of the cross, and began to pray.

As his soft, deep murmurs of the Our Father rumbled through the sacred chamber, she hesitated.

Latin?

Not that she should be surprised. Given the title he would one day inherit, in his youth he would have been taught Latin and French, along with several other languages that would serve him in his future dealings.

After finishing the Paternoster, her betrothed started anew.

Gwendolyn squeezed the bottle in her hand as she leaned forward. Why would he repeat the prayer? Her skin tingled with each word, more so when, after he finished the prayer, he started once more.

Against her will, she felt a connection to the man who knelt, head bent before the altar, as if he too searched for answers in these tumultuous times.

Perhaps the good Pieres had suggested lay within him was truly there, which would explain her own baffling pull to her betrothed.

Her foot started to go numb. Gwendolyn shifted and lost her balance. On a gasp, she caught herself on the door, and the aged wood gave a soft squeak.

Lord Balfour stilled. In the somber light, cold eyes narrowed on her. Like a panther, he unfurled his muscled body, his hand smoothly withdrawing his dagger as he stood. "Whoever is there, show yourself."

Chapter 3

The soft glow of candles exposed Lady Gwendolyn as she stepped into the light. Despite the relative darkness, her hair gleamed with warmth, and her dress fluttered around her womanly curves.

God's sword, what was she doing here? Cailin and Rónán were to join him at any time. If she'd listened in on their conversation, 'twould have put all their lives in danger.

"Why did you not show yourself when I entered?" he challenged, irritated he hadn't noticed her when he'd stepped inside, nor taken a moment to inspect the chamber.

Defiance flashed in her eyes. "I owe you nay explanation for my presence in *my* chapel."

She damn well did, a fact they both knew. From their first meeting in the stable, she'd held her ground, exposed her stubbornness, but that did not excuse her impropriety. "Why were you spying on me?" he demanded, thankful 'twas only prayers she'd overheard.

"I wasna spying."

He stepped toward her.

Gwendolyn stiffened. "Stay where you are!"

At the nervousness in her voice, he paused. Never would he cause her harm, except that she believed he was Bróccín, a warrior renowned as a brutal leader. Regardless of the man's reputation, he couldn't pretend to possess that level of cruelty. She was a pawn, a move to play, no more.

"I will not hurt you," Aiden assured her.

She didn't move.

"You are afraid of me," he said.

As if poking a badger with a stick, her eyes flared with warning. "I fear nay man."

Memories of the brutality he'd witnessed in war slammed through his mind. "Then you are a fool."

"You know naught about me to make such a judgement, but know this: I am far from a weak-kneed lass you can intimidate." She angled her jaw. "I agreed to Lord Comyn's request to wed a man of his choosing only to ensure my people's safety, and to protect my home. I assure you, if I had a full contingent of knights to keep my castle secure, our marriage would never take place."

Her face flushed with anger, her blond locks framing narrowed gray eyes, she looked like a defiant fairy and, to Aiden, the lass couldn't have been more beautiful. Irritated by the shot of need sliding through him, he focused on his mission. He and his men couldn't risk raising suspicion during their brief stay. Neither could he allow her rebellious nature to interfere with their plans.

"Your people and home will be cared for." By which side was another matter. "As your betrothed, you will obey me. I will not tolerate your defiance."

"I will be your wife," she stated, "but never will I capitulate to being an observer when it comes to my people's needs."

He shoved aside his growing admiration for the fierce lass, damned yet another innocent was harmed in Lord Comyn's bid for power. Nor, with the stakes so high, could this be helped.

Aiden folded his hands over his chest. "So long as you follow my orders, we shall be comfortable with each other."

"I await the day you ride off to battle," she said.

"Nay more than I." And more than she understood.

The door opened. Cailin and Rónán entered.

After a surprised pause, Rónán shut the door. The knight's gaze shifted from Aiden to her. "Is something amiss?"

Aiden unfurled his arms. "Lady Gwendolyn was just leaving. My lady, I will see you at supper."

She stiffened, and he could all but see the angry thoughts whirling in her head. She gave a curt nod. "My lord." She strode past his men, slammed the door in her wake.

"God's blade," Cailin said, "the lass is angrier than a wounded bear."

"She is, and rightly so." Aiden met his friend's gaze. "I despise talking to her with such disdain. She is a strong and proud woman, but a stubborn one as well."

"What happened?" Rónán asked.

"I had begun prayers when I heard a sound from behind the statue." Aiden walked behind the figurine, frowning at the bottles of oil on the floor and a small door cracked open. He pushed it wider, impressed by the array of oils lining the hidden shelf. "'Twould seem I caught her replenishing oils and herbs, but after I entered, she didna make her presence known. For the short time we are here, we must be careful. I willna risk her interference."

"We need the lass's aid to discover whether a secret tunnel to the castle exists," Cailin said.

"As much as I agree, given the tension between us, I doubt the time exists to gain her trust." Aiden stowed the bottles she'd left, then closed the small door. "For the few days we will remain, all we must do is allow her to continue to believe I am her betrothed. If somehow I can convince her to divulge the location of the secret passageway, so be it."

His men nodded.

Aiden continued, "Given her reluctance to marry, she willna seek me out and we can explore unheeded. Once it is dark, come to my chamber and report your findings; then we will discuss our next step."

"How will you warn us if there is trouble?" Cailin asked.

"I will rub my thumb across my jaw." Aiden paused. "Any other questions?"

His men shook their heads, then departed.

Aiden stepped toward the door. At the entry, he glanced back to the altar.

Lady Gwendolyn wouldn't marry Bróccín, but she would wed a man chosen by the Bruce. Latharn Castle's strategic location was too important to allow the lass to live without the protection of a noble loyal to King Robert.

Nor was her desire to remain unwed of any matter. War demanded its own dictates, all within its own boundaries, often sacrificing one's dreams for the sake of power. A fact he well knew.

Yet she wasn't a warrior, but a maiden ensnared within the turbulence of war.

Sympathy for her plight swept him. Her fate could not be helped. He wasn't a noble who could offer her aid, but a Knight Templar.

No, his life in the Brotherhood was over.

Aiden's hand tightened on the entry at thoughts of King Philip's duplicity against the loyal order that had protected the sovereign over the years. Desperation and greed had pressed the king's hand, neither of which excused the royal's betrayal of warriors who had displayed the highest ideals and principles for nearly two centuries.

Aiden yanked the door open, the golden rays of the late afternoon sun far from warming the chill blackening his heart.

Almost a year had passed since he and the other Templars had sailed beneath the shield of night from the port of La Rochelle. He regretted those they'd had to leave behind, the many brave men who had been tortured or killed since.

Aiden strode toward the keep. By God, their sacrifice wouldn't be for naught. This night, he and his men would begin gathering the information King Robert needed for the attack on Latharn Castle. Thoughts of a lass had no place in war, something he must never forget.

* * * *

The lingering scent of venison, herbs, and onions filled the air as Gwendolyn finished the last sip of her wine, relieved the tedious meal was over. Except for Lord Balfour's initial reserved greeting, when he'd sat beside her on the dais, throughout the meal he'd remained quiet, his cool demeanor far from a surprise after their confrontation in the chapel.

The entry to the keep opened. Illuminated by torchlight, Sir Pieres stepped into the great hall, a sealed writ in his hand.

Mary's will, what news did he bring? Fingers trembling, she set aside her goblet. Please God, let it not be a warning that the Bruce's men were nearby.

Her trusted knight strode to the dais, handed her the slim, tied leather pouch. "This just arrived from Rome."

"Rome?" Relief swept her that 'twas not a report concerning King Robert. As she accepted the document, she caught her betrothed's interest. Mouth tight, Gwendolyn broke open the seal, unrolled the missive, and scanned the lines. Her fingers tightened on the parchment.

Lord Balfour raised a brow. "What is wrong, my lady?"

Wrong? An understatement. Pressure tightened in her chest as she reread the damning lines and then lifted her gaze to his. "'Tis a request for Father Iames to sail for Rome immediately."

With a shrug, her betrothed emptied his goblet. He set it on the table, motioned for the lad nearby for more. "I see no issue with the priest's departure."

She damned this unwanted turn of event. Nor did he understand the consequence. "In the missive you delivered, Lord Comyn instructed we would marry within a fortnight after your arrival. Father Iames is to perform the ceremony."

A bored expression settled on Lord Balfour's face as he took a sip of his wine. "A directive easily fulfilled. We will send for a nearby priest."

Gwendolyn struggled to accept that the time to adjust to his presence, to find a way to tolerate him within her life, was lost. "There are nay other clerics nearby."

"Then at the end of the period in question, we shall handfast."

"I would agree," she said, cursing the tremor in her voice at thoughts of the Scottish practice of marriage through oaths pledged to the other, "but Lord Comyn's directive states our vows are to be given by a priest."

His eyes widened for a fraction of a second, then grew unreadable. She frowned. Panic? Nay. Lord Balfour was anxious to wed, to enter a union that would bring him the title of the Earl of Hadington, along with Latharn Castle. "A ship awaits Father Iames in the harbor. Once he has performed our marriage ceremony, he will leave."

* * * *

Aiden forced his expression to remain calm, at odds with the alarm raging inside. Married this night? God's sword, no! From the corner of his eye, he caught Cailin watching him from a nearby trestle table, his expression curious. Aiden rubbed his thumb across his jaw

Eyes widening, Cailin leaned close to Rónán, whispered. Both men sat back, covertly watched for his next signal.

"Sir Pieres," Gwendolyn said, "instruct Father Iames of the change in plans posthaste."

Worry lined the knight's brow. "Aye, my lady." He bowed, then hurried out.

Gwendolyn's eyes leveled on Aiden. "'Twould seem," she whispered, her voice icy, "that you will have my castle this night."

Heart pounding, Aiden fought rising panic. Blast it, there must be a way to avoid saying their vows.

With her guard filling the castle, he and his men couldn't slip away unseen. Nor could he allow her to see his concern. God help them if 'twas discovered they were the enemy.

Through sheer will, Aiden set the goblet on the table as if the news hadn't shattered his composure, then met his bride-to-be's fierce gaze. "Don a gown fitting for our marriage, then return."

Her eyes blazed with anger, and he muttered a silent curse. The last thing he wanted was to involve the lass further, much less toss her into this sham of a marriage.

Gwendolyn fled to the turret.

On unsteady legs, Aiden rose. With herculean will, he stepped off the dais. His stride easy, as if his entire life hadn't been tossed into chaos, he walked over, halted before his men. "We need to speak in private."

Nodding, his knights followed him down the corridor.

Once inside the solar, Aiden shut the door. The scent of fresh rushes melded with the warmth of the summer night, at odds with the anguish roiling in his gut.

Cailin narrowed his eyes. "What happened?"

Unable to believe the turn of events, Aiden rubbed the tension in the back of his neck. "'Twould seem Lord Comyn dictated our marital vows are to be given by a priest."

"A common occurrence," Rónán said.

"I agree, but Father Iames has been called to Rome and sails this night, and there isna another man of the cloth nearby. Thus Lady Gwendolyn and Lord Balfour are to wed immediately," Aiden said, the words screaming in his mind.

Cailin's face paled. "God's blade, you canna marry the lass!"

"Dinna you think I know that?" Aiden spat, praying that at any moment he would awaken and find 'twas naught but a nightmare.

"God's truth," Rónán breathed, "we must leave now."

"Nay, we would be seen if we tried to take our mounts and go," Aiden said. "Nor have we gathered the information necessary for King Robert."

Cailin gave a rough exhale. "Then what are we going to do?"

A question Aiden had asked himself a hundred times since she'd broken the news, yet each answer had collapsed in his mind but for one.

Duty.

The reason they were at Latharn Castle.

An objective regardless of the risks they must achieve.

However much he loathed the idea, he resigned himself to the choice he must make, one involving a stubborn lass with gray eyes whose actions had shown him more of a spine than he'd expected.

"The details we gather are critical to King Robert's capturing this stronghold, a fortress he must seize if he is to unite Scotland," Aiden said, his voice grave. "We have bits of information, but far from what is needed to ensure our sovereign's success."

Rónán eyes widened. "God in heaven, you are actually going through with this farce?"

A hard ache pounded in his head. "I have nay other choice. When we have the information we need, in a day, two at most, we depart as planned.

Once we reach the Bruce's camp, I will send word to Lady Gwendolyn that Lord Balfour has died."

"God help us if she learns that you are not her betrothed before we escape," Cailin said.

Confident in this regard, Aiden shook his head. "She willna. And any vow I swear under Bróccín's name will not be binding."

Brows furrowed, Rónán walked to the hearth, turned. "What of the lass?"

"What of her?" Aiden asked.

"She believes 'tis her wedding night," his friend replied. "She will expect you to bed her."

Aiden stilled. In the chaos, he hadn't considered the possibility of their sharing a chamber, or the repercussions of that intimate setting. He recalled how her face had paled at the prospect of an immediate marriage, and the pounding in his head eased. "Given Lady Gwendolyn's dismay at the news of our imminent marriage, I doubt she will be troubled if I dinna share her chamber."

"With the celebrating after your vows," Cailin said, "and more than likely the revelers following you to her chamber, I dinna think you will have a choice of where you sleep this night."

God's sword, their being alone was never to have been an issue. Except the priest's imminent departure had laid waste to his plans.

For an instant, his body hardened at thoughts of the sheer loveliness of Lady Gwendolyn's curves. In different circumstances, he couldna deny he would be interested in exploring her alluring form. Yet he couldn't ignore his greater duty, or that he wasn't her betrothed. When he used a false name for the upcoming marriage, he would not be her husband.

Though she was beautiful, and regardless if she intrigued him, or that he'd never met a woman like her before, with ease he could keep his distance. How many nights had he spent in the desert with naught but a blanket to cover him, or sailed with a galley of knights preparing for an attack. Sleeping in a chamber with the lass was naught but another obligation.

"Given the earl's renowned dictatorial manner, she will expect a quick bedding," Cailin warned.

A muscle worked in Aiden's jaw. "Bedamned with what Lord Balfour would have done. I refuse to make a mockery of the sanctity of marriage any more than necessary."

But his friend's words held wisdom, ones he damned. She would expect his sharing their marriage bed, but based on her reaction when she learned their wedding would be this night, intimacy was something she loathed. A fact he would bend in his favor.

Aiden refused to ponder her naked curves or soft sighs. Instead, he thought of what was within his control. "Once the bedchamber door closes, I will devise a reason to allow her to sleep alone."

"What of the well-wishers who will camp outside the chamber and demand proof of Lady Gwendolyn's innocence?" Cailin asked.

"A simple task to take care of, which doesna involve her."

Rónán arched a brow. "And she will comply with your deceit before her people?"

"I believe she will, at least for the few days we are here," Aiden said. Based on their prolonged silence, neither of his men seemed convinced of his plan.

A shout, then laughter echoed from the great room.

He frowned. "We must return before Lady Gwendolyn arrives." With his men on his heels, Aiden exited the chamber and strode to the dais, anxious for the time they could depart.

* * * *

Torchlight filled the great room as Lady Gwendolyn stood before Father Iames, noting the way his cassock hung from his reed-thin frame, and the deep lines of worry creasing his brow.

Through her dread, she forced herself to smile. She refused to add anguish to a man she'd known all her life, one who was more than the priest of this stronghold but a friend, one who knew of her reluctance to marry.

Heart pounding, she faced her betrothed, aware of his eyes lowering to her ivory silk gown with a scowl. Let him be irritated by her choice. After her first marriage, she refused to wear white. Though elaborate, this attire wasn't crafted for a wedding. 'Twas a gown her father had gifted her with months ago as a surprise for an upcoming trip to meet with Lord Comyn.

Weeks after, he had died.

She slid her thumb over the embroidered gold detail at the edge of one of the long sleeves, appreciating the elegance of the gown, of how the simple ivory top narrowed at the waist, then opened in a vee to the floor to expose a delicate weave of golden flowers. For that momentous occasion, every detail had been considered, from matching panels sewn into the exposed sleeves to the ivory pearls and gold beads threaded into a Celtic pattern that surrounded her neck. But most of all, she had loved that her father had taken the time to select a dress for her of such elegance.

Tears burned her throat as she remembered how she'd learned he'd died, how she'd collapsed on her bed and wept until she had no tears left. Heartbroken, she'd stowed the gown deep inside a chest, never again to be seen, the gift given out of love naught but a reminder of his death.

Today, she found this garb a fitting reminder of dreams shattered.

Numb, she took in the pride and joy on the faces of her men filling the great room when all she wanted to do was scream with outrage at this marriage.

Lord Balfour shifted beside her.

Gwendolyn stared straight ahead, refusing to acknowledge his presence until decorum dictated the commencement of this horrendous act.

Like a death knell, the peals of the chapel bell announcing Vespers sounded.

The priest nodded to Sir Pieres, and the knight called the crowd filling the large chamber to silence, but she caught the anguish in his eyes at her marrying another man. However much she did not want this marriage, she wished that one day her friend would find a woman deserving of his love.

The scent of roast venison and herbs filling the air, Father Iames opened the Bible. Strains of Latin echoed around her as the sacred ceremony began, holy words that would forevermore bind her to a man she detested.

As the priest made the sign of the cross, Gwendolyn averted her gaze to the flames in the hearth, the whirl of black soot spiraling upward, so like her life, charred of hope.

"Do you," the priest began, "take Bróccín MacRaith, Earl of Balfour, as your lawfully wedded husband?"

The vicar's deep voice echoed within the great room, and her stomach lurched.

At her silence, a frown worked its way across the priest's weathered brow.

Too aware of the pride-filled faces around her and refusing to dishonor her legacy, she steadied herself. "I—I do."

The priest's gaze shifted to Lord Balfour. "And do you, Lord Balfour," Father Iames said, his aged voice rough with emotion, "take Lady Gwendolyn Murphy as your lawfully wedded wife?"

At his silence, she looked up.

Green eyes penetrated hers with such intensity, like a warrior set to conquer, and she shuddered. "I do," he replied, his deep, his confident burr rolling through the chamber as if staking his claim.

Her knights within the great room exploded into cheers. Tankards of ale were passed around with fervor, and men raised their cups in toasts to the occasion before downing the brew.

Amid the merriment, she lowered her gaze. Gwendolyn stared at the man she'd never wanted, and fought to accept the fact that at this moment her life had changed.

The earl's strong arm wrapped around her. She stiffened as he turned with her to face the crowd. "May I present my wife, Lady Gwendolyn!" Another round of cheers roared within the great room as servants refilled pitchers of ale and trays of roasted meat, bread, and sweets to celebrate the occasion. One by one, those within filed past to offer their congratulations. Wanting to escape, she thanked each person as she fought to keep her smile in place.

Eyes cool, Sir Pieres stepped forward. "Lord Balfour, I congratulate you on your marriage."

The earl nodded.

Her friend moved to stand before her. "My lady... Know that I will protect you always."

"A task *I* will undertake," Bróccín said with soft warning. "Your loyalty to my wife is something I applaud. Faithfulness, I welcome into my ranks and expect no less from anyone within my protection."

Sir Pieres's face grew taut. "Aye, my lord." He turned and walked away.

She did not miss the way the earl watched her knight's departing form with a critical eye. "We have been friends since childhood. He is a man I trust with my life."

"A fact I well understand, but I tolerate naught but his complete fidelity." Anger slid through her. "Sir Pieres is a man of honor."

"Of that I have nay doubt. But his protectiveness exposes that his feelings for you extend beyond those of a loyal knight."

Deciding 'twas prudent to change the subject. "You may release me."

"The way you are trembling," he whispered, the grim smile on his face never wavering, "if I let you go, you would collapse."

Humiliated that her legs were indeed unsteady, she remained silent.

A tall warrior with a shock of red hair and eyes as blue as the ocean stepped before her, the man Bróccín had introduced earlier as Sir Cailin, gave a deep bow.

"My Lady Gwendolyn, I congratulate you on your marriage." The formidable knight knelt before her and lowered his head. "I swear to you my loyalty and, if necessary, I will protect you with my life."

The earl's other knight, his brown hair secured behind his neck with a strip of leather, knelt beside the other warrior. He lowered his head in deference, and repeated the pledge.

Humbled, she cleared her throat. "I thank you, Sir Cailin and Sir Rónán."

The knights rose.

Sir Rónán's eyes filled with appreciation, but sincerity as well. "Know this: Your husband is a stern man, but one you can trust."

Though a stranger, she found comfort in the warrior's claim, and prayed 'twas true.

Shouts followed by laughter filled the chamber.

Inside, emptiness swelled with a painful ache. She wished her father were there; then this entire mess would never have taken place.

Overwhelmed, exhausted from the chaos of the day, she glanced up, unnerved to find Bróccín's gaze on her. "I refuse to stay here to celebrate a lie."

He arched a skeptical brow. "Are you so anxious for the bedding?"

Mary's will, in the mayhem she'd momentarily forgotten this unwanted event.

This night he would come to her bed.

Chapter 4

Gwendolyn fought for calm at her husband's alarming reminder of their upcoming wedding night, of his expectations, of the role she must play.

She stared at the celebratory crowd, the blur of smiling faces, toasts, and laughter, wished she was leagues away, anywhere to avoid climbing the steps to her chamber and to her fate.

"Lady Balfour," Father Iames said, his voice rough with concern as he halted before her, "your face has grown quite pale. Are you ill?"

Lady Balfour, proof of the deed done, confirmation her coveted freedom to live the life she chose was gone. Wanting to shout her outrage, she forced herself to smile at her friend, refusing to add to his concern. "I admit being a bit tired."

At her side, Lord Balfour's gaze shifted to her, and his mouth hardened into a frown.

Disapproval narrowed the priest's eyes as he glanced at him, and her throat tightened, humbled the cleric would, however subtly, dare censor this fierce warrior. Well she understood the expectations of her this night.

"I thought you had left, Father."

"I went to pack. Before I departed, I wanted to say good-bye." The cleric slanted his gaze toward her husband, cooled. "Take care of Lady Gwendolyn."

Lord Balfour gave a solemn nod. "I swear to you that she will be well cared for."

The elder's shoulders relaxed. "I thank you. Once my business in Rome is done, I will return." Father Iames gave her hand a gentle squeeze, then the elder wove his way through the crowd until the flow of his black garb was lost within the mill of bodies.

Moments later, the entry to the keep opened, and her chest squeezed tight as her ally slipped into the darkness.

Her husband took her hand. "'Tis time we went upstairs."

The hours ahead, secluded with this stranger who now ruled her life, crashed through her in an unnerving rush. Needing a moment more to compose herself, she glanced at the earl. "I would like to remain a while longer."

He leaned close to her ear. "I willna linger until those well into their cups haul you upstairs like a marital offering to our bed."

Heat stroked her cheeks at his reference to the drunken escort many a newlywed bride received to her bedchamber.

Lord Balfour tightened his grip and guided her toward the turret.

"They are leaving!" a deep male voice called from behind them.

"Dinna let them go without us!" another man shouted, and the crowd roared with laughter.

Her husband cursed under his breath, and scooped her into his arms. She gasped. "What are you doing?"

"Saving us both an awkward scene." Bróccín sprinted up the steps.

Cradled against his chest, she swore she could almost hear his heart pounding through his garb. Was he as unsettled as she?

On the second floor, he paused. "Which chamber is yours?"

"At the end."

The slap of footsteps and shouts rose from the turret.

On a curse, he bolted past paintings of the castle's founders, the torchlight scraping across his taut expression without mercy. Once inside, he kicked the door shut, set her down, and then slid the bar into place.

Drunken calls and laughter grew in the corridor. A moment later, banging sounded against the wooden entry.

She held her breath.

So did he.

Their gazes met and she caught a glimmer of awareness in his eyes that made her heart thump anew.

"I dinna think they will let you in, Nigel," a slurring voice called.

Muffled laughter rang out.

"Did someone bring the wine?" a man yelled. "We could be here for some time."

* * * *

Amid the calls for drink, the lewd suggestions of the drunken men in the hallway settled into errant shouts, bawdy songs, and laughter.

Silently cursing the pallor of Gwendolyn's elegant face, Aiden released her, then took a careful step away from the door. As if he bloody wanted to be cloistered with her this night. A role he must play as she believed their marriage was real, and that in the hours ahead he would claim his marital rights.

His gaze lingered on her soft curves, and another burst of heat shot through him. To distract himself, he glanced around the room, taking in the elegance and warmth.

A fire blazed in the hearth. The shimmer of flames entwining with candles placed around the room illuminating the chamber within their golden glow. Several chests carved with intricate Celtic designs sat along the far wall, and drawings of birds hung above. On a corner table lay a basket filled with bottles of wine, a selection of cheese, a variety of apples, and a loaf of bread.

Aiden fisted his hands as he caught sight of the sturdy oak bed. Swaths of green satin fell in luxurious folds from a polished circular mount overhead to accent an intricately carved frame. An ivory comforter, embellished with gold flowers woven around the rim, draped over the bed, the corner near the pillows turned down in silent invitation.

Bawdy laughter had him glancing toward the entry. With a slow exhale, he unfurled his fingers. "'Twould appear our well-wishers are settling in for the night."

Wary eyes held his. "So it seems."

He dismissed the slight quiver in her voice, her nerves expected. God's sword, with the door blocked he couldn't leave, and given the falsehood of their marriage, neither would he bed the lass. Somehow, he needed to find a way to calm her without straying too far from Bróccín's demeanor.

Aiden walked to the table and poured two goblets of wine, brought one to her. "'Twill ease your nerves."

Her gaze flickered over the breadth of his shoulders, and her fingers tightened around the crafted gold stem. If possible, her face paled further.

From the rumors he'd heard about the callous man Lord Balfour had become, the earl would have slaked his lust without care of Gwendolyn's feelings. Bile twisted in his gut at thoughts of such brutality. Never would he touch the lass without her welcome.

A fact she didn't know.

In one gulp, Aiden downed the spiced liquid, shoved the cup onto the nearby stand, then crossed to the open window. A soft breeze tinged with a hint of the sea washed over him as he stared into the night.

Beyond the full moon, stars glittered in the heavens like flickers of hope, although he found naught encouraging about this entire situation. All for king and country. A mumbled curse tore from his lips, mingled with the faint rumble of waves below.

In the distance, where the sea met the sky, the sail of a departing cog shimmered beneath the moonlight. How he longed to be aboard, or anywhere except trapped in Gwendolyn's chamber on their supposed wedding night.

Still, this wasn't the first time he'd been forced to complete a task through unconventional means.

A rueful smile tugged at his lips. So caught up in the chaos, an important point he'd overlooked. This was a hindrance, no more.

In regard to the mission, naught of importance had changed. This unfortunate pretense would last but days, and throughout he would leave the lass untouched.

The runner he would send to announce Lord Balfour's death would give her freedom. At least until the Bruce seized Latharn Castle.

Tension ebbed from his body, and he focused on the benefits of the situation. He could ask questions of the servants without raising suspicion, and view the castle and ledgers as he pleased. As for the lass, instead of dreading the upcoming hours, he'd use the time to nurture her trust.

Aiden turned.

Gwendolyn hadn't moved, but watched him with suspicion from the opposite side of a table topped with candles, the shifting of light exposing the concern in her eyes.

And why wouldna she be unsettled? She was a virgin. God knew what tripe the women within the castle had told her about the marriage bed. Her believing him a hard, callous warrior wouldn't ease her disquiet.

To calm her fears and play true to who she thought he was, he must know what she'd been told about Balfour. "What kind of man do you think I am?" Aiden demanded.

Gwendolyn's brows drew together. "Why?"

He strode to the table and poured himself another cup of wine. Aiden took a sip and met her eyes over the rim of his goblet. "We know little of each other, except what we have been told, rumor or otherwise."

"'Tis said you are a fair man."

The stubborn admission tempted him to smile, which he smothered. "And...?"

She slid a finger along the goblet's rim as if coming to a decision. "That your men trust you."

"Anything else?" he asked, frustrated that each bit of information she gave him was like a battle won.

She shot a quick glance at the bed, and her expression darkened with dismay.

God's sword, he would end her worry. A few drops of blood would appease the crowd outside when they inspected the sheets in the morning. Aiden stormed to the bed, unsheathed his blade. At the slide of steel in his wake, he whirled.

Gwendolyn stood before him, proud, defiant. Nerves darkened her eyes, but the grip on her dagger remained firm. "I know my marital duties and will yield to your touch, but I will have your promise that 'twill not be done with a brutal hand."

However much he admired her spirit, he doubted Lord Balfour would have tolerated such defiance. "Sheath your blade," he ordered.

On a hard swallow, she again slanted a wary look toward the bed before leveling her gaze on him.

Frustration chipped away at his calm. "I *told* you to secure your weapon."

Her fingers whitened on the handle.

With predatory steps, he crossed the room, his ire building with each step. "Do you believe displaying your *sgian dubh* will scare me?" Before she had a chance to reply, he seized her wrist.

She twisted hard to break free.

Aiden reached out to catch her, but she turned her body, throwing him off balance. They started to fall. Keeping a firm hold of her arm, he shifted to place himself between her and the floor, grunted as he hit, her landing square on top of him.

Outrage flashed in her eyes. "You bastard!" Her knee took precarious aim.

With an oath, he flipped and pinned her, securing her wrists. "Release the dagger."

"You willna take me like an animal!" she hissed.

"Had I wanted to bed you," he said, his voice icy, "the deed would have been done."

Her breaths coming fast, she struggled against his hold.

The stubborn fool. He pressed the weight of his full length against her, ceasing her ability to move. This close, the scent of woman and night teased him. Too aware of how his body fit against hers, Aiden hardened beneath her soft curves. As if of its own will, his gaze slid to her mouth a breath away. The soft lips seemed to beckon him, and he wondered at her taste.

What was he bloody thinking? He tore her blade free from her grip and shoved to his feet.

Eyes wide, she scrambled back.

Aiden let her go, more than ready to put distance between them. Furious that she had the power to tempt him, he turned to the bed and his original intent. With a quick slash, he cut a small line in his palm, tossed the sheet back, and smeared blood on the fine linen.

After wiping his blade clean, he secured his weapon, turned. "The deed is done."

The crackle of flames melded with the soft breeze tumbling into the chamber, playing cadence to the moment as Gwendolyn stared at him in disbelief.

Blast it! Aiden strode over and refilled his goblet, shoved the spirit aside. He downed the cup, doubting he could drink enough to blur his mind from his unexpected and unwanted thoughts of her this night. He grabbed the bottle and poured until wine gurgled to the brim.

"W–why did you do that?"

At the shocked disbelief in her voice, he shot her a cool look, his gaze traitorously straying to her full breasts. A spike of desire slammed through him, and he emptied the goblet. If the situation wasn't so serious, he would have laughed at his adolescent inability to control his body's urges. "Which one, tackling you or smearing my blood on the sheet?"

Though trembling, she held her ground. "The first."

"You drew a knife on me. In the future, never pull your blade on me, or any warrior, unless you are prepared to defend yourself."

On an unsteady breath, she wet her lips.

Aiden's gaze narrowed on the slide of her tongue, cursed the spear of heat. "And the blood on the sheet?"

"I dinna take an unwilling woman," he snapped.

"I see."

By the skepticism in her voice, he doubted she did. Nor would he explain further. "I suggest you finish your wine and then retire to your bed."

"What of you?"

"I will make a pallet by the fire."

She watched him for a long moment, her eyes guarded, as if trying to assess the situation.

A fate they shared. Turning, Aiden crossed to where a stack of blankets lay folded, grabbed two, and knelt before the hearth.

"I heard you were a ruthless man."

He looked back, oddly amused that she would find the need to reply to his earlier question. Mayhap a peace offering? Doubtful. Regardless the reason, her initiating the dialogue bode well.

He spread out the first cover. "I can be, given the right incentive." As when he'd witnessed unarmed Christian pilgrims being slaughtered for their faith in the Holy Land. Outraged by the barbarians' heartless act, he'd cut them down without hesitation, their spilled blood a fitting penance for the peaceful travelers they'd murdered.

"And 'tis said you rule with an iron fist."

Frustrated, he again glanced over, too aware of her blamelessness in this blasted situation. She held naught but fears and rumors of the man she now believed her husband. Neither could he forget the softness of her body beneath his, of how her blond hair had spilled out to frame her face, her mouth slightly parted.

He smothered the dangerous memory. Though he must remain in Bróccín's character, she did not deserve to fear him. That he could give her.

"Many things are said about warriors who achieve power," Aiden said. "Some are true, others fables that grow with the telling."

"Either way, know this," she rasped, her voice cool, "I willna be cast aside in my own castle, treated like I am a scullery maid fit only for bedding."

He held her gaze, her bravery stealing his breath. God's sword, the lass was a woman to admire. "Except for the duties the lord of the castle holds, your place at Latharn Castle willna change. When I vowed to the priest that I would take care of you, I meant what I said."

She again skimmed her thumb along the goblet's rim, a habit he'd noted when she was in deep thought.

Flames wavered in the hearth, casting a wash of gold over her face, highlighting her cheekbones, the softness of her skin, and the lush curve of her mouth. However beautiful, and a lass that would intrigue any man, with his soon rejoining the Bruce, she wasn't a woman he could ever have as his own.

Her breath exhaled in a soft rush as she watched him, and satisfaction filled Aiden that Lord Balfour would never touch her with cruelty or disrespect.

Although she'd drawn her blade against him, fear had driven the act. She wasn't a simpering lass, but a woman who held her own, one he could admire and, more, respect.

"Though we are strangers, I swear you have nay reason to fear me."

At her silence, deciding 'twas a strategic place to end their discussion, he turned and stripped off his forest-green tunic with its band of Celtic designs woven at the end of each sleeve. He folded the top over the chair, settled on the pallet, and then tugged the other blanket up to his waist. "Sleep." Too aware of her, Aiden stared at the flames, doubtful he'd rest this night.

* * * *

Gwendolyn studied Bróccín's prone form, unsure whether she was more embarrassed by the ease with which he'd disarmed her or her husband's decision to leave her untouched.

A simple man, no. With his quickness, the way he made decisions without hesitation, and his attention to detail, he was a warrior who lived and died by his blade. Though he dismissed some of the stories told about him as myth, after the memory of his swift but painless retrieval of her weapon, she wasn't convinced.

Neither was she swayed by the fine cut of his jaw, the green eyes stunning in their brilliance, or his muscled body as if carved by the gods. Though handsome, to her, a man's loyalty meant the most.

His claim that he wouldn't harm her echoed through her mind. Keeping a close watch on him, Gwendolyn walked to the other side of the bed, opposite from where he'd stood moments before.

Firelight shimmered over his broad shoulders as they rose and fell with his every breath, the inherent power of this fierce warrior one he'd sworn never to use against her.

Her gaze shifted to his muscled arms, relaxed at his sides. Arms that had swept her up without hesitation and carried her away from the inebriated knights celebrating their wedding, arms that had held her as he'd twisted to protect her from falling and taking his weight on the hard floor. As well, 'twas concern for her safety that had him hauling her from the mare's stall during the birthing.

Gwendolyn lay her hand upon the comforter, traced a gold embroidered flower. Her life ahead had been simpler when she had believed Bróccín to be a cold, hard man.

Hard, aye. A necessity as a warrior, but he wasn't cold, more a man who evaluated his thoughts before he spoke. Fair came to mind, intelligent and thoughtful as well. What else had she missed, and how had she misjudged him so completely? Known for her ability to discern the worth in a person, 'twould seem in regard to her new husband, she had erred.

Or had she?

For the first time in her life, she found herself floundering in her assessment of a man. Did it matter? With their vows given, he now owned everything she loved.

She glanced at the slash of red on the opposite side of the bed, an action to appease those who sought proof of her innocence.

Guilt rose within her. Odd Lord Comyn hadna informed him that she'd been married before. Perhaps embroiled in war against King Robert, her liege lord had forgotten or found the detail irrelevant. Nor, with his short time here, had he gleaned word from her people of her previous husband. As if a man focused on war would find interest in scraps of gossip.

Gwendolyn scraped her teeth across her lower lip. Should she admit the truth? If she did, would her admission bring him to her bed?

Unease ripped through her. No, she'd tell him in the morning, before he departed the chamber. She refused to allow him to be humiliated before those who served him by permitting him to display supposed proof of her bedding.

Was one night too much to ask to regain her much-needed composure? She wasn't a coward, but she needed time. With an unsteady sigh, Gwendolyn tugged up the sheets, closed her eyes, and prayed that by some miracle she would sleep.

Chapter 5

At the soft scrape of the door, Gwendolyn stirred from sleep and rolled over in her bed, struggling to identify an insistent warning in her head.

Failed.

She forced her eyes open.

A shaft of torchlight streaming through the entry outlined Bróccín.

Like fog lifting, memories rushed in. Their marriage. Bróccín leaving her untouched. How she'd withheld the fact of her widowed state, that she wasn't an innocent.

Bróccín's body blocked the light as he shifted to step into the hallway.

Mary's will, he couldn't leave without knowing the truth! Frantic, Gwendolyn half-climbed, half-fell out of bed, tugging the covers around her as she scrambled to her feet. "Wait! Close the door!"

His hand stilled, and his cool gaze leveled on her.

Pulse racing, Gwendolyn fought for coherent thought as she held the warrior's ferocious gaze. Her plans of waking before him, devising a logical explanation crumbled. With her mind blurred by exhaustion, she floundered for even pitiful rationality.

With slow purpose, he closed the door. A muscle worked in his jaw as he leaned his muscled body against the sturdy frame and then folded his massive arms across his chest.

What a mess! "T-there is something I must tell you."

A drunken shout sounded from the corridor.

Broken laughter followed.

Her heart sank as she glanced out the open window at the streaks of dawn slicing through the sky. 'Twas morning already? She looked toward him, noted his stern demeanor remained unchanged. Gwendolyn swallowed hard. "The well-wishers are still out there."

"Unfortunately," he growled. He unfolded his arms and pushed away from the door. "What is it you wished to speak of? 'Twould seem we have time."

Legs unsteady, she stepped away from the bed, the setting too intimate for her admission. She halted beside the chair where he'd folded and placed his blankets, proof of his generosity in giving her time to adjust to their marriage in his belief in her innocence.

She braced herself for his outrage. 'Twas far better he learned now than to discover the truth from another. "I was married several years ago. My husband died a month later in battle."

His nostrils flared as his gaze cut to the smear of blood upon the sheets, then narrowed on her. "Why did you not inform me last night?"

"I wasna aware you didna know until you cut yourself."

"Yet," he growled, "you said naught."

"I..."

"'Tis done!" He curled his fingers into his damaged palm. "Sit."

Spikes of terror pierced her, yet she straightened her shoulders and walked to the edge of the bed, turned to face him. Her gaze unflinching, she lifted her chin. "Do you wish me to disrobe now, my lord?"

"Just *stay* there!"

She stiffened.

The steady tap of boot heels sounded as he stalked across the floor.

Confused, she watched him as he paced, his mouth carved into a fierce frown.

She fought back a shiver as her husband reached the hearth for the third time.

He knelt, his back to her.

The size and width of the man's shoulders took her breath. She envisioned him atop her, his weight pressing her into the mattress. Another shiver swept her, and she drew the blanket closer around her body.

Bróccín tossed several pieces of wood atop the ashes from last night's fire. Flames wavered beneath the crush of dry tinder and then slowly crept up the bark. He stood. His shoulders tensed, but he did not turn. "I willna touch you," he said, "but I shall remain in the chamber."

An unsteady breath escaped as she raked her gaze down his formidable length. She glanced to the side, where a large curved chest with three forged iron hinges securing the top lay shoved against the wall. Filled with naught but clothes, 'twas easy to move, a necessity if ever she needed to escape into the secret tunnel hidden behind.

In the future she might tell him of the hidden passageway. As her husband, 'twas his right to know the location of every one hidden within the castle. Now, regardless of his title or the kindness he'd shown her, they were still strangers, their marriage vows still raw in her heart.

His vow, aye, but not even a kiss.

She frowned at the thought. Not that she was complaining.

At his silence, tension within her built. His reserve was odd for a powerful noble, one who'd led men into combat. With his battle-hardened body equally designed for war as a woman's bed, no doubt he'd tumbled many a lass. In truth, if she hadn't been forced into marriage and had met him some other way, she would have found him handsome to look upon.

Unbound hair as black as a raven's wing proved a perfect foil for green eyes that could ignite a woman's desire. She could envision women charmed by his powerful gaze, his confidence, and the powerful play of his muscles. A man like him would know how to make love to a woman, to touch her and make her tremble, not the fumbling touch of a lad.

She couldn't help but compare him to her late husband, who, while pleasing of feature, did not parallel Bróccín's masculinity and air of command.

In the bedroom, though she and Luke had been intimate, he'd only touched her at night with the express intent of getting her with child. His gentleness had eased her fears, the expectedness of the act with each joining adding its own relief, more so when, after he was done, he'd always turned away and left her alone.

What would it be like with this man?

Memories of his body pressed atop hers came to mind, of how she'd fit against him with aching clarity, and of how his hardness had wedged intimately against her. With a simple touch he could have...

She gasped. Mary's will, what was she thinking? He did not care for her. He was a warrior, a noble who'd wed her for one purpose—to claim Latharn Castle.

A fact she must never forget.

Now he was leaving her untouched, the reason brutally clear. After her admission of having shared a man's bed 'twas naught out of kindness, but irrelevance. To him, like the stronghold she loved and protected, was she little more than a possession?

Regardless his reason, she should be thankful for the reprieve. Nor could she forget that if he changed his mind, he could claim her as his right.

"Gwendolyn."

At his deep burr, she stiffened. "Aye?"

"Come here."

"Why?"

Hard eyes held hers with soft warning. "Because we need to talk."

Relief rolled through her. Talk, not intimacy. From his cool manner, she should have guessed, not that she wanted him. "I can hear you fine from here."

Dark brows narrowed. "Then, I will come there."

Closer to the bed? No!

On unsteady legs, Gwendolyn crossed the room and lowered to a chair, wishing she had her dagger. A ridiculous thought. Hadn't his unarming her with ease last night demonstrated that even if she carried a weapon, she far from posed a threat to him? As well, he'd given his word that he wouldn't harm her.

With the stealth of a panther, Bróccín strode over, settled in a nearby seat.

Gwendolyn studied his face, the hard plains unsettling, the intelligence in his eyes more so. She knew little about him. What did he know of her? "Did anyone tell you anything about me or my life?"

He shook his head. "Lord Comyn bid me to wed you; a command I followed."

"I see." Except she did not. Gwendolyn looked away. Throughout her life, she'd damned that women were little more than chattel for men's desires. Never had she considered that men were manipulated in plays of power as well.

'Twould seem that like her, Bróccín was naught but a pawn. Except, by complying with Comyn's dictate, in addition to taking a wife, he'd received a strategic stronghold. Still, he was a man of war, his life one of wielding his sword, of taking orders and issuing them as well.

She glanced over. The fire crackled in the hearth, creating a cocoon of intimacy around them, casting his features in an almost unearthly shade. His intense gaze held hers, and for a moment, 'twas as if he could see straight to her soul.

Shaken by the sense of connection, she swallowed hard. "There is little for us to say to the other."

"Why?"

The rumble of his deep voice left her further on edge. "You have every right while I... While I have my home...if even that."

Sadness flickered in his eyes, throwing her further off balance. "Is that what you believe?"

"Believe?" She gave a cold laugh. "Tell me, what rights do I have in a man's world? When I married before, my vows were given at my father's request," she said, her frustration poured into her words, and she found herself caught in the flow of anger. "Luke and I were friends, our marriage tolerable. When he died, I mourned a friend. After," she whispered, "I foolishly believed my father when he told me that my life was my own, and never again would I have to marry unless 'twas my choice."

"What happened to change that?"

She hesitated, confused he would ask or care. "My father died."

"I am sorry."

The genuine sincerity in his voice caught her off guard.

In the silence, Bróccín leaned forward, shoved a piece of wood deeper into the fire. Sparks spit out, danced within the curl of smoke, and then disappeared up the chimney. Face taut, he sat back, a pondering expression darkening his handsome face. "'Tis difficult to lose those we love."

The roughness of his voice, how his lower lip tightened when he spoke, betrayed an inner pain, reminding her of the priest's disclosure. "'Tis." Gwendolyn gave a slow exhale. "I am sorry as well."

His brows narrowed. "Why?"

"Before he left, Father Iames explained that you had lost your family."

* * * *

Aiden's heart slammed against his chest. Gwendolyn knew about his family? Had the priest recognized him? Panic churned as the repercussions stormed his thoughts. No. Had the priest known, Aiden would have been arrested prior to the ceremony, much less been allowed to gain access to Gwendolyn's bed.

Easing the tension from his shoulders, he glanced at her, noted the curiosity in her eyes. "What exactly did the priest tell you?"

"How your father died several years ago, and your brother some years later." Her gaze slid to the hearth, paused before shifting to him. "And of how your mother became ill and passed away this spring."

Relief swept him. She spoke of Bróccín's family.

"Several months have passed since I lost my father," she said in a broken whisper. "Yet I still grieve."

A flush slid across her cheeks, as if she hadn't meant to share. Nor had he intended their discussion to deteriorate into something so personal. Unlike her, he'd lost his family when he was a lad. The years had blurred the pain of his loss. Still, 'twas a mistake to allow the conversation to continue.

Aiden stood and stepped away from her. The last thing he wanted was to find common ground with the lass. At least during her time of strife, she was surrounded by people she loved, those she could turn to.

He, on the other hand, hadn't experienced the luxury of being with people he knew, those who cared. A homeless lad without family, he'd lived off the land by his quick wit until the Knights Templar had taken him in. A life with the Brotherhood he loved, or had until King Philip had betrayed the men who'd protected him over the years.

He smothered the burst of fury for France's king. The bastard would pay. Upon the royal's death, 'twould be *His* judgment the sovereign would face.

"In time," Aiden said, his jaw tense, "memories of those you love will fade. Then, you will nay longer feel the pain."

She frowned. "How can you believe such when your mother died but months ago?"

He silently cursed himself. "I was thinking more of the death of my father and brother. However hard, the hurt at their loss has faded to where I can think of them with warmth."

Gwendolyn's mouth pressed into a thoughtful grimace.

Blast it, he did not want to be having this discussion with her, to strengthen their tenuous tie to any degree.

She stood, moved before him. "I shouldna have pressed. I understand how difficult 'tis to speak of those you have lost, those whom you loved."

Furious at her compassion when he was feeding her naught but lies, Aiden started to move past her.

She stepped before him. "Bróccín?"

Trapped, he faced her.

Shrewd eyes held his, and then she slowly exhaled, as if coming to a decision of great importance. "We are wed, though a choice neither of us wished; mayhap we can become friends."

A cold laugh welled in his throat. If only she knew their marriage was false. He hadn't wanted to respect her. Yet like a thorn, she was determined to work her way into his life. An action he couldn't allow.

But the harsh words he formed to drive her away wilted on his tongue. Last night, he'd pondered how to gain her trust. If he pushed her away now, any bond between them, however tentative, would be severed, and valuable information could be lost.

However much he despised deceiving her, however much she unsettled him in numerous ways, he must continue to use her ignorance to his benefit. With the lives of many Scots loyal to the Bruce at risk, an opportunity he must take.

He forced his expression into a fierce scowl. "I am not an easy man," he warned, lowering his voice to a hard timbre.

She angled her jaw. "I, too, have been known to be less than traditional."

Aiden damned the soft challenge in her voice, the way her eyes flashed with defiance. Blast it, she and her foolish dreams weren't his to choose.

"I am a man of war. I know how to defend a castle and the intricacies of running a stronghold. Though I demand much from those who fight by my side, I am fair." He paused, wanting her to ponder his comments before he continued, to believe his next words hard won. "So, I have a proposition for you."

"A proposition?"

"Aye. Neither of us sought this marriage but agreed to comply with those to whom we give our fealty."

Gwendolyn gave a hesitant nod.

He took a step closer. "I willna force a woman."

Red swept up her cheeks, but she didn't move. "For that I thank you."

"But," Aiden said, aware he could push the limit of expectations only so far, "I want an heir."

Her eyes flared with apprehension, but she remained silent.

"Those beyond this chamber will believe we have consummated our marriage. Once weeks have passed and you are ready," he said, confident such a time would never arrive, "you will join me in my bed."

Relief washed over Gwendolyn's face. "I never..."

Her blush deepened, and guilt slid through him at his duplicity. "For now, we willna speak of this further." He turned, but she lay her hand on his arm. Aiden froze, willed away the awareness burning inside him. "What?" he demanded without looking back.

"I misjudged you."

He shrugged away her hand. "Then we are even." Mouth tight, Aiden strode to the window, needing distance, needing air, needing to blasted be out of this chamber. Nurturing their friendship played into his strategy, but he hadn't expected to like her or, worse, have to speak of when he would bed her to complete his damnable plans.

Blast it, he refused to think of Gwendolyn's slender body, curves that would make a man beg, or her full lips that he could too easily imagine crushed beneath his. He must focus on the fact that he'd found a way to gain her trust.

The air, ripe with the scent of the sea, filled the chamber as the rays of the rising sun spilled into the pinkish-blue sky.

Aiden closed his eyes, relished this time of morning when, if only for a little while, peace descended upon the madness that had become his world. The habit a fragment of survival from his childhood that he'd hoarded over the years.

With a grimace, he rubbed the back of his neck and scoured the swells far below, watched as the gulls soared on the air currents, their lonesome cries entwining within the rumble of incoming waves. Near the shore, sea fog clung to the surface, thick and unyielding. How many times had he and his men damned the thick swath of white that could shroud the enemy or offer their foe a safe haven?

"'Tis my favorite view."

He stiffened as Gwendolyn stepped to his side, not wanting her close enough so that he could smell the scent of woman and heather. "I enjoy the beach," he said, forcing the roughness from his voice.

"As I. 'Tis where I go to think, to be alone." She slid her thumb along the sill, her tone querying, almost gentle. "There is something soothing about the roll of waves upon the shore."

Yet another thing they shared.

"Mayhap we—" She gasped.

Aiden glanced over. Surprised by the shock on her face, he followed her gaze seaward, stilled.

The tip of a mast bearing an English flag cut through the top of the thick bank of white. A breath later, another appeared. With each moment, more masts came into view.

God in heaven, enemy ships! The possibility of a skirmish rushed through him.

"Why are English ships here?" she asked, her surprise confirming she hadn't anticipated their appearance. She frowned. "Were you expecting them?"

How should he answer? Was Lord Balfour privy to the ships' arrival? Worse, with the numerous masts streaming into view, 'twas more than a few ships. God's sword, 'twas a blasted fleet!

An anchor splashed into the depths from the nearest cog. A short distance away, crewmen hurled their anchor over the side, and another shot of water erupted from the sea.

Alarm screamed in his gut as the obvious cause for their arrival blared in his mind. With the Bruce sweeping across the Highlands with devastating ferocity, in his desperation, Comyn must have requested aid from the English king.

Mayhap he was wrong, but a sinking feeling in his gut assured him 'twas the only reason that made sense. Aiden grimaced. "I must meet the captain." Let the lass deduce his answer however she wished. He strode to the door. He must inform Cailin and Rónán. King Robert must be warned!

Chapter 6

Sunlight streamed through the stained-glass windows, casting shades of blues, reds, and purple within the solar as Aiden hid a dirk beneath his garb. He nodded to Rónán and Cailin standing opposite him. "As lord of the castle, I will take Sir Pieres and several men with me to meet whoever leads the English force." He secured another dagger into the side of his boot. "Once I depart, you both will leave. Rónán, once out of sight of the castle, head to the Bruce's encampment and inform him of the situation."

Rónán nodded.

"Cailin," Aiden continued, "round back and find cover where you can keep watch over the stronghold. When you see that I have safely arrived at the keep, return, and I will share what I have learned. After, you will ride to King Robert with a report."

Rónán slid his thumb across the hilt of his sword. "And if anyone asks where we are going?"

Aiden slipped a third dagger onto his belt. "Say you are off to hunt."

"A sound reason," Cailin said, leaning his shoulder against the wall. "If the English are staying for any length of time, more food will be needed."

With a nod, Aiden tugged on his cloak. "Let us hope they willna remain. I despise the thought of being trapped inside this bloody castle playing Lord Balfour to the Sassenach." He glanced toward Cailin. "If anything goes awry and I am taken prisoner, inform the Bruce."

The Templar straightened and nodded. "I pray all goes well."

"I assure you, I await the day we are leagues from here. A life shackled to a lass, however false, is not a part I wish to continue playing."

"Mayhap," Rónán conceded, "but if you are to be constrained in marriage, 'tis fortuitous to be bound to such a beauty."

"Beautiful and guiltless. She didna ask to be wed, but was cast into this position, one she accepted with dignity and grace. And," Aiden added with disgust, "Lord Comyn is a fool to exploit an intelligent and astute woman with such disregard. Obviously, he hasna met Gwendolyn; if he had…" At the surprise flickering in his men's eyes, he paused.

A smile brushed Cailin's mouth. "If Lord Comyn had met Lady Gwendolyn, he would have what?"

"At a loss for words, Aiden? Hers is a fate that, upon our arrival, seemed of little concern to you. Yet now, 'tis important?" Mirth flickered in Rónán's eyes. "I find myself curious to learn the reason."

His friends broke into laughter, and Aiden shot them both a fierce glare. "Given the severity of the situation, our thoughts should be on the unexpected arrival of the English force, not tawdry banter!"

Their laughter faded.

Embarrassment seared his gut. He rubbed the back of his neck, shot his men a wry smile. "We are all tired and the stakes are high."

Rónán's shrewd gaze held his. "Lady Gwendolyn is a lass to admire."

"Aye," Cailin agreed.

Soft voices sounded from beyond the chamber.

Rónán placed his finger to his lips, crept over, cracked open the door. With a quiet push, he shut the entry, returned. "'Twas naught but knights walking past."

"Were you able to see how many ships are in the fleet?" Cailin asked.

"Nay," Aiden replied, thankful his men hadn't pressed about his feelings toward Gwendolyn. "By the number of masts I discerned through the fog, 'tis a sizable force. If the ships are filled with soldiers, which I suspect as I saw warriors in the galleys closest to shore, there could be several thousand troops."

"God's blade!" Cailin hissed. "A contingent of such enormity marching east would not only divide King Robert's men but leave his forces without access to reinforcements."

Aiden grimaced. "Aye. Another reason 'tis imperative to discover the Englishmen's intent."

"What will you tell the lass?" Rónán asked.

The intensity, sincerity, and passion that had simmered within her pewter-gray eyes as they'd spoken throughout the night flickered in his mind. However unwanted, they'd forged a fragile bond. Nor could he forget how once the revelers outside her chamber had dispersed, she'd procured fresh sheets while he'd destroyed the bloodstained ones.

He smothered the blistering rush of need at her remembered scent entangled in the bedsheets, how he'd crumpled the linen between his hands in a pathetic attempt to crush the desire smoldering inside.

"When the time comes," Aiden said, "I will deal with Lady Gwendolyn. If the Englishmen are here to join forces with Comyn, we must stall their departure."

Cailin grunted. "The bastards are not likely to stay put."

A wry smile curved Aiden's mouth. "Mayhap they will."

Rónán stared at him as if he had two heads. "Are you daft? There is bloody little you can do to prevent thousands of troops from marching east to confront our king."

"If they are here to support Comyn, a move I believe the Earl of Balfour played a part in arranging, then there is a way." Impatience whipped through Aiden, and he began to pace. At the hearth, he paused, turned. "I shall explain to whoever commands the English that King Robert's troops are on the move and headed toward an unexpected position. That Lord Comyn has relayed, through me, a request for them to remain here. Once Comyn has the Bruce's location, he will lead a force here to plan an attack against Scotland's king."

Rónán grunted. "You think Lord Balfour's arrival was a strategic maneuver?"

"Indeed," Aiden replied. "The marriage strengthens Comyn's power, positions a noble skilled in the ways of battle to unite with the English."

"Given Lord Balfour's fierce loyalty to Comyn," Cailin said, "the tactic makes sense."

A frown lined Rónán's brow as he glanced from one man to the other. "Except the earl didna carry a missive for the English."

Aiden gave a slow nod. "Easily remedied, my friend. Given the sensitivity of the mission, I will explain that Comyn ordered all plans to be passed only through word of mouth."

"Which blasted makes sense." Cailin walked to the window, looked out, turned. "How long do you think you can keep them here?"

"A fortnight, mayhap more. Long enough for the Bruce to gather his forces and make a retaliatory plan." Aiden glanced at Rónán. "I have changed my mind. I canna risk something going wrong and our sovereign being uninformed. Leave now."

The Templar nodded.

Voices in the corridor grew louder. A knock sounded at the door. "Lord Balfour, the guards you requested are ready."

"'Tis Sir Pieres," Aiden whispered. "My thanks," he called out." He met each of his men's gazes. "Stay alert. God help us if we fail."

* * * *

Hours later, the details of his meeting with the English pouring through his mind, Aiden entered Gwendolyn's chamber. A fire blazed in the hearth, spilling wavering shadows along the walls and the arched beams overhead, much like the anger now fracturing his calm.

He shoved the door closed. God's sword, the situation was worse than they'd believed. He strode to the small table, poured a glass of wine, and downed the drink in one gulp.

Two short raps sounded at the entry.

With a muttered curse, he shoved the goblet aside, strode over, jerked open the door.

Cailin hurried inside. "Before you ask, the serving maid informed me you were here. As for your wife, she is in the bailey."

Fresh rushes swirled on the floor as Aiden closed the entry with a firm snap. "Good."

"Do you think anyone aboard ship recognized you?" the Templar asked.

"After the many countries I have traveled through, I worried that might happen, but I dinna believe so, but I canna risk further contact with the English crew." Aiden paused. "Rónán?"

"Is safely away." Cailin gave a dry smile. "I returned with four rabbits. Not much, but 'twill squelch any suspicions of my departure's intent."

"Did anyone question Rónán's absence?"

His friend shook his head. "With the servants busy preparing for the incoming Englishmen, I doubt whether anyone noticed he did not return."

"Still, if anyone inquires," Aiden said, refusing to take any chances, "inform them Rónán pursues a stag in the forest."

"I will."

A slow pounding throbbed in his head, and Aiden poured two goblets of wine. He handed one to his friend. "The English force is led by the Duke of Northbyrn."

The Templar muttered a curse. "I have heard of him. A nasty lot."

"Brutal on the battlefield but a shrewd warrior, and a prudent choice to lead a force against the Bruce," Aiden said. "Last spring he came close to routing King Robert west of here. Our sovereign willna be pleased to learn his nemesis has returned to Scottish soil, more so leading over five thousand well-armed men."

Cailin's fingers whitened on his goblet. "Over five thousand. God's blade, the Bruce will be angry."

"He will." Aiden swirled the ruby liquid, took a sip. "Besides being armed with the finest weaponry, the duke bragged that they carry enough supplies to build several trebuchets."

His friend's face paled. "How did he respond to the supposed instructions from Comyn to remain at the castle until he arrives?"

"He was livid. But"—amusement lifted Aiden's lips—"the plan we discussed earlier worked well. I was able to convince his grace that Lord Comyn must confirm the Bruce's position, as well as investigate rumors of Welsh archers joining the king's forces before he makes any plans to attack."

"Superb." Cailin paused. "What have you told Lady Gwendolyn concerning the English?"

"That once Comyn has completed his inquiry on the Bruce's activities, he would travel here to meet with them."

"And her reaction?"

"Surprise, as you might expect, which shifted to concern when I explained that the Duke of Northbyrn and his nobles would be residing at Latharn Castle until Comyn's arrival."

Cailin lifted his goblet in a toast. "In the meantime, an attack will come, except 'twill be the Bruce storming this stronghold." He lowered the cup. "What will happen to the lass?"

"Before the assault, I will ensure she and those loyal to her are hidden to keep them safe."

Cailin grunted. "Is there such a place when a castle is under siege?"

A twisting wrenched Aiden's gut. In the heat of battle, even the best laid plans could go awry. "With the size of this fortress, I am confident secret passageways exist for such situations." He prayed he was right.

"How are you going to convince the lass to divulge such information?" Calin asked.

The slow pounding in Aiden's head built. "A challenge, to be sure." He downed the remainder of his wine, set the goblet on the table with an exasperated hiss. "Mayhap 'tis prudent to beseech the king to consider another tactic."

Cailin frowned. "Such as?"

Aiden rubbed his thumb against his temple, irritated by his concern for her. Blast it, what happened to Gwendolyn was never supposed to matter.

He stilled as an idea came to mind. "Our initial plan to collect information on the stronghold still stands."

His friend gave a slow nod.

"However, against the duke's sizable force, instead of allowing the English to remain here, I will wait a sennight, then craft a supposed missive from Comyn, requesting their presence. 'Twill lure the men away and prevent the English from using the stronghold as a defense, and Latharn Castle, along with her people, will be spared."

Calin nodded. "A logical solution." He downed the remaining drink, set his empty goblet on the table. "I will pass your recommendations to King Robert. Once our sovereign has decided on a strategy, I will return with further direction."

A heavy weight settled in Aiden's chest as he glanced toward the window. He walked there, unhinged the panes, shoved. Sunlight illuminated the land, the shimmer of golden rays glistening upon the breakers as far as he could see.

On a sigh, he turned. "Leave now, my friend. You will need every hour of daylight."

"Aye," Cailin replied.

Aiden clasped his hand. "Godspeed."

The Templar strode across the chamber, pausing at the door. "Take care of the lass. She is, after all, your wife." With a chuckle, he slipped into the corridor.

Shouts and the clash of blades from arms practice echoed from the bailey.

Aiden glanced at the combatants. His plans to manipulate the duke and his men was critical to King Robert's intention to unite Scotland. Nor did he take lightly that Gwendolyn was an unknowing pawn in this deadly game.

Hooves clattered from below.

Astride his bay, Cailin glanced toward the tower. His gaze met Aiden's a moment before he cantered beneath the gatehouse.

Aiden made the sign of the cross and prayed his friend reached the Bruce in time.

Worries of the upcoming meeting with the duke and his knights weighing heavily on his mind, Aiden gathered the few belongings he'd left there the previous night, crossed the room, and tugged open the door. He stilled.

Paces away, her face flushed, stood his wife.

* * * *

Her pulse racing, Gwendolyn lowered the blankets in her arms and stared at the stranger she'd wed. A man who confused and tormented her, a noble at odds with the warrior Sir Pieres had described.

Except there was no denying that, due to her husband's involvement, an invading force had moved into her castle.

Her knees weakened by his commanding presence, how he dwarfed the space around him, leaving little room to put much-needed distance between them, confines that in the dark of the night left the setting too intimate.

"My lord husband. The Englishmen from the ships have filled all the available chambers."

"Which means…?"

She frowned, irritated to have to explain the obvious. "This morning, in preparation for Lord Comyn's arrival, I readied the chamber I had promised you for him."

"Your point?" he pressed.

The words scraped her throat, his formidable presence piling atop her omission like a weight as she glanced at the few items in his arms. "Regardless of both our wishes, your other possessions have been moved into my chamber for the duration of his stay."

For a moment he did not speak, though his eyes flared with unreadable heat. "I see."

To Hades with him for being able to intimidate her. 'Twas her home. More important, there were bigger issues to deal with, those that involved her people. "Our food stores are inadequate for the additional men."

With a shrug, Bróccín placed the contents in his arms atop the remainder of his belongings, then walked to the window and leaned against the frame. He glanced out for a long moment, then faced her. "I will lead a hunt."

She forced her frustration aside. Her husband wasn't from this locale, nor had he time to review the ledgers to understand the seriousness the extra mouths presented.

"Due to the years of war, much of the wildlife and crops are depleted. The few homes still standing have long since been raided, leaving little for those who remain."

Bitterness iced his gaze as he shoved away from the window. A pace away, he paused. "There is naught fair in war. 'Tis a violent clash for power. Few win in their lethal quest, for the path to victory is riddled with the bodies of the innocent."

His impassioned words cut through her. Shaken, she fought to refocus her thoughts. Any belief she carried of his indifference to the carnage spawned in battle dissolved on her blistering breath and further chipped away at the wall she'd built around her heart.

Fighting to control the riot of emotions, she walked to the chest. Hand trembling, she flipped open the top, dumped the blankets inside, and then secured the top. She turned. "Earlier this morning, I sent out several fishermen. Their catch will add to whatever game you and the men return with."

Her husband nodded. "Sir Cailin returned a short while ago with several rabbits."

"I thank you." Swallowing, she lifted her chin. "I am surprised you didna mention the duke's coming arrival at our first meeting."

"Why?" he asked, his brow raising as if with a careless afterthought. "The Englishman's arrival or that of his force has naught to do with you."

The arrogant ass! "When my home is infiltrated by the *English*," she growled, "by men who will deplete our already strained resources, and possibly pose a threat to those I protect, it has *everything* to do with me."

Irritation darkened his gaze. "The time the English will remain at the stronghold will be brief."

How dare he dismiss her concerns? "They are here *now!*"

Hard eyes held hers. "You dinna like the English?"

"I am loyal to my liege lord," she said, her voice unapologetic, "a Scot. But I struggle to condone the presence of warriors in my home who are loyal to a king who seeks to claim Scotland as his own."

"The Hammer of the Scots is dead," her husband said with soft precision as he watched her. "His son isna a man driven to war, to collect lands or power for his own vain purposes."

She scoffed. "Yet Edward of Caernarfon sends troops to my castle. Why?" she asked, her voice rising. "To kill Scots in the guise of aiding Lord Comyn in his bid to bring King Robert to heel."

"'Tis traitorous words," her husband softly warned.

Fear curled through her. Aware she took a great risk, she couldn't help but speak her mind about a king who'd so far proven untrustworthy. "However loyal I am to Lord Comyn, I canna trust England's sovereign."

Silence fell between them.

She awaited his displeasure, the roar of a threat.

Instead, the hard lines of the earl's mouth relaxed. Without warning, the moment shifted, and his gaze darkened with awareness. "'Twould seem you are as courageous as you are beautiful."

At the appreciation stroking his words, heat slid through her. Floundering at the flare of desire, and needing to shift to safer ground, Gwendolyn touched the cross hanging at her neck. "I have been known to speak my mind."

Her husband folded his arms across his massive chest. Genuine amusement flickered over his handsome features. "A trait I have noticed."

Warmth crept up her neck as her gaze lingered on his muscles, noticing the raven-black hair on his chest peeking from beneath his tunic. Her fingers bit into the cross as she fought to smother the scorching sensations unlike anything she'd ever experienced.

Blast this man to Hades and back. She focused on their conversation, however dangerous, safer than her body's traitorous yearnings. "Neither will I curb my tongue."

"Nor would I expect such." In a swift movement, he stepped forward and lifted her chin. His fingertips warmed the skin where he touched. "I canna tolerate a weak lass, nor one who blindly follows dictates."

His somber admission swept over her like a caress. This close, she reveled in the mesmerizing depths of his eyes, the dark flecks of gold, sinking further into the emerald warmth reflected back.

He leaned toward her, his scent of man and heat wrapping her within their potent embrace. On a soft gasp, her mouth parted.

His shoulders stiffened. As if scalded, he lowered his arms and strode toward the door.

"W-where are you going?" she stammered as she struggled against her body's traitorous recoil.

"To gather men to hunt," he snapped.

"Bróccín?"

His intense gaze leveled on her.

A tremor ran though her as she remembered his request for an heir. Her breathing grew shallow and warmth swept her cheeks. Gwendolyn cleared her throat. "I… I pray you have good luck."

Eyes narrowed, Bróccín strode across the room, each step stealing the air around her, caging her as if bound. "That isna what you meant to say," he stated, his throaty challenge leaving her further off balance. "Where is your courage now?"

Her pulse slammed in her chest. "I was thinking," she rasped, "that mayhap we can overcome our differences."

Nostrils flaring, he scoffed. "Overcome our differences?" His gaze swept to her mouth, lingered. "Is that what you wish?"

The raw need of his question slashed her defenses. Never had she been so aware of a man. Aye, she'd endured Luke's touch, but never had he ignited such longings.

In stunned realization, she stared at the warrior. For the first time in her life she craved to please a man, to garner his favor.

"Nay," he continued in a sultry burr. "I think what you want between us is far more."

Overwhelmed by her body's intense response to him, she stumbled back. "Nay!" She had to get away from him before she did something foolish—like invite him to her bed.

Eyes dark with heat, he stalked toward her.

* * * *

Aiden's body roared its demand as he caught Gwendolyn's wrists, stroked his thumb across the silkiness of her lower lip. "I think—" He skimmed his mouth atop hers in a soft caress, "that we could—"

"N-nay," she breathed.

He was pleased at the flush pinking her cheeks, by the way her breathing shallowed, and how against her will she'd leaned closer. Her pulse raced beneath his fingers, pleasing him more. Aye, just one kiss, 'twould end the question of how she would taste, allow him to push thoughts of her aside.

He pressed his body against hers and, with slow intent, sealed his mouth over hers. An explosion of feelings blinded him to his cause until he lost himself in her sweet taste.

A low moan rumbled in her throat, and she deepened the kiss, demanded more, igniting a fierce, primal need that shrouded rational thought.

His blood pounding hot, Aiden backed her up against the door, his hands gliding over her curves as his mouth devoured. He shoved aside her garb, needing to touch her, to cup her soft flesh in his hands, to strip her until—

Stunned by his loss of control, Aiden jerked his head back. God's sword, never had a woman made him lose control! He scowled at her mouth, swollen from his kisses, her rumpled garb exposing a hint of her tempting breasts, and her eyes dark with need that seduced him into crossing every line he'd ever drawn.

Damning his weakness, Aiden whirled and strode away, before he did something reckless, like take her.

Chapter 7

Hues of soft golds, purples, and reds shimmered upon the clouds in the western sky, announcing the oncoming night. Pleased with the several deer the hunt had provided, Aiden halted his mount on the rock-strewn knoll and peered at the sea of grass coating the summer-warmed land, Latharn Castle but a speck down the coast.

Sir Pieres drew to a halt on his right. "Is something wrong, my lord?"

My lord. He stifled a grimace at the reminder of his duplicity. "Nay. Take the men and return to the castle. I will follow shortly."

"With King Robert's troops about, 'tis unsafe for you to be without escort."

"If not for a fleet of English troops sitting off shore, I would agree."

A frown creased the stocky knight's brow. "'Tis possible the Bruce's men havena sighted Lord Comyn's reinforcements."

"Scotland's king is one not to be underestimated," Aiden said. "'Tis my belief he has men hidden along the coast to report any unusual activity, and they have already passed the arrival of the English to the Bruce."

"Mayhap the dense fog shielded the fleet from the king's men?" The stalwart knight shrugged. "Regardless, if the Bruce's men havena seen the English ships, with the size of the Duke of Northbyrn's force, 'twill not be long before they do."

"Indeed." Aiden's fingers tightened on the reins. "Leave me."

"I will see you at the meeting with the duke this night." With a nod, the knight nudged his steed to rejoin his men.

A smile curved Aiden's mouth as the hunting party, bearing proof of their day's success, cantered toward the stronghold. Aye, with Rónán and Cailin on their way to inform the Bruce of the English troop's arrival,

King Robert would soon know. A crucial fact Sir Pieres and the Duke of Northbyrn would discover too late.

His smile faded. Far from anxious to return to his enemy's fortress, he stretched in the saddle. Throughout the morning, however much he'd tried to erase thoughts of Gwendolyn's kiss, the sweetness of her mouth lay etched in his mind, her lips designed to lure a man, to invite fantasies that would drive him mad.

Leather reins bit into his palms as Aiden's fingers tightened at memories of her soft moan, and of how her lips had moved beneath his, demanded more. Aye, he remembered, cursed the clarity of the kiss that seeped into his every pore and haunted his every thought.

God's sword, how had he convinced himself that 'twas prudent to touch her? His plan to create distance between them had failed, miserably so. It had taken sheer will to not bed her then. From the desire in her eyes, intimacy she'd wanted as well. As if her wanting him blasted helped anything?

He kicked his steed into a gallop. The thrum of hooves upon the turf wove within the steady breeze as he guided his mount down a well-worn trail. In the distance, swells tumbled ashore to storm the beach with relentless fury. White-tipped swirls smothered rocks, enveloped the jagged shore, and then slid back.

Blast it, he had been attracted to her from the start, and with the way her strength and intelligence intrigued him, he should have considered the possibility that his feelings for the lass would grow.

Over the years as a Templar, he had faced many problems, however difficult, challenges he'd overcome. 'Twould seem Gwendolyn was such a trial. Regardless of the feelings she inspired, she was a temptation he would resist.

Nor could he forget she believed him to be Bróccín MacRaith. Thankfully, the arrival of the English fleet had turned their disaster of a marriage into a boon, one he would use to his advantage.

At least she would never learn of his duplicity. Once the Bruce had seized Latharn Castle, she would receive word that Lord Balfour had died, and never would she see him again.

Aiden guided his steed toward the cliffs. The vastness of the ocean drew him, and he inhaled the salty tang. What if his worries were for naught? Although she'd responded to the kiss, mayhap her actions weren't out of desire but duty? Previously wed, she understood the expectations of marriage. Hadn't she stated as much?

Relief slid through him, and his body relaxed. Gwendolyn hadn't responded to the kiss, nor had he seen desire in her eyes, her reaction only what she believed was required, a prelude to the expected bedding. An intimacy that would never occur.

The error of kissing her he could forgive, but with her believing him to be Lord Balfour, he refused to allow familiarity between them to go further.

A cool breeze battered his face, and he glanced skyward. Dark gray clouds moving in from the west brought the threat of a storm. With a sigh, he glanced toward the fortress. He couldn't linger. Much remained to be done. Meeting with the duke and culling information to pass on to the Bruce. As for the lass…He grunted. With her on edge about the upcoming night, no doubt she would avoid him.

Confidence in his plan restored, and with his men safely on their way to King Robert, Aiden reined his mount toward the stronghold.

* * * *

"Lord Balfour arrives," a guard called from the tower.

Heart pounding, Gwendolyn shifted her gaze past the battlements to where, against the fading ball of sun on the horizon, Bróccín cantered toward the gatehouse. Forcing an expectant look on her face, she tamped down the fear and walked to the turret. However much she wanted to bolt down to the bailey to meet him, she refused to raise suspicion.

Hurried steps echoed from below. Torchlight wavered with violent shadows as an English guard appeared, rushed past.

Thank God he hadn't stopped. Alone, she quickened her pace. Pulse racing, she exited the keep, moved across the sun-dried turf, praying those watching attributed any signs of nervousness were due to her being a new bride anxious for her husband's arrival.

Bróccín cantered beneath the arched stone entry with the confidence of a warrior, his air unapproachable, and his stalwart bearing commanding respect. For the first time since they had met, Gwendolyn found herself grateful for his daunting presence.

He drew his steed to a halt before her. Eyes unreadable, the earl dismounted, handed the reins to an awaiting lad.

Forcing a smile on her face, she rushed forward. "Welcome home, my husband," she said loudly, forcing cheer into her voice. "Put your arms around me as if you welcome my presence," she whispered, "then draw me close as if to kiss me."

His entire body stiffened. "Wh—"

"Do it," she ordered, leaning in.

Green eyes narrowed, then strong hands wrapped around her waist, pulled her flush against him.

Gwendolyn lifted on her toes and pressed her mouth against his. A fraction of a second passed. On a soft groan, his arms tightened, and his mouth claimed her, hot and hard. A shudder ripped through her as his taste, touch, poured through her until her mind blurred.

Until she almost forgot why she had initiated this demonstration.

Almost.

Heart pounding, she broke off the kiss and leaned her head against his shoulder. "That should appear believable," she murmured. "Dinna look around, but cup my chin as if in affection."

He complied.

"We are in grave danger," she whispered. "The duke has seized the castle."

His thumb slid along her lower lip as his gaze covertly skimmed the stronghold and then shifted to her. "Explain."

The calmness of his voice belied the fury blazing in his eyes, an anger that matched her own. "This morning, after I saw to the health of an elder in a nearby crofter's hut, I returned to the keep. As I walked down a corridor, from an open door ahead, I overheard the duke informing one of his nobles that my guards were taken care of and Latharn Castle was now under English control. Worse"—she rasped, damning the tremor in her voice—"he stated that his hosts could now be disposed of."

Bróccín's jaw tightened, and he skimmed his mouth along the curve of her jaw. "Why would he betray Lord Comyn?"

"I canna be sure."

"Thank God you are safe." Her husband lifted her face, his gaze intense. "You should have escaped and then tried to find me."

Though she'd once dreaded his existence, she couldn't help feeling comforted by his presence. "I needed to warn you."

His hands slid down her back, pressed her body fully against his, nor did she miss the flash of heat in his eyes. "What of Sir Pieres and the knights who went on the hunt with me?"

"I met with Sir Pieres in the stables upon his return. In brief, I advised him of the situation and ordered him to leave with the men. I warned, if anyone asked the reason for their departure, to explain they needed to hunt further. But, once out of view, to return and enter through the secret tunnel, hide there, and await further orders."

His brow arched with interest. "A secret tunnel?"

Before she could reply, the entry to the keep thudded open.

On a nervous breath, she stepped back, forced a smile, then tucked strands of hair that had come loose from her braid into place.

A portly man, a scowl darkening his face, waddled toward them.

On a nervous breath, she clasped her hand within Bróccín's. "The Duke of Northbyrn is headed this way," she whispered with urgency.

"Where is the entry to the secret tunnel?" her husband whispered.

"My chamber." Now wasn't the time to hesitate at revealing secrets, especially those he had a right to know.

"Good. Trust me," he said, his eyes holding hers with fierce intent. "Whatever I say to the duke, agree."

"I will," she promised, and for the first time since she had realized the duke had seized her home, had a glimmer of hope that she and her people had a chance of surviving.

* * * *

Jowls sagged on the duke's face, his eyes dark with condescension riveted on Aiden.

Far from intimidated by the arrogance pouring off the noble, Aiden held his hard glare. He'd met his kind before, born into wealth and a formidable title without proving his worth. Aye, the warriors who served him were dutiful, not out of admiration but likely from fear of repercussion if their lord perceived a slight.

The rotund duke halted before them, his well-tailored garb tinged with the stale stench of sweat. "Lord Balfour, you mentioned that once Lord Comyn confirmed the Bruce's latest position, along with his suspicion that Welsh archers had joined his cause, he would travel to Latharn Castle."

"Indeed," Aiden replied.

Coldness flickered in his eyes. "The situation has changed."

Gwendolyn's hand tensed in his, and Aiden gave her fingers a calming squeeze. Aye, 'twould seem the situation had changed because the bastard had seized the castle. Why? With Lord Balfour's well-known loyalty to Comyn, no doubt plans to unite with English forces had been made months before.

Had King Robert's military success across the Highlands forced Edward of Caernarfon's hand to seize control of the remaining critical strongholds loyal to Comyn?

The reasoning made sense.

With the Bruce's tactical strength increasing, Comyn could offer little retaliation to the duke's coup.

But this meant the information Rónán and Cailin rode to deliver to the king was moot. Blast it, he had to warn the Bruce.

"Once we sup," the noble continued, "you and Lady Gwendolyn will join me in the solar. I have important news to impart."

Of that he had no doubt. Nor did Aiden dismiss their fortune in not being arrested on the spot. He owed the blunder to the duke's arrogance. With the stronghold in his control, the bastard was doing naught but toying with them for his own perverse amusement.

"I learned you and Lady Gwendolyn were recently married." The duke's lecherous gaze slid over her with insulting slowness, and his nostrils flared. "If I had a wife of such beauty, I would not have allowed her out of my bedchamber for at least a fortnight."

Well aware the duke baited him, Aiden smothered the urge to drive his dagger into his chest. "'Twould seem, Your Grace," Aiden said, his voice icy. "England's definition of what is proper discussion in the presence of a lady far from meets the standards of Scotland's."

The noble's face reddened.

Before he said something to incite the noble further, Aiden nodded. "As you said, we are just married, and I wish to be with my wife. If you will excuse us." Without awaiting a reply, he led her across the bailey, his hand ready near his blade.

Several paces away, Gwendolyn's gaze narrowed on Aiden. "The cur is fortunate I didna drive my blade into his heart."

"Or mine," Aiden agreed. The bastard would die before he touched her. "We will talk more in your chamber."

In silence they walked, and with each step he noted the changes around the castle. The number of guards posted at the entry, as well as upon the wall walk, had increased. Englishmen carried goods into the castle, along with weapons into the guardhouse.

A short while later, thankful to have reached her chamber without incident, Aiden shut the door behind them, slammed the wooden bar into place.

"Do you think his grace will wait until this evening to arrest us?" she asked, nerves edging her voice.

On a deep breath, he stowed his anger. With the decisions ahead, he needed a clear mind. "I believe so. We must be gone before then." He scanned the chamber. "Where is the entry to the secret chamber?"

She crossed to the wall, pushed aside the chest, and pressed her finger into a hidden indentation in the stone.

A portion of the wall slid open, exposing a black void.

Aiden strode over, the deep, rich scent of sea air from the tunnel strong. "This leads directly to the shore?"

"Aye. It also branches off to several paths beneath the castle."

He nodded. "Tunnels we will use when we return to reclaim the stronghold."

Eyes dark with worry held his. "How? The knights Lord Comyn sent to guard the castle have been killed. We have naught but you, myself, and the handful of knights I sent with Sir Pieres. And the two knights who rode in with you." Her face was pale. "Mary's will, they—"

"Are out hunting," Aiden finished. "I will tell Sir Pieres to warn them not to return."

She gave a shaky nod.

"Once we meet with your guard, I will decide the best course of action. That we still have the element of surprise gives us an advantage. Hurry; gather the few things you must have with you."

As she rushed about the chamber, he grabbed a basket of bread, wine, apples, and cheese, and set them in the tunnel.

Gwendolyn lit a candle. "After I overheard the duke, I used a tunnel that has a concealed exit in the kitchen to hide extra food stores where Sir Pieres and his men will meet us."

"Excellent."

Eyes blazing, she angled her jaw. "'Tis our castle we retake. Whatever I can do to aid our cause, I will!"

Aiden's breath caught as he took in his warrior wife standing strong and fearless beside him, as fierce as any knight. Aye, they would seize Latharn Castle, though for a purpose far from what she believed.

He clasped his dagger's handle, scanned the chamber one last time, his gaze pausing on the bed. Hours before, too aware of Gwendolyn, her taste, the softness of her skin etched in his mind, he'd worried about the night ahead. Now, foolishly, he yearned for the uninterrupted hours lost.

A dangerous thought. Whatever bond they'd built was constructed upon a foundation of deceit.

He must keep his mind on his mission. "We have to hurry."

The candle flickering in her hand, she clutched her bag in the other and looked one final time around the room, as if memorizing it. Eyes filled with determination met his; then she stepped into the tunnel.

Mouth tight, he followed, sealed the entry behind him.

* * * *

Guided by the flicker of flames, Gwendolyn allowed herself a moment of despair as she made her way through the twists and turns of the passageway. Though Bróccín believed they could reclaim the fortress, doubts battled the glimmers of hope.

An ache built in her chest, and she struggled against thoughts of never seeing her home again. The last time she'd seen her father, she'd promised to do whatever was necessary to keep her legacy safe. Now, regardless that she'd wed the noble chosen by Lord Comyn, however fierce a warrior, a real chance existed she would fail.

A drip of water dropped in the blackness ahead, the scent of the sea growing stronger with each step. As she rounded the next turn, the crash of waves echoed in the distance.

"How much farther?" Bróccín's deep voice reverberated in the gloom.

"A short way." On a steadying breath, she stepped down several strategically placed rocks. Behind her, the steady pad of boots sounded, the thrum of confidence in his every step.

What if her husband was wrong and they couldn't recapture her home? She shook her head with disgust at her doubts. When had she become a spineless fool who surrendered at the first sign of adversity? Bróccín was a man of war, one trusted by Comyn to defend her, a man who in the brief time she'd known him had earned her respect.

If he believed they would retake her home, regardless his plan, she would give him her trust.

The faint waver of torchlight illuminated the scarred walls ahead, and through an opening, she caught shadows moving about. Her shoulders sagged with relief. "My men are there." She led her husband into the large chamber. Twenty knights rested near chests filled with blankets and the food she'd left there earlier.

Hand clasping his sword's hilt, Sir Pieres jumped up from a rock cropping. Recognition flickered in his gaze, and he released his weapon. "Thank God you were able to escape. The state of the castle?"

"'Tis under the duke's control," she replied, "except he doesna know we have slipped out."

"A fact he will soon discover when we dinna appear to dine," Bróccín said.

Face grim, Sir Pieres sheathed his blade. "Now what?"

Pride filled her as she gazed upon her husband. "We make plans to retake the castle."

A short while later, as Sir Pieres and his men moved out into the darkness, Gwendolyn's chest tightened at the danger of their mission ahead. "I pray they can recruit enough locals to aid us in our task. With the Bruce having gained control of so much of the Highlands, many have shifted their fealty to him."

Her husband hesitated. "Once we return with reinforcements," he said at last, "we will add whatever men Sir Pieres has found to our ranks. For now, we must warn those faithful to you to burn their fields, then flee."

Bile rose in her throat; she despised the distressing news she would bring her tenants. "My people have endured so much," she rasped, "the thought of asking them to burn crops they have nurtured since the last time troops swept through and devastated their harvest breaks my heart."

A muscle worked in his jaw. "'Tis a necessity to ensure the duke's men canna use them. Once the castle is secure, we will help the tenants to replant their fields and rebuild their homes."

"Aye," she said, sadness weighing her words.

Bróccín picked up a water pouch. "The alarm announcing our escape will soon sound. We need to be long gone before then."

She glanced down the blackened tunnel, angled her jaw. By God, when they returned, they would recapture her home!

Chapter 8

Exhaustion weighing heavy on his mind, Aiden shook the farmer's hand, the elder's weathered face lined with grief but determination as well. "I thank you for your loyalty to Lady Gwendolyn. Move your family to safety. Stay hidden until the castle has been recaptured."

"We will, my lord." The man's gaze softened as it shifted to Gwendolyn. "Take care, my lady. We are thankful, knowing you are protected by such a valiant warrior."

Eyes dark with worry, she squeezed his hand, then stepped back. "Godspeed."

Though her expression remained somber, Aiden caught the tremor of her lips.

The man climbed onto the wagon, sat, then snapped the reins. The swaybacked mare plodded toward the woods, the cart tethered behind her loaded to the brim.

"I pray they are safe," Gwendolyn rasped.

Aiden moved to her side and gave her hand a gentle squeeze. "Away they have a chance. If they had remained, they would have died."

"I know," she said, anger sliding into her voice. "I canna believe Lord Comyn could ever trust the English."

"Why?" he asked, keeping his tone casual.

"It isna important."

Her upset over her liege lord ignited Aiden's hope that he could sway her fealty to the Bruce. "I admitted earlier that I have had doubts concerning Lord Comyn's decisions of late. It wasna as if your words will convince me otherwise."

She slanted him a measuring look. "My concern with my liege lord arises due to his ties to King Edward I. England's former sovereign proved himself over and again a ruler not to trust. From his declaring himself Scotland's overlord after King Alexander's death, to forcing John Balliol to abdicate the throne, and in his final push for power he went to great lengths to ensure Scotland was excommunicated."

Indeed, Aiden silently agreed. A religious exclusion that had allowed King Robert to offer all Knights Templar within his realm impunity, a sanction that no doubt had England's former king turning over in his grave.

"Edward of Caernarfon doesna have his father's drive to conquer," Aiden said.

"Mayhap," she agreed, and withdrew her hand from his. "but he is still king, one who is susceptible to the influence of the powerful nobles advising him. As well, though King Edward I is dead, his father's influence still lingers." Rubbing her brow, Gwendolyn shook her head. "Forgive me; fatigue loosens my tongue. I rarely discuss my feelings on such topics."

Her distrust of England's monarchs pleased him, and he stifled the impulse to share his loyalty. The time would come, but 'twas too soon now. Stepping away, he lit the torches in the hearth, handed her one. "Let us finish."

Lips pressed tight, she nodded.

Once they'd burned the crofter's hut, they ran to the edge of the knee-high oats swaying in the breeze. Bitter remorse ripped through him as he set the fertile crops ablaze.

Sparks flared, caught on the sun-dried stems. A gust breathed life into the fire, nurturing the flames until it consumed the surrounding stalks and raced down the field with lethal intent.

Smoke churned into the sky as the blaze grew, devouring the fields that had held the promise of feeding the family for the winter, a promise lost against the need to keep the harvest from enemy hands.

Aiden cast his torch into the sweltering inferno and glanced back.

Soot smudging Gwendolyn's cheeks, she trailed her tallow-dredged torch across a swath of oats. Flames consumed the leaves. Wiping away tears, she stumbled back, her face forlorn, her steps faltering.

Aiden took her torch, tossed the weapon of destruction into the field. Sparks ignited, then a wavering orange-red grew until only a vague outline remained. Thick clouds of smoke and soot billowed into the late afternoon sky as the fire destroyed all within its path, leaving naught but charred waste.

"I hate the English," she rasped, her rough words dampened by tears. "Damn that Comyn made a pact with the bastards, an act I will never understand, or forgive." Aiden drew her against him, damning the necessity of destroying this field, this home, along with the other crofters' huts. "He is desperate," he said, comprehending too well the decisions of such men, a desperation that had swayed France's king to betray the Knights Templar, men who had protected him for years. "I pray Lord Comyn will one day learn that the Sassenach canna be trusted."

On a sob, Gwendolyn looked skyward. The smoke-smeared rays of sunlight underscoring her dirt- and soot-streaked face, and the grief haunting her eyes.

"This is far from over," he ground out. "We will reclaim Latharn Castle. That I promise!"

Eyes dark with fury met his. "Aye, we will."

He clenched his hand to staunch the urge to sweep back the blond lock lying across her sweat-drenched cheek. Yes, by God, beneath the Bruce's lead he would reclaim the stronghold for this courageous woman.

"We must leave. If the English havena seen the smoke from the fields by now, they will have discovered our absence." Aiden gestured toward a depression on the far horizon, clogged with bushes and downed trees. "Though not deep, 'twill provide adequate cover as we depart."

She nodded.

With long strides, he headed toward the ditch; she followed.

Hours later, though they had long since journeyed beyond the lands surrounding the castle, on foot they had far from traveled a safe distance. Mounted, the English could cover significant ground. Another day, mayhap two, then if they saw no sign of the English, he'd believe they'd escaped. Safe was another matter.

Lord Comyn's men roamed the woods in search of the Bruce and his supporters. God help them if he and Gwendolyn were discovered. She might believe her lord's men were honorable, but too often he'd seen warriors who, with the right incentive, strayed from morality. She was a beautiful woman, a fact that could lure warriors to make vile, lust-filled decisions.

Thunder rumbled overhead. A drop of rain hit his face, then another. Aiden glared at the swirl of angry clouds. God's sword. A storm would complicate everything.

He looked back. Rain splattered the pale curve of her cheek, exhaustion rimmed her eyes, and loose tendrils of hair escaped her braid in disheveled tangles around her shoulders. "We will soon rest."

"I am fine." Gwendolyn stumbled over a wet clump of mud, belying her words.

Far from it, nor with her stubborn attitude would she admit such. In the murky light, Aiden scanned the rocky ground, the dark patches of terrain inundated with shadows. All offered some protection, but not enough to safeguard her. "As you are familiar with the land, is there a place close by where we can hide?"

"Aye, there is a waterfall with a hidden cave about two hours ahead." Her hand trembled as she wiped her brow. "Except 'tis farther south and puts us too close to the Bruce."

Thunder rumbled nearby.

The thrum of rain upon the leaves increased. A gust of wind swept past, and droplets splattered to the earth with a hard slap.

Blast it. However necessary to put more distance between them and the English, he couldn't risk pushing her. "'Tis too far. We must find shelter before it begins to pour." A jagged streak of light illuminated a copse of firs to their right. Thunder slammed in its wake.

He gestured toward the trees. "We will shelter there for the night."

Gwendolyn gave a weary nod.

Soaked by the driving rain, Aiden slipped his hand around her upper arm, pulled her along with him over the rocky terrain, an overwhelming need to protect this woman burning through his veins.

She stumbled, fell against him. "Steady, lass," he whispered. However much he cursed the weather, 'twould slow the English as well as wash away any telltale signs of their passing.

The fresh scent of fir filled the damp air as he shoved aside a large bough. "Climb under." Gwendolyn crawled beneath and he followed, lowering the thick, bristled limb into place to shield them from the storm.

Another slash of lightning streaked across the sky, illuminating the roll of the land. A blast of thunder followed.

Her body shivered against his.

Aiden removed a blanket from his pack and draped it over her shoulders. "Better?"

"I-I thank you."

The patter of rain melded with the howl of the wind as he scraped together the weathered needles below the limbs, shaping them into a soft, level mound.

"What are you doing?"

He wiped off his hands, spread the woven material atop the heap, and then sat back. "Making our stay more comfortable. Until the storm breaks, 'tis best to remain out of sight."

"We have seen no sign of the English."

Despite the hope in her voice, he refused to give her false assurances. "They are out there. After discovering us gone and the crofters' huts and fields burned, they will suspect we have learned their true intention." He spread another blanket atop the one covering the makeshift bed. "Climb under and try to sleep."

Worried eyes held his. "What of you?"

Aiden scanned the murky, storm-fed surroundings. "I will keep guard."

Needles crunched and the scent of pine lifted as she settled into place. She handed him the coverlet he'd placed over her shoulders. "Here, t-'twill offer you protection."

"I thank you." Her teeth chattered, and he frowned. With the storm intensifying and night quickly approaching, it had grown cold. She was drenched and clearly exhausted, a dangerous combination. With a beleaguered sigh, Aiden lifted the makeshift cover, removed his cape, and crawled in next to her.

She gasped. "W-what are you doing?"

Working to ignore her soft body pressed against his, he pulled the cover over them. "The heat of our bodies will keep us warm."

Long seconds passed. She lay stiff against him. "I wish we could start a fire."

"As I do. Even if we had dry tinder, given the circumstances, 'tis unwise."

Lightning flashed overhead. Thunder boomed.

She jumped, and Aiden lay his hand on her shoulder. "'Tis naught but a storm."

"Thunder always makes me nervous," she whispered. Another blast shook the earth, and she caught his hand. On a sharp exhale, she released him. "You must think me foolish."

"Nay."

Another slash of lightning severed the blackened sky; thunder raged around them.

"When I was a child, my father would tell me stories to try to calm me." She exhaled a shaky breath. "He would explain how knights battled in the heavens, the great sounds naught but the warriors' broadswords' clashing."

He arched a brow. "An intriguing tale."

"One of many," she said, the hint of a smile in her words. "My favorite memories are of the walks my father and I would take along the shore. At the last moments of day, when the intricate maze of oranges, reds, and golds faded on the horizon, he would tell me stories of the fey. He explained that sunset was the most magical time of day."

Moved by the love in her words, the tenderness, he swallowed hard. "They are wonderful memories."

"They are. Now," she replied, sadness edging her voice, "when the last rays of light flicker in the sky, I catch myself looking at the horizon and making a wish." She paused, the steady sound of rain against the boughs a somber backdrop. "'Tis foolish, I know."

"Nay. You are fortunate to have had such a loving father."

"I-I miss him so much."

Memories of his four sisters swam into his mind, their laughter, teasing, and that they were fortunate that, like Gwendolyn, he and his siblings had been raised with affection. "'Tis hard to lose those you love."

She settled her head against his shoulder. "What of your father?"

A smile curved his mouth, the steady beat of her heart matching his. He stroked her damp hair. "He was a proud man, one with high expectations."

"Those he shared with his son?"

"Aye," he admitted. "He had plans laid out for me. Yet I chose a different path. You had nay brothers or sisters," he said, shifting the discussion away from painful thoughts of his past. "It must have been lonely."

She shrugged. "I had many friends within the castle. And my father would often take me with him on his travels."

Intrigued, Aiden paused. "Your mother allowed you to go?"

"Aye." She shifted, her warm breath caressing his skin. "Often, she would join us. Do you like to sail?"

"When I was young," he replied, fighting back the crush of memories, the unbearable loss of a family he had loved.

For a moment, she remained silent, and then her hand rested over his chest, where his heartbeat thudded. "What happened to make you despise the sea?"

Wind howled as rain slashed against the branches. Lightning illuminated the sky and thunder shattered around them.

Water droplets slid down Aiden's face, and his mind stumbled back to his twelfth summer, to the crash of waves slamming against the bow with merciless force, and his father's shouts to his family to remain below. Not believing he would ever be harmed, Aiden had slipped away and climbed up the ladder.

A move he regretted to this day.

As he had stepped on the deck, the moans of the ship savaged by the sea merged with the screams of the passengers. The cog had plunged into the next trough. Terrified, he had clung to the ladder as water had rushed over the bow, ripping crates free as the turbulent force flooded the weathered planks.

On a demonic shriek, the ship had angled up. Massive waves of churning white crashed over the side, and several men who had fought to secure the cargo vanished.

Wind screamed past like the howl of death. Once again, the ship dove into the oncoming trough. The wall of water rushing down the deck tore him off the ladder.

He had opened his mouth to scream but gulped seawater instead. Helpless against the brutal flow, he'd been swept overboard. Tossed about in the storm-fed water, by sheer luck he had caught the edge of a plank.

In the darkness, he'd clung to the wood, prayed for help, for any sign of life. Hours had passed, and with each his hope that somehow the cog had survived, that his family had lived, faded. Exhausted, numb from the cold, sometime during the night he had been overcome.

Fractured memories poured through him of being hauled into a fishing vessel, of the sailors prying his fingers from the water soaked board. In those devastating moments, he'd learned that the ship had sunk.

Days had passed, and with them his hopes that his family had somehow escaped a watery death faded. In the end, naught was retrieved except wood strewn along the shore, one plank bearing the ship's name.

Another burst of thunder jerked Aiden from the horrific images of his past. With a shaky hand, he wiped away the water streaming down his face and damned the memory, one he hadn't allowed to surface in years.

"Bróccín?"

"Aye?" he rasped.

"What happened to cause you to despise the sea?" she repeated.

Despise? Too tame a word for his family, who had been torn from his life. A void he'd smothered beneath duty as a Templar, a loss he'd never meant to revisit. Except she'd made him think, made him remember, made him hurt.

"I simply tire of the days of seeing naught but the endless sea and sky," he said, evading the truth. "I yearn to walk on land, to smell something as simple as the scent of grass on the breeze."

She shifted her body to face him, her hand pillowed beneath her cheek. "Did you often accompany your father on his business travels?"

"Aye." The simple answer, one she would expect. "I know you are exhausted. Try to sleep. I will let you know when 'tis time to go."

"And what of you?" she asked on a yawn. "You are as tired as I."

"Once we reach the cave and I have ensured nay one is about, I will rest."

The distant rumble of thunder echoed, and she gave a slow exhale. "I should stay awake with you."

He stroked her cheek, his fingers hesitating below her jaw, aching to lift her mouth to his. A mistake. "Go to sleep." At her silence, he tucked the blanket tighter around them. The pounding of rain ebbed into a steady thrum and, however wrong, Aiden savored her presence. Another mistake; soon his time with Gwendolyn would end.

* * * *

The first rays of dawn cut through the murky sky as voices sounded nearby.

With a silent curse that he'd missed the Englishmen's approach, Aiden pressed his finger over Gwendolyn's mouth. "Dinna move," he whispered. With stealth, he eased up, crouched behind the limb.

Her eyes widened, and she nodded.

Through the branches, thick fog clung to the land. Streams of dawn slipped through the sheen of white, crafting faint outlines of trees and rocks.

A horse whinnied.

He glanced toward the sound.

Hooves clattered upon rock, echoed in the eerie silence. Within the murky swirl, the vague outline of several knights rode into view.

His hand clasping his dagger, Aiden watched as the warriors searched their surroundings with slow efficiency.

"Do you think they have traveled this far?" one of the riders asked, his accent marking him as English.

"Aye," the knight in the lead replied. "His grace believes they are headed to warn Lord Comyn."

"We still do not know if they are traveling by horseback. If so, they could be leagues away."

The leader halted his mount, his body shifting as he took in the landscape. "We will travel farther east. I had hoped to pick up their trail by now, but if they are on foot, last night's storm has washed away any tracks." He kicked his mount forward. "Nor will we give up. If the men ahead of us have seen no sign of their traveling through, I will have them circle back and retrace our steps while we continue on. Whatever it takes, Lord Balfour and his wife willna reach Lord Comyn."

One by one, the Englishman disappeared into the thick fog.

Aiden turned back in time to see Gwendolyn shudder as she stared at the fog-tainted woods. He sheathed his knife. "We are safe." For now. He glanced up. Clear skies hung above the thick shroud of white. "Once the sun begins to rise, the fog will clear."

She scraped her teeth across her bottom lip. "We must reach Lord Comyn posthaste."

"Aye, but 'tis safest to take a more southerly direction, one the English willna expect."

"But that will place us closer to where the Bruce's men are believed to be camped. Do you think 'tis wise to take such a risk?"

"I believe 'twill serve us best. While the duke's men search for us, the Bruce willna be aware we are nearby." At least not until Aiden led her into his camp. "Let us continue to the falls. They will provide adequate shelter this night."

Gwendolyn's eyes, filled with trust, held his; she nodded. "Then we can head northeast to Lord Comyn."

"For now, 'tis crucial to put distance between us and the duke's men." Impatient to tell the Bruce of the English duke's arrival and treacherous plan, he pushed aside the thick boughs that had kept them safe.

Her soft hand touched his arm. "Bróccín…"

Aiden turned.

* * * *

The fierce expression on her husband's face had Gwendolyn lacing her fingers with his. "I wanted to thank you for last night," she said, off balance at how this man made her feel, his gentleness hours before meaning more to her than he could imagine. "For your kindness."

His mouth flattened into a frown. "I did naught but offer protection."

A warrior, he'd view his actions as such. Yet he'd gone beyond the role of protector and had offered her comfort. Why was it that at every turn he wasn't the man she believed him to be? The man she was coming to know cared and had a kind heart.

Before, she'd cursed Lord Comyn's directive to wed the Earl of Balfour. Now, incredibly, for the first time in her life, she was deeply attracted to a man.

Shaken by the way he made her feel, by the desires he evoked, she stared up at her husband, unsure at which moment he had torn down her defenses.

When he offered his hand to help her up, she stood, deliberately pressed her body against his. Embraced by the thick fog, she lifted her gaze.

Green eyes held hers, darkened.

Fingers trembling, she raised her hand to his face, but he caught her wrist. Bróccín slowly lowered her arm, but he did not let go. "Nay," he whispered.

Nay? Her eyes narrowed, but she caught the unsteady pulse at the base of his neck. He wasn't unaffected by her, so why was he pushing her away? Frustrated, she leaned closer.

He stepped back.

Heat washed her cheeks, and she struggled to pull away from him. "Let me go."

"You dinna understand."

The roughness of his voice had her narrowing her gaze. "Then tell me why you dinna want my touch?"

He swallowed hard and looked away, his face taut, as if he was fighting an inner demon.

Hurt, she pulled her hand free, stormed past him. "I see." But she did not. "Come; 'tis unwise to linger."

Chapter 9

Aiden shoved aside a low bough and headed east, too aware of the annoyed woman behind him.

Tell me why you dinna want my touch.

Gwendolyn's anguish-filled question flowed through his mind. Want her touch? God's sword, will alone kept him from hauling her body against his and burying himself deep inside her slick warmth.

'Twas best if she was angry with him, believed he did not want her. He needed as much distance as he could get away from her combination of sorcery, beauty, and grace. Never had a lass scaled his carefully built walls with such ease, a woman, who if he allowed, could become important in his life.

"Hurry your pace," he ordered over his shoulder.

Her unladylike grunt, despite their dangerous circumstances, made his lips quirk.

Throughout the day, he'd used the sun's position to keep them headed southeastward toward the Bruce's camp. Several times, the nearby whinny of horses or knights' calls forced them to hide. Aiden cursed the sinking sun, mocking the fact that they'd far from covered the ground he'd intended.

He pushed through the thick tangle of brush and then continued. The harsh curve of ground angled up, the dense canopy of leaves overhead shielding the sky. They crested the next brae, and he stilled, his breath catching in his chest.

Sunlight cut through the clear skies, shimmering over the rough cut of the Highlands. The colorful blooms framed by the forest and rock swayed in the thick grass, the fragrant rush on the soft afternoon breeze igniting memories of his youth. The sort of summer day he'd enjoyed as a lad.

Gwendolyn halted at his side. "'Tis beautiful."

A lump swelled in his throat as he stared at the stunning landscape, one torn from his childhood. "We should find shelter soon."

"The falls are just beyond the ridge," Gwendolyn said, her voice cool as she pointed ahead.

He nodded. "I—"

A horse snorted nearby.

Blast it! He hauled her to the ground and shoved her forward. "Move under that brush!" She crawled under the dense tangle of branches and leaves; he scrambled in behind her.

Leaves scraped into place, shielding them as several Englishmen cantered into view. Paces away from where they'd stood on the rocks moments before, the riders paused.

"Bedamned, I saw fresh tracks a short distance back," the lead rider growled, whirling his horse in a tight circle. "They must be close." He nodded to the man on his right. "Sir William, ride back. Tell the others to rejoin us as we have picked up their trail."

"Aye." Hooves scraped against rock and turf as the man galloped away.

With a grunt of disgust, the leader again scoured the rough landscape. "Before daylight fades, we will return to where I last saw their trail and then spread out."

"Their moving southeast does not make sense," another man said. "Loyal to Lord Comyn, why would they head toward where we were informed the Bruce is camped?"

Gwendolyn stiffened, and Aiden pressed his finger over his mouth to remain silent.

She nodded, but gray eyes darkened with concern.

"They are not traveling there," the lead rider said, his voice smug. "'Tis but a tactic. They think we will avoid riding too close to King Robert's forces. Before long, they will double back and then travel northeastward toward Lord Comyn's stronghold." He grunted. "The fools believe they will outsmart us, but they will not escape, especially not on foot." He dug his boots into his steed's flanks, and his men fell in behind him as he rode into the dense woods.

Aiden grimaced as the last horse faded from sight.

"We are too close to Scotland's king," she said, nerves edging her voice, "and must turn northeast now."

"'Tis too dangerous, and a move our pursuers expect. Scotland's sovereign is a fair distance ahead, and we can start northeastward long before we reach any sign of his camp."

She gave a shaky nod. "Now what? They know we are on foot, and soon the rest of their contingent will join them."

Blast it, whenever possible he'd kept them traveling over the rocks, but with the ground soft from the rain, the knights had caught sight of impressions from their steps.

He crawled from the cover, helped her to her feet. "We continue to the cave. Walk in my footsteps." He chose firm surfaces when available but damned the delay as several times he was forced to walk back to erase any imprints in the drenched earth.

Aiden wiped the sweat from his brow as they topped the next brae. He glanced down, noted the sheen of perspiration on her face, her mouth grim with determination. However tired, the lass held her own.

The stand of trees around them grew denser, the thick cover overhead embracing them within its cool shadow. He walked on any fallen trees and sticks littered upon the ground, scanning their surroundings for any sign of movement, the glint of steel or scrape of hooves upon stone.

Again, the ground angled up. The churn of water ahead grew, smothering their labored breathing. At the top, the trees fell away.

Below, boulders jammed with brush lining the bank guided the rush of water below. In a violent play of might, the churn of white collided against the rain-swollen banks before plummeting over the ledge.

Above the pool, sunlight collided with the droplets hurled into the air by the pounding water, like the fey caught in a wild dance.

With a sigh, he rubbed the back of his neck, irritated by the errant thought. He wasn't an innocent lad intrigued by stories of the wee folk from the Otherworld. The days of his youth, of time given to thoughts of fancy, were long past.

After a thorough scan to ensure the English weren't about, he worked his way down the steep slope. As his feet hit the soggy earth surrounding the bank, he glanced back.

Gwendolyn moved with caution, choosing her every step with care. She paused, glanced up and met his gaze.

"The cave?" he mouthed against the thundering roar.

She nodded, eased past him.

He caught her sweet scent, and his body tightened with need. Ignoring her effect on him, he kept pace.

Gwendolyn detoured into the dense thicket. Several steps later, she knelt before moss-coated rocks and twigs. A smile tugged at her lips. "Watch." She settled her palms atop the earthen cover, shoved.

Foliage gave way as what had first appeared a solid boulder shifted, exposing an entry.

He crooked his brow. "Clever." He knelt, followed her through the narrow opening, his forehead bumping against the sensuous curve of her derriere. He gritted his teeth, fought to stifle the unwanted surge of heat.

She turned, her body but a hand's breath away. "There are handles inside the cover. If you lift them as you pull, the stone enclosure will settle back in place."

Aiden turned, caught the forged grips, and secured the door. Darkness encased them as he stood, and then his eyes slowly adjusted to the dim light.

The muted rumble of water grew as she led him deeper into the tunnel, the passageway brightening with each step.

After a short distance, they entered a small chamber. In one corner, water roared in a violent spill past a stone opening. The sun's rays glistened off the deluge, casting the cavern in a prism of light.

Gwendolyn walked to where several rocks were shoved together, pushed one against the wall, and then removed a small chest. From inside, she withdrew a candle, flint, and clumps of dried grass. With a deft hand, she struck the iron, and the tinder sparked to life.

Once the candle was lit, she smothered the grass, stored the items, then gestured to a blackened passageway at the back. "'Tis where we will stay until we leave." She paused. "We are protected here. These chambers were designed so that even if we light a fire, it willna be detected from outside."

"Who else knows about this cave?" he asked, impressed.

"Nay one." Flickers of yellow light wavered over the stone walls as she led him into the darkened corridor. "My great-grandfather oversaw the building of this refuge. 'Twas made if ever our family needed to escape. Only I know of its existence, and now you."

"How is that possible?"

"Those who helped craft this sanctuary have long since died."

Aiden nodded. In the future, if ever the need arose, 'twould be a perfect location for the king or the Templars to meet in secret.

The roar of the falls faded to a muted rumble as they stepped inside a large cavern.

Beneath the shimmers of light, he scanned the chamber, amazed to find benches, a table, and several chests within. His gaze lingered on a bed centered along the back wall. His body tightened. Blast it; the last thing he needed to think about was her lush body pressed against his.

"The workmanship is impressive," he forced out.

Pride shone in her eyes. "According to my father, it took more than five years to complete every detail in the original plans. Tunnels were dug to connect several natural chambers, including the passage we used to enter."

My great-grandfather oversaw the building of this refuge.

Oversaw? Not, designed. Something niggled at him as Aiden glanced toward her. "Who devised this cavern?"

A frown wrinkled her brow. "I dinna know, which is odd."

"How so?"

"Throughout the written history of Latharn Castle, the details of my family, every corner of the keep, and additions to our stronghold have been meticulously documented," Gwendolyn explained. "But to my knowledge, there is nay record describing this place."

"That this complex was built as an escape could explain why naught was ever recorded," he suggested.

"I would agree, except that in a family ledger I keep hidden, the secret tunnels above the castle and the hidden chambers below are noted. I have always wondered, why those details and none of this?"

"Hidden chambers?" he asked, remembering those constructed below Avalon Castle, the complex designed and built by the Brotherhood, one now under the control of his friend and fellow Templar, Stephan MacQuistan. He stilled. God's sword, had the Templars played a role in the design of both strongholds? 'Twas unthinkable.

Or was it? Unease crawled up Aiden's spine. Whoever had planned this secret complex had a proficiency held by few. The design was anything but simple, considering the quiet of the room so close to the thunder of the falls, and the intricate craftsmanship of the entry. He'd known several stonemasons accomplished enough to design something of such caliber, all Knights Templar.

The Grand Master was known for his complex planning within the Brotherhood. Nor could Aiden forget another fact known by few: Scotland's king was secretly a Knight Templar.

Before France's sovereign had disclosed his arrest order for the Brotherhood, word of King Philip's nefarious plan had reached the Grand Master. A deed that had unsealed a secret pact, one drafted between Jacques de Molay and King Robert Bruce years before to serve as a haven if ever the Brotherhood was forced to flee.

More important, 'twas Bruce who had ordered Stephan MacQuistan to seize Avalon Castle. Once captured, the stronghold had turned out to have important ties to the Brotherhood.

God's sword, had King Robert sought the capture of Latharn Castle for the same reason? If so, 'twould explain why Robert Bruce had chosen him, Cailin, and Rónán, all Knights Templar, to scope out the fortress in preparation for an attack.

He slanted a hard glance at Gwendolyn, noted she watched him with confused interest. She had stated that Latharn Castle had remained in her family, but she'd also mentioned documentation of every addition to the stronghold had been kept over the years, which was another Templar habit.

Reeling from the prospect, Aiden again looked around. 'Twas not an artless chamber. The detail involved, the years necessary to construct this compound, hinted at more—if one but looked.

He yearned to see whether Latin inscriptions were tucked into discreet locations within this room or passageways within the complex.

"Is something wrong?" she asked.

"Nay," he said, forcing lightness into his words. "Rest. I will make a pallet by the entry and keep guard."

"There is nay need. They willna find us."

If indeed this place had been designed by the Templars, he would agree. Still, with his thoughts in turmoil, his earlier fatigue had faded. He needed time to think, to explore the rest of the cavern alone.

"Through the break in the side of the waterfall," he said, "there is still enough light to keep watch to see if the English have picked up our tracks."

She nodded, lit a second candle, then handed it to him. "You may need this."

"My thanks."

* * * *

Gwendolyn's shoulders sagged with exhaustion as her husband departed. Alone, she withdrew several blankets and smoothed them over the bed. Thankful the rush of water and depth of the room inside the cliff smothered any chance of the scent of smoke being detected, she started a fire. As the tinder caught, flames rose up, offering comforting warmth.

Though summer, the cool dampness of the cavern had her wrapping a blanket around her shoulders. She stared at the flickering light, pondered the many times she and her father had stayed here over the years.

She'd enjoyed their time together, whether on a walk, a hunt, or on their way to a destination. His laughter echoed in her mind, as did his recollections of her mother, and the tender way he'd spoken of the woman she missed with all her heart.

The stories of how her father had wooed his wife drew a smile. Every day he'd brought her mother a gift, each one more special than the one presented the day before. At first, she'd ignored his attempts to catch her interest, but in the end, her father's determination had won her mother over.

One day, she hoped to find the same closeness her parents had enjoyed. How would it feel for a man to want her so much?

On a weary breath, she tugged the blanket up to her chin. For the second time she'd wed for duty, but in this union, though her husband was a stranger, he was becoming a man she could admire.

Except, she grumbled inwardly, for the way he had pushed her aside earlier, when she'd confessed her attraction...a draw even she did not quite comprehend. Though she agreed, the timing had been poor.

The distant rumble of water had her glancing toward the exit illuminated in the flicker of flames where Bróccín had departed a while before.

Guilt edged through her. After helping her tenants flee, setting fire to the homes and fields, they'd spent hours getting away. They were both exhausted.

However much he pushed her away, by the flare of desire in his eyes when he looked at her, he was far from immune to her touch. To be fair, 'twasna desire that had him keeping her at a distance. Given their dangerous surroundings, his decision came from the need for preservation.

Shame filled her. Lured by need, however brief, she'd ignored the danger. On a sigh, she lay several sturdy limbs across the fire. Flames engulfed the dry wood, and she rubbed her hands against the building warmth.

Legs unsteady, she shoved to her feet and retrieved her satchel. She cut wedges of cheese, smoked meat, and bread, then arranged them on a piece of cloth. Gwendolyn filled two cups with wine. Wiping her hands, she headed into the tunnel to invite him back to eat.

But he wasn't at the edge of the waterfall. Surprised, she scanned the area, frowned at the faint light shining from the passageway by which they'd entered. Curious where he'd gone, she headed down the tunnel. As Gwendolyn neared, she paused, watched as Bróccín, on his knees, slowly moved a candle along the forged steel door half-opened at the entrance.

Aware the rush of water would smother her voice, she walked up and tapped him on the shoulder.

At her sudden touch, he whirled, and then his body relaxed as his eyes met hers.

She leaned closer to be heard without having to shout. "What are you searching for?"

Face unreadable, Bróccín lowered the candle. "I was curious as to the design."

Too tired to be intrigued, Gwendolyn glanced back to where water spilled with a ferocious roar. "I have laid out food for us in the cavern."

He shifted. "Return to the chamber and rest. Once the sun has set, I will join you."

She nodded and turned to leave, then hesitated, glancing at him over her shoulder. Guilt had Gwendolyn kneeling beside him. "Earlier, after we climbed out from under the shrub, I shouldna have become upset when you stepped away from me. We were in danger, and..." Heat swept her cheeks. "I was wrong to have wanted to kiss you."

In the wavering of yellow light, intense green eyes locked with hers. "You have naught to apologize for."

"But I—"

"As I stated before," he cut in, his voice solemn, "I willna rush you into my bed. And I agree. With danger about, 'tis unwise to invite intimacy."

She should be pleased by his unexpected understanding. Only too aware of him, she ached for his touch, to lean forward and press her mouth against his.

"Once we recapture Latharn Castle," he continued, his voice devoid of emotion, as if they weren't but a breath apart, "then we can allow our thoughts to turn to the need for an heir."

* * * *

A man's shout had Aiden glancing to the ledge above.

Several knights moved along the bank at the top of the falls.

Blast it, he'd been so shocked by Gwendolyn's innocent words, he had missed the men's approach.

"They have followed us here," Gwendolyn gasped. "How?"

"Persistence," he muttered. With the stakes so high, nor was he surprised.

She gave a sharp inhale. "Look to the left!"

Across the river, several more knights emerged from the dense forest. Moments later, he caught sight of a large contingent riding into view. Several men dismounted, and the others followed suit.

Aiden cursed as soldiers began to set up tents. Candlelight wavered across her face as he slid the entry back into place, muting the roar of the falls. "'Twould seem they are planning to remain here through the night. Is there another way out besides this passage?"

Face pale, she shook her head. "Nay."

Chapter 10

Though Gwendolyn believed that aside from this passage there wasn't another way out, Aiden disagreed. If this cavern had been designed by the Templars, there would be more than one means of escape. For now, though, time to discover more about this cavern did not exist.

"If the English havena left by morning," she said, "we could try to slip out tomorrow night."

He shook his head. "We wouldna get that far. Their leader believes we are close, and he will have posted significant guard around the entire area."

"We dinna have time to sit and wait until they move on," she said, nerves edging her voice. "Lord Comyn must be warned."

"Indeed." Except the warning would be shared with King Robert. Aiden damned the delay. On horseback, by now both Rónán and Cailin had reached their sovereign. God's sword, he must reach the Bruce before he ordered forces to Latharn Castle!

A short while later, the soft crackle of flames filled the silence inside the secluded chamber as Aiden leaned back in a chair of crafted oak. He swallowed another bite of bread, then cast a covert glance toward her.

Heat stormed his body at Gwendolyn's slender frame outlined in the firelight. Pale hair the color of ripened wheat shimmered within the fire's glow, the length spilling over her shoulders taunting, demanding he sink his hands into the silken depths. He silently groaned as his gaze lowered to her soft curves.

Irritation filled him at the draw, that however much he tried, he couldn't erase the memory of their kiss. He glanced at her untouched food. "You need to eat."

"How can I when I fear for those trapped within the castle?"

He tore off another piece of bread. "With the Englishmen's focus on war, I doubt them foolish enough to harm those preparing their meals or tending to the stronghold."

Hope flickered in her gaze. "Is that a common decision by the victor who seizes a fortress?"

"'Tis prudent for anyone in charge to weigh the consequences of his decisions." Aiden chewed the fare, swallowed. "Many who seize a stronghold demand fealty from all within."

"I pray the Duke of Northbyrn will show such leniency."

Despite the hope in her voice, Aiden refused to utter false assurances that her people would remain safe. Too many times, he'd witnessed horrific consequences brought against those loyal to a previous lord.

He refilled her goblet, then pushed the wine toward her. "Drink; 'twill help you relax."

"After our hard travel, you would think I could consider naught but sleep," she said, her voice breaking into a rough whisper, "but in addition to my worry for my people, I am haunted by the devastation on my tenants' faces." Trembling fingers tucked away strands of hair that had fallen on her cheek. "The homes they built, the fields they labored in over the years, all lost."

He refilled his cup. "Scotland must unite under one leader."

Gray eyes darkened.

Aiden smothered the urge to assure her they'd flourish beneath the Bruce's reign. Until the clans united beneath his sovereign, naught would exist but war.

"I fear for my liege lord as well," she said. "Instead of the English joining with him, his forces will be gutted by those to whom he has foolishly given his trust." Her eyes widened. "Mary's will, what if Lord Comyn is killed during the attack?"

"Gwendolyn," Aiden said softly, "there is nay more we can do this night. On the morrow, and with us both rested, we will decide our next move."

Tired lines creased her brow as she set her goblet aside. "You are right." She crossed the chamber, leaned against the timeworn stone and stared out. "What if after everything we canna reclaim my home, and"—tears pooled beneath her lashes—"I have failed my people."

His fingers curled into a fist beneath the ache inside him for her anguish. Time and again she'd proven herself a woman of honor. Instead of her own safety and possessions, her greatest worries were for those who served her.

Humbled by the depth of her caring, moved by this woman any man would be blessed to call his wife, Aiden shoved to his feet and walked over. "Never could you fail them."

Wisps of blond hair framed eyes raw with emotion. "Mayhap," she whispered, "I already have."

"What could you have done?" he demanded, furious she'd blame herself. "'Twasna as if you knew of the Duke of Northbyrn's strategic arrival. Even if you had, believing he was in league with Comyn, when his ships dropped anchor in the bay, you would have allowed the traitor entry into your castle. And," he continued, one palm rising to stop her when she opened her mouth to argue, "what if Comyn had arrived before the English fleet? With the duke having seized your home, do you think King Edward's man would have allowed Comyn to live?"

The little color in her face fled.

On a muttered curse, Aiden brushed away a lone tear glistening on the curve of her cheek, the silkiness of her skin in stark contrast to her fierce will. "However terrible the circumstance, your courage to face the challenges, to press on, astounds me."

Anger glittered in her eyes and she turned away.

Moved by her passion, by the complex woman who made him want beyond what was safe, he caught her shoulders and turned her to face him. "You made the best choices you could!"

She stiffened. "W-What if they are not enough?"

"Blast it, I refuse to allow you to condemn your decisions. Your every action is given with care, goodness, and honor." He released an unsteady breath, and spoke from the heart. "You are the bravest woman I have ever met."

"If I was brave, instead of leaving, I would have confronted the duke and driven my blade through his treacherous heart."

He grunted. "Had you tried, with your guard greatly outnumbered, you would have been captured if not killed."

"Mayhap, but the Sassenach would be dead."

Aiden crossed his arms. "Aye, and another English noble sent by Edward of Caernarfon stepped into his place."

Red sweeping her cheeks, Gwendolyn strode across the chamber, whirled. "I hate war."

"As do I," he agreed, the scrape of blades melding with screams of death of the battles he'd fought over the years still raw in his mind. He stepped toward her. "I despise each day, each life I or my men take, and will thank God once the last sword is sheathed. But to not confront evil or halt the threat is to empower those who wish us dead."

She stared at him a long moment, the struggle for calm in her expression, her acceptance of the pain, and the upheaval of the past few days, easy to read. With a frustrated exhale, she shook her head. "Now what?"

"We finish eating."

She scrutinized him as if performing her own internal evaluation, then a sad smile touched her mouth. "As simple as that?"

Aiden nodded, suppressed the burning ache to cradle her against his chest. "For now, we canna do more. On the morrow once we sneak out, with the duke's men in search of us, 'twill be a dangerous journey. We need all of the rest we can get."

"Then we should finish the fare."

At her sigh, his gaze lowered to her full lips, and her belief that he hadn't liked her kiss sifted through his mind.

Liked?

A colossal understatement.

He wanted, no, he craved her touch. Her soft sweetness beckoned, destroying his hold on logic, on his purpose for being here, and muddling his brain until he wanted to haul Gwendolyn against him and help her forget the atrocities of this day.

His reactions toward Gwendolyn went beyond the usual. Her beauty, her character and courage all appealed to him more than any woman he'd ever met. In this mayhem they were bound, each aching from wounds not yet healed. Yet, however much he wanted, he couldn't pursue a deeper relationship now.

Or ever.

At his silence, she frowned as her eyes searched his. "What is wrong?"

"This, us, I..." Aiden stepped out of reach, the depth of his desire for her shaking him to the core. "Our kiss earlier this day," he breathed, damning his words, yet overwhelmed by the urge to give her something when she'd been stripped of her home, and the life she loved. "You pleased me greatly. However much 'twould be wise, I canna pretend indifference."

A delicate blush crept up her cheeks. "We are nay longer in danger, and hours lay ahead until dawn."

Heat stormed him at thoughts of hauling her to him. Given the situation, a mistake. He started to turn away, but caught the sadness in her eyes. Bedamned, had she not been hurt enough?

On a sharp curse, Aiden closed the distance and cupped her face, damned the warnings blaring in his mind. "We have time, but 'tis sleep we need."

Anguish-filled eyes held his. "With all that has occurred over the past few days, can you rest?"

The torment in her voice twisted his gut. "We must try." His hands not as steady as he would have liked, he willed himself to release her.

"I think this will serve us both better." Before he could move away, her eyes dark with need, she lifted on her toes and pressed her mouth against his.

Her sweet taste poured through him obliterating logic. Aiden fought to think, to remember the reasons why he must keep away from her, failed. On a muttered curse he hauled Gwendolyn against him, filling his hands with her soft curves, tormenting in their lushness. Just a blasted taste, then he would set her aside, no harm done.

Heart pounding, he skimmed his mouth over hers, savoring until his every breath was filled with her. At her moan, he took the kiss deeper.

Gwendolyn slipped her hand beneath his tunic, and he hardened with anticipation as her fingers slid lower, searching, caressing until he burned to have her.

Pulse raging, Aiden backed her against the wall. His breaths coming in sharp rasps, he wrenched down her top filling his hands with her glorious breasts. He skimmed his thumb against their firm tips, leaned down to suckle.

Her body shuddered as he took, nipped her sweet flesh, doubting he'd ever have enough. Lost to all but her, he knelt before her, shoved aside her garb and exposed her to his view.

"You are beautiful," he whispered as he opened her slick folds, leaned forward to taste. Her moan drove him as he took, tasted until her gasps surround him in a heady bliss.

"Bróccín," she cried out as her body shuddered her release.

His mind pounding out its demand, he swept her into his arms and laid her upon the bed. Cool air brushed across his exposed stomach, and he glanced down.

Gwendolyn's sure fingers released the last tie, dipped lower.

God's teeth! He caught her hand before she touched his hard length, and pinned her wrists against the sheets. What in Hades was he doing? Sweat beaded his brow as he dragged in a deep breath, then another, fighting back the need storming him. Blinded by desire, had she stroked him, guilt piled atop his doubts that he would have stopped.

With a muttered curse he fought to rein in his desire. How had he convinced himself that one touch of her would be enough? "We canna do this," he rasped.

Confused eyes dark with desire held his. "But...we are wed. Though you were gracious to offer me time to adjust before we shared a bed"—a sultry smile curved her mouth as she slid her arms around his neck—"I want you now." Gwendolyn skimmed her gaze down his every inch, then lifted her lids, and pinned him beneath scorching intent.

Bloody hell! With but one hand he could strip her naked and fulfill his every fantasy.

Except their marriage was a lie. However much he craved her precious offering, he wasn't the man who she believed him to be.

Aiden damned his own wretched weakness. Once he departed and she received news of Bróccín's death, she'd mourn the loss of another husband.

However much he despised continuing this charade, for the sake of duty, 'twas his only recourse. "I do want you— God's sword, so much it hurts... But"— he pushed to his knees, the ache inside him screaming against unspent lust—"I willna have our first time together be on the floor of a cave. 'Twill be in a real bed, upon silken sheets, with firelight caressing your skin."

Her lips parted on an unsteady breath.

Control eked in slow, pathetic spurts through his veins as he skimmed his hands over curves. "When we make love," he whispered, his teeth nipping along the curve of her jaw, "I will revel in touching you, kissing your every glorious inch for hours. No rush. No worry. No intrusions. Even that willna be enough. We shall remain in our chamber for days," he said as he kissed a path down her neck, her taste threatening to undo his steel will. "When we are not asleep, I will have you over and again until you beg me to cease."

Eyes dark with challenge, Gwendolyn wrapped her fingers around his hardness. "Mayhap 'tis you who will be pleading when I kneel before you and slide my lips over your impressive length."

His eyes crossed as he moaned against her tight hold, striving to smother his body's demands, to not strip her and drive into her heat. "Nor will I be gentle."

Gwendolyn gave a throaty laugh. "I am counting on that, my lord, but"—she skimmed her lips over the curve of his mouth, then began to edge down his body—"I dinna need to wait. We can—"

Merciful God in heaven! On a rough inhale, Aiden flattened his hands against her shoulders. "I have given you little," he growled. Her breathy moan shoving the control he'd worked so hard to rebuild down another notch. "'Tis my wedding gift to you," he said between clenched teeth.

"The waiting will allow us to learn more about the other, increase of our awareness, and give us the ultimate pleasure upon our joining."

Skepticism stared back from a bewitching bewildering pool of gray eyes.

"Give me this," he pressed, her heady scent, taste, eroding his will further. He unwrapped her fingers from his length. God's sword he needed air.

For a long moment she held his gaze.

As if possessing a maddening will of its own, his hardness flexed against her belly. He bit back another groan,

"I agree," she whispered, her eyes alight with mischief. "unless *you* decide otherwise."

Aiden sucked in a sustaining breath, stepped away as he secured his garb. He could do this. He had no other choice.

If they'd met under different conditions, Gwendolyn was a woman whom he'd pursue. Given their circumstance, the graveness of the situation, God's teeth the very reason for his presence here, she was the one thing he could never have.

Now.

Or ever.

* * * *

Gwendolyn stilled, stifling her disappointment. Though she'd lain with a man, never had she experienced the raw desire Bróccín's touch inspired.

She shuddered at the erotic promises he'd whispered, ached at thoughts of how he'd touched her, kissed her until she'd fallen over the edge. Aye, he was right. With the way he made her feel, a night making love with him wouldn't be enough, doubted mere days would sate the feelings he inspired.

A smile touched her lips as she held his gaze. They'd known each other but days. That he could evoke such intense feelings for him in such a brief time was amazing.

Instead of a short-lived burst of intimacy, her magnificent husband offered gallantry. Heat surged through her at thoughts of sharing his bed, but more, a sense of hope, of peace in their years ahead.

Though renowned as a fierce warrior on the battlefield, 'twould seem few knew the man she'd vowed to spend the rest of her life undressing in their bedchamber. However much she wanted him, how could she not savor the thoughtfulness of his request?

She would wait.

With her heart in her throat, and feeling as if never again would her life be the same, Gwendolyn stood, unashamed of her near nakedness. From this day on they would be man and wife, but not the artificial life she'd first believed.

Images of their children flickered in her mind, and her smile grew. Look at her spinning fancies from his simple request. No, 'twas naught simple about what he'd asked. A man did not make the moment of their first joining special unless he wished for their marriage to be more than mere compliance with a noble's dictate.

He'd obviously asked the delay to bed her because he cared.

She trembled at the realization. Overwhelmed by the unexpected gift, for both their sanity, she tugged up her garb. Gwendolyn laid her fingers within his outstretched hand and fought to keep her voice smooth. "Aye, let us finish our meal."

Then they would find their bed, except unlike before, they wouldn't sleep apart. They wouldn't make love, but she hadn't promised to leave him untouched. With the boundaries drawn, heat poured through her at thoughts of the infinitely wicked ways she could tease him.

Throughout the meal, she enjoyed their animated discussion, impressed by his vast travels. With each moment they spent together, she found herself relaxing more, and if only for the few hours ahead, ignored the perils beyond the cave. The morning and the danger ahead would come soon enough.

Nor could she dismiss the underlying current between them, awareness she intended to fuel. Gwendolyn stowed the uneaten food, stood. "I will find my bed now."

Bróccín nodded.

She walked over to the pallet, knelt and turned down the blanket. "Are you not tired?"

"I..."

Embraced by the fire's glow, she saw his hands fist at his sides. Gwendolyn smiled. "Our boundaries are set," she whispered as she loosened the ties of her gown. "'Tis but your warmth I seek."

Jaw tight, on an unsteady breath he remained still. "I—"

She pulled the last tie, nudged the woven cotton into a puddle around her feet. A simple white chemise clung to her curves. Pleasure swept her at the hungry flare in his eyes.

He cleared his throat. "Mayhap us sleeping together isna wise."

Gwendolyn laughed, enjoying herself. "I far from think a simple woman like me is a threat." Gwendolyn slipped beneath the covers, leaned forward until the top of her cleavage threatened to spill out. "Come now, my lord. You are not frightened, are you?"

Lines of strain deepened across his brow. As if a momentous task, Bróccín turned. With his back to her he stripped to his trews.

Warmth slid through her body as she took in the play of his muscles, the hewn perfection, and savored the memory of his hard length within her hand.

Her husband turned. His eyes met hers, narrowed. "I thought you were going to sleep."

"I will," she said, stroking her finger across the generous swell of her breasts. "I was but admiring the way you move, and envisioning how soon you will move inside me."

His throat worked.

Empowered by her affect over him, she edged the blanket lower. "I canna believe nay one has ever told you that you have a fine body, one any woman would want, one I canna wait to—."

"Move over."

Pleased by his brusque manner, she shifted to give him room, but not too much. If she were to suffer in their delay to make love, she would ensure he experienced the same wanting ache. And if in their play he decided to take her, Gwendolyn believed she could find forgiveness for his transgression as well.

Bróccín moved beneath the covers, and then rolled over to lie on his back.

A smile touched her mouth as Gwendolyn shifted so her entire body pressed against his. "Neither of us will be cold this night."

Bróccín grunted, and then tugged up the cover. "Go to sleep."

Her smile grew as she ran her finger along the curve of his arm, resisting a laugh at the sudden tensing of muscle. "At every turn, just when I believe I am starting to understand you, I discover you are not the man I initially thought."

Silence.

"When we first met," she continued, far from dissuaded, "I was put off by your brusqueness, had pegged you as a cold man, uncaring about everything except war."

He remained quiet, but the pulse in his throat raced.

"Now with each passing day," she continued, caressing his broad shoulder, "I find you caring, a man who doesna make decisions in haste." She lingered as she reached his lower back. 'Tis said you are a warrior who inspires devout loyalty. Now," she said, slipping her hand lower, "I understand why."

The cover rustled as he faced her. He clasped her hand within his. "You understand naught."

"I believe I do," she said, "and am surprised the fact makes you uncomfortable."

"You dinna worry me."

"I think," she said as she skimmed her free hand down the lean muscles across his chest, enjoying the play of thick hair upon his taut skin, "that I do."

His brows narrowed as he leaned over and caught her other wrist, leaving him on his elbows but a breath above her. "Good God, lass, go to sleep!"

"Will you dream of me?" she asked in a sultry whisper.

"Nightmares, to be sure," he said, the brusqueness in his voice lost beneath a strained groan. He scowled. "I havena figured out why you intrigue me."

"I do?" she asked, pleased.

"Aye," he said on an exasperated exhale, his expression growing tender. "You are unlike any woman I have ever met."

She shifted closer so her breasts slid across his chest. "How so?"

A muscle worked in his jaw. "Do you plan on badgering me all night?"

Her gaze lowered to where the mat of hair disappeared beneath his trews, the thought of him thrusting her warmth shooting thrills through her body. "If you dinna feel like talking, you could kiss me. Or," she said at his pained look, "you could answer my question."

"Will you go to sleep after?"

"After what, the kiss or your answer?"

He muttered a curse.

Enjoying their banter, she pressed her lips against his neck and nibbled her way down. "That isna an answer," she purred, relishing the salty-sweet taste of him.

"And that," he said, releasing her and shifting to his side, "isna listening."

At the movement, firelight illuminated a Celtic cross design on his opposite shoulder. Pigments of pewter gray and black ink crafted the symbol with jade stones at the end of each tip.

Curled around the upper cross was an emerald dragon of the finest quality she'd ever seen, the wings wrapped around its body like a royal cape, as the head lay resting upon the center of the cross.

His brows narrowed. "What?"

Intrigued, she sat up. "Never have I seen such fine work, or a dragon paired with the church's most powerful symbol."

"'Twas done years ago."

"Where?"

"Far away."

Undeterred by his vague answer or lack of interest, Gwendolyn leaned closer.

"What are you doing?" he snapped.

She glanced to where her breast grazed his chest, and if she leaned but a whisper closer, her lips would be on his. "I wanted to get a closer look."

A hard frown edged across his mouth.

Breathless, she forced her gaze to his shoulder.

Without warning, her husband caught her arms. "God's sword, lie down!"

"If I do, I will find myself distracted," she said, remembering their discussion of moments before. "Is one simple kiss too little to ask?"

He released a frustrated sigh. "Then will you go to sleep?"

"Aye, but this time, you have to kiss me back."

He shot her a dark scowl. "I should ignore your request."

"But you willna," she said, empowered that he hadn't set her away.

"Nay."

Without warning, he shifted, rolling her beneath his powerful body, his hard length pressed against her thigh. The fierceness of his expression delighted her.

"You demand much," he softly warned, "when I have stated my intent."

Far from intimidated, she arched against him, savored the intimate pressure and how his eyes narrowed with a combination of frustration and lust. "Then there is naught to be worried about in our going too far."

"Fine, then," Bróccín hissed. On an oath, his mouth skimmed across her lips, teasing, moving with soft seduction until she moaned. He lifted his head, held her gaze, his own intense. "Say you want me."

Blood pounding hot, excited by his assenting, what she wanted him to do to her this night screaming through her mind, Gwendolyn angled her head to give him greater access. "Aye," she rasped, "I want you."

His mouth covered hers, slow, savoring, as his tongue tangled with hers. As if a prayer answered, his hand cupped her breast and then stroked her nipple until she shuddered.

Like a man possessed, he edged down, took her nipple between his lips, suckled.

Her body on fire, on a moan she tried to rub against his hardness, but he rolled to her side and drew her firmly against him. "What are you doing?"

"You asked for a kiss but you didna say where. 'Tis done. Now go to sleep."

Stunned, she stared at him with anguished need. "You canna kiss me like that and then stop."

"I can and I did." He grunted. "At least we will both suffer this night."

Chapter 11

A shiver swept through Aiden. Wrapped within the tangles of erotic dreams, he reached for the covers. His arm brushed warm flesh.

Through the groggy haze, he forced his eyes open.

Gwendolyn lay against him, her gentle breath feathering his chest.

The muffled roar of the falls sounded in the distance as he struggled against the rightness of this moment, of how natural it felt having her cradled in his arms. Contentment settled in his chest, a peaceful serenity he'd never experienced before. 'Twas like coming home, finding peace, and being wrapped within the miracle of such, of belonging.

He sucked in a deep breath. 'Twas wrong to think of her in any regard other than that of duty. God's sword, last night hadn't he weighed every reason why allowing her close, in any way, was wrong?

On a soft exhale, she shifted and rested her cheek in the crook of his neck.

Heat shot straight to his loins. Her moan of ecstasy as he'd taken her over the edge last night stormed his mind. 'Twould be effortless to awaken her with a kiss, touch her until she arched against him, and then bury himself deep inside her.

On a hard swallow, Aiden eased her head onto the blanket. However tempted, he wouldn't be foolish enough to tread down that dangerous, sensual path.

Last night's teasing her had left a heavy price. For hours he'd feigned sleep, each one enticing him to awaken her to make love.

Within the shimmer of firelight, her thick lashes flickered and then stilled.

An ache built in his chest as he watched her, savoring this unguarded moment before she awoke.

On a quiet sigh, Gwendolyn's lids lifted. Gray sleep-laden eyes met his. Confusion, then a slow smile curved her lips. "Good morning, Bróccín."

Bróccín. Aiden's gut wrenched. "Good morning." With a scowl, he shoved to his feet, dragged on his garb, and then crossed the cavern. He tossed several pieces of wood atop the waning fire, damning his foolish thoughts. "While you break your fast," he growled, "I will look to see if the duke's men have departed."

Silence.

He glanced back.

Confusion and hurt darkened her gaze.

Aiden took a step toward her. On a muttered curse, he turned and strode into the tunnel. Several paces down the passageway, he leaned against the damp, timeworn stone. He dragged in a deep breath, the cool scent of water and earth far from smothering the burn of desire.

God's teeth, they couldn't remain here. Last night had been torment, pure and simple. Wanting her, yet not succumbing to her seduction was tearing him apart.

Aiden pushed from the wall and headed toward the exit. Sunlight drenched him as he pushed aside the disguised entry and then crawled to where he had a clear sight to the side of the falls. He scoured the surroundings.

Naught.

Far from convinced that the entire English force had departed, he crept to the other side of the hillock.

A movement at his side had him glancing over. Gwendolyn. A muscle worked in his jaw as she halted beside him.

"I see nay one," she mouthed.

He worked his way to a higher position, her on his heels, the rumble of water softer now. He paused. "Nor I, but I suspect the duke has left a few of his knights behind to continue their search. Before we go, I need to locate the positions of the remaining guards."

"I will accompany you."

He shook his head. "'Tis too dangerous. Stay inside the cave until I return."

Gray eyes narrowed. "And you decide this because..."

"As your husband 'tis my right," he stated, finding her outrage preferable to the tenderness that made him want.

Her brows narrowed. "When you go, I will be by your side."

Blast her! "You willna defy me."

"Outnumbered and given my skills with a knife and a sword, one would think you would welcome my accompaniment." She angled her chin. "Nor will I remain."

He clenched his fingers, unsure if it was with the need to strangle her for her stubbornness or to pull her against him and kiss her.

Shaken by fierce desire slamming through him, too aware of how at this precise moment he was on dangerous ground, Aiden leaned toward her with a fierce scowl. "You will accompany me. If for naught else, to save the time 'twould take to return for you."

"How noble," she said, her voice dry.

Jaw tight, he moved back, aware if she touched him now, asked him to make love, he would likely be unable to deny the blaze burning between them.

"I will retrieve the few supplies we will need." Gwendolyn stormed off.

Aiden rubbed the back of his neck. That had gone blasted well. Aye, her temper should help keep his mind on his mission, where it should have remained from the start.

A short while later, she returned.

The rumble of water roared around them as they slipped into the dense cover. Aiden held up his hand. Alone, he crept to the ledge above, peered through the clutter of brush, rocks, and grass.

A small contingent of men was camped on the opposite side of the clearing.

Aiden climbed down to where Gwendolyn was hidden.

"Did you see anyone?"

"Aye. They are some way back from the falls, the reason we didna spot them from below."

Gwendolyn's face paled. "We must find a way past them and reach Lord Comyn."

"'Tis too dangerous to chance our course now. For now, 'tis safest to continue southeast and follow the river."

After a brief hesitation, she nodded.

The tension in his body eased a bit. "If you see anything as we travel, tell me." After glancing at the morning sun to get his bearings, he started down the incline. As before, he kept to the rocks whenever possible.

Masculine voices sounded ahead.

Aiden waved her to follow him behind a dense fir. Squatting, he caught his breath as he parted the needled boughs. Ahead, a sizable force was riding along the bank.

"They are too close to the river for us to sneak past," Gwendolyn whispered.

"Aye. We must go inland and then farther south." A move that would suit his plans even better.

"But we overheard the duke's man say King Robert's camp isna far."

"Trust me, all will be well." For the Bruce, aye. As for Gwendolyn's attitude toward him once she learned the truth, that was another matter.

Though her eyes had darkened with worry, she nodded. "I trust you with my life."

Guilt welled within him. However much he despised the thought of breaking her faith in him, of never seeing her again, he would find comfort in knowing the Bruce would ensure that she was well cared for.

Before he muddled his mind further with dangerous thoughts of her, Aiden refocused on their escape.

A warm breeze rustled the leaves overhead at midday as he halted beneath an overhang of rock shielded by trees. "We will rest here to eat. Though we havena seen English troops since this morning, we must be careful."

* * * *

Stifling a groan at her sore muscles, Gwendolyn settled on a smooth stone, appreciating the sun's warmth. She unpacked a loaf of bread and cheese, sliced off a wedge of each, and then handed him both. After taking a portion for herself, she stowed the fare.

Clouds slid over the sun, enshrouding the earth within a murky gloom.

She grimaced against the doubts creeping through her resolve. Was the loss of her father, as Latharn Castle, the death knell of the way of life she loved?

Gwendolyn glanced at Bróccín. Hope blossomed, and a small smile creased her lips. No, all hadn't gone awry. In the mayhem, he had promised to reclaim her home. How he'd tried to dismiss her help this morning smothered the warmth, a potent reminder of how little she knew about him.

"What are you thinking?" he asked.

She took a bite of bread layered with cheese, swallowed. "After wanting me to hide within the cave like a foolish lass, I find it odd you would think me capable of thought."

Green eyes narrowed. "My intention was to keep you safe. When I tell you to do something, I expect you to obey."

She stiffened. "I am not one of your men to order about."

"Nay," Bróccín said, his gaze sliding along her curves, lingering before lifting to again meet hers. He gave a rough breath with a decidedly disgruntled male look. "That you are not."

The appreciation in his voice caught her off guard, more so the tinge of regret. Confused, she watched his throat work as he swallowed a bite of bread. Memories of last night, of how she'd shuddered beneath his touch, returned tenfold.

Aye, he wanted her, but after their confrontation this morning, 'twould seem his logic did not extend beyond intimacy. How had she misjudged him to such a degree?

Or had she?

The cold warrior this morning was the arrogant earl she had first met

So, who was the man last night, the one who had left her body burning with need, the one who, if he hadn't stepped away, she would have given herself to without hesitation?

Nay, they were one and the same. Between her unwanted marriage, her home being seized by the English, and with them desperate to reach Lord Comyn, 'twas her mind that had twisted her thoughts into believing more existed between them.

A rueful laugh threatened to escape her. If naught else, their desire for the other put them on an even plane. Despite their situation, her body still responded to his potent masculinity.

Gwendolyn again searched their surroundings. Though most of the duke's contingent had moved on, she and Bróccín were still in danger. Neither had a night's sleep given either of them the rest they needed.

She grimaced. A night's sleep? Far from it. She'd dozed a bit. After he'd taken her over the edge with his touch, and with the memories of how right his body had felt pressed intimately against her, how could she have slept?

"With the Bruce raising forces to overwhelm Lord Comyn," she asked, shifting the topic to safer ground, "do you think Scotland will ever find peace?"

Her husband wiped his hands, lifted the water pouch. "'Tis a possibility."

Mayhap, but she heard the tension in his voice. Like her, he had doubts.

He took a long drink, then offered her the pouch.

"Nay, I have drunk enough." A slow pounding started in her head. She closed her eyes and focused on the sun's warmth falling across her face. Her thoughts wandered back to soothing memories of walks along the beach, of listening to the waves tumble ashore. How she yearned to feel the slide of sand between her toes, to run into an oncoming swell and dive beneath, and, if only for a moment, to lose herself within the rolls of white.

"Come," her husband said, severing her thoughts, his voice sharp, "'tis time to go. The clouds grow dark; a storm is coming."

With regret and slight resignation, she stood, reminding herself of all that was at stake.

* * * *

Rain pelted Aiden, and he pushed branches aside to allow Gwendolyn to pass, as he had for the last several hours. "I intended to travel farther before we stopped for the night," he said over his shoulder, "but we must find cover before it grows dark."

"If only the English hadna blocked our path," she said, a little breathless as she followed, "we wouldna have had to go even farther south before turning east to follow the river."

Nor had that been their only brush with the enemy as they'd traveled. Several times, they'd spotted small contingents of English knights, their aggressive search in the foul weather a testament to the duke's determination to catch them before they reached Lord Comyn.

Another gust of wind howled through the trees. Rain stinging his skin, Aiden glanced back, proud of how she had followed without complaint.

Blond hair clung to her wet face and smears of dirt shadowed the dark circles beneath her eyes. Mouth tight, she pushed on. However strong she tried to appear, he'd seen her stumble earlier, and tiredness was reflected in her eyes. He wouldn't push her much farther.

As he reached the next brae, the pounding water of the swollen river surged past. He searched the bank for a safe crossing, scowled.

The raging water collided against the lash of grass and rocks as it hauled limbs and small trees within the strangled rush.

Wiping her brow, she glanced at him. "I see no place to safely cross."

"Nor I. We will find something ahead." Frustrated, he started down the incline, half-slipping with each step. "Take care," he called back, "'tis treacherous."

The cool slap of rain filled the air as they followed the bank. Around the next curve, he halted.

White water churned around rocks and slammed against a fallen tree, mired in the river, long since dead.

He pointed toward the weathered trunk extending over halfway across the powerful torrent. "Once across," Aiden said, "we will stop for the night."

She nodded.

Rain slid down her face, her sodden clothes clinging to her slender frame, but to him she had never looked more beautiful. Aching to reach out and draw her against him, he trudged forward, prayed that the downpour had washed away their trail before any of the Englishmen rode past.

As they neared the roots of the downed tree, he frowned at the violent swirl of water. 'Twas stronger than it had appeared from above. "'Tis still too dangerous." Aiden smothered his frustration, pushed on.

A short distance ahead, the roar of water grew. Aiden stepped up on a thick slab.

Gwendolyn moved to his side, gasped. "A waterfall."

Another delay. "A small one. At least," he said as he slanted a look toward the sky, "the clouds are thinning. Mayhap we will see a bit of sun this day."

A weary smile creased her mouth. "I doubt 'twill be enough to dry our clothes."

"We can hope." He climbed down the bank, reached up to take her hand.

"There!" a man's deep voice boomed.

Aiden whirled.

On a distant knoll, one of several mounted knights was pointing toward them.

"Run!" Brush slapped his face, cut at his arms as he led her toward the falls. Gasping for breath, at the bottom of the knoll, he glanced back. "Blast it!"

Frantic eyes followed his gaze, widened. "They are going to catch us."

"Nay." He caught her hand. "When I tell you to, jump."

Her face paled. "You want to go over the falls?"

Aiden refused to voice his own doubts; they had little choice. "'Tisna far, and the pool is deep. Once you surface, if we are separated, swim with the current and allow it to carry you downstream. Though on horseback, they canna keep up." He paused, silently cursed. "Can you swim?"

With a wary eye, she studied the white water colliding against the boulders and the half-fallen tree as it rushed down the river. She swallowed hard. "Aye."

Thankful, he exhaled. "Keep your feet together when you hit the water below." Damning his decision, he laced his fingers with hers. "Whatever you do, keep hold of my hand."

Fear flickered in her eyes, but she nodded.

"Jump!"

Together, they leaped.

Mist-driven air rammed down his throat as Aiden flailed his arm to help balance their fall.

A blast of frigid water erupted around them, tore her from his grasp. Fighting panic, the surge of bubbles erasing her from his view, Aiden kicked to the surface. Gulping a deep breath, he scanned the churn of white.

Water splashed as Gwendolyn surfaced nearby.

Angry shouts from above had him glancing up.

Several riders peered down from the rocky ledge they'd stood on moments before.

Bedamned! With several hard strokes, he reached her, hauled her against him. "Are you hurt?"

"Nay," she gasped.

Thank God. "Swim toward the center of the river." The spray from the falls splattered them as they worked in unison to guide themselves into the main flow. "Remember, once the current catches us, dinna fight it, but let it carry you. Use your hands to push yourself away from anything dangerous. Once the banks widen out, the flow will lessen and we can swim to shore."

She nodded.

After two more kicks, the rush of water sucked them in. "Hang on!" Fingers entwined with hers, Aiden matched his strokes with hers as they swam, thankful the deep water kept them well above the rocks.

As they were carried around the bend, Aiden caught the fury on the Englishmen's faces before they disappeared from sight. The rough terrain would buy them distance and time. He prayed both were enough.

Water swirled around them as the current cast them about with ruthless glee. The bank raced past. Muscles burned in his arms as he fought to keep them afloat.

"Look ahead," she shouted.

Amid the roar, plumes of white surged in towering blasts as waves slammed against a large tree jammed in the middle of the flow.

"I am going to try to get hold of a branch as we pass," he yelled. "Once I have a firm hold, climb over the trunk and move to shore. I will be just behind you."

A hand's length away, Aiden grabbed a slick branch, braced himself as Gwendolyn rushed past; her body jerked hard. Water streamed down her pale face as the powerful flow threatened to break his hold. "Wrap your hands around me!" he yelled.

She reached out.

The branch snapped.

* * * *

Gwendolyn screamed as water sucked her under. Fighting the wash of panic, she kicked hard.

Strong hands caught her wrist, dragged her upward. She resurfaced, gasping for air.

Bróccín pulled her against his chest. "Hold on!"

She caught his forearm as they rushed down the torrent.

The greens and browns of the shore streaked past. An unexpected shift in the current threatened to rip her from Bróccín, and he tightened his hold.

By slow degrees, the current weakened. In unison, she swam beside her husband, avoiding the outcrops of rock, limbs and other debris that had fallen prey to the river's merciless bite.

Around the next curve, the bank again narrowed and the current increased.

"Bedamned!" her husband cursed.

Bedraggled hair slapping her face, she followed his gaze. Gasped.

Within the violent swirl, clusters of boulders loomed ahead. Large waves hit the massive rocks, erupting into powerful columns of white.

Bróccín's muscles coiled, and then he shoved her sideways. "Swim hard to the left," he shouted over the roar.

Her body aching and exhaustion weakening her arms, Gwendolyn fought against the tireless churn. An eddy ripped her free and threw her into the violent surge, and with a scream, she was hurled upward.

His hand clamped hard on hers. "Hold on!"

Fighting for each breath as she tried to keep hold, a dip in the flow again tore them apart. "Bróccín!" Flailing to keep afloat, Gwendolyn searched the water for her husband.

Past the white tips of the waves ahead, she gasped in horror. Caught in the water's rage, he was speeding toward several rocks jutting from the river.

"Watch out!" she screamed.

He slammed against the rocks. Shoulders slumped, he bobbed within the batter of waves.

Fighting back terror, pain cramping her muscles, she swam hard toward him.

The current swept them around a corner, with him several lengths ahead.

The banks widened, and the flow flattened until the riotous mayhem of moments before calmed to ripples.

Heart pounding, she caught his arm. Fighting the weight of his sopping clothing, she hauled him against her. His eyes were closed, a deep gash lay across his head, and blood streamed down the side of his face.

"Bróccín!"

He moaned.

Thank God he was still alive. She trod water. "Can you swim?"

Silence.

Her hold tight, she swam toward shore. Gwendolyn's foot hit silt, and she could have wept with relief.

She continued kicking until her toes hit solid ground. Through will alone, she dragged him onto the bank, then collapsed at his side.

Muscles aching, her breaths coming fast, and exhaustion blurring her thoughts, she glanced around, unsure how far they had gone. With the time they had remained in the river and the speed of the current, they should have traveled quite a distance. Given the rough terrain, even on horseback, 'twould take the duke's men hours to reach them, if not a day. Time enough for them to be long gone.

She shoved to her knees. Body trembling, she touched his shoulder. "Bróccín."

Silence.

Gwendolyn smothered the surge of panic and shook his shoulder.

His head lolled to the side, and an ominous stream of red trickled down his pale cheek.

God help her, she needed to stop the bleeding. First, she had to get him out of the open. Pulse racing, she scanned the area. Along the shore, mud-caked grass lay smeared against the earth, outcroppings of rocks ending where thick fir towered before the forest.

Her throat tightened as she stared at the dense swath of trees. On horseback 'twould be a difficult trek. On foot, an even greater challenge.

Legs shaking, she got to her feet and lifted him to a sitting position. Gritting her teeth, she slid her arms beneath his shoulders, tugged him with her as she staggered back.

He slid a hand's width.

Again, she pulled. On the fourth try, her legs gave and she sprawled backward into the muck. As if mocking her efforts, mud-stained droplets rolled down her face.

Tears burned her eyes, but she refused to give up. Bróccín needed her, and after all he'd sacrificed, by God, she'd do whatever it took to take care of him.

With a hard shove, Gwendolyn pushed to her knees. A sense of being watched shivered up her spine, and she glanced around. Stilled.

Across the short clearing, several mounted knights watched her.

Breaths coming fast, she jerked her dagger from its sodden sheath, stood. "Stay back!"

Anger clouded the closest rider's face, a tall, muscled warrior, his long brown hair secured by a leather tie at the nape of his neck. "Move away from him!"

Far from relieved by the Scottish burr, too aware of their proximity in regard to the Bruce's encampment, she searched his garb and the others for a sign of his loyalty.

Naught.

"To whom do you swear fealty?" she demanded.

The daunting knight gaze narrowed on her. "King Robert."

The enemy!

"And you?" the fearsome warrior demanded.

Pulse racing, she fought for calm. There were only three men. If she allowed their leader to come near, she could fight him with her blade, toss the dagger hidden in her boot into the second warrior, and, with luck, grab the third knight's weapon and end his threat. Then, she and Bróccín could use their mounts to escape.

"King Robert," she forced out, the name vile upon her tongue, but to save their lives she would say what she must.

With a grunt, the first knight guided his destrier toward her.

Gwendolyn tightened her grip on her blade.

The fierce man halted his mount.

Mary's will, he was still too far away for her to throw her dagger, nor could she leave Bróccín unprotected. Her *sgian dubh* raised, Gwendolyn moved before her husband.

"Lower your weapon, lass. We willna harm you."

She scoffed. "And I am to believe you?"

"I dinna lie," the warrior ground out.

Dark brows pulled together, and the knight gave her a curt nod.

The squish of mud sounded a moment before strong arms caught her from behind. With ease, her captor ripped her blade free, and then pinned her against his muscled body.

"Release me!" she shouted, twisting against him.

"Cease," her captor warned, his arms tightening around her like bands of steel. "If you continue to try to escape, I will tie you up."

She stilled, furious she hadn't heard him. Nor was she a lackwit. If they bound her hands, 'twould end any chance of escape.

"As Sir Quentin stated," the man holding her continued, "we willna harm you."

Far from trusting the word of her enemy, she remained silent.

Sir Quentin shot her a warning look, dismounted, then knelt beside Bróccín. "Aiden, wake up."

Through a daze of exhaustion and fear, she frowned. Why had he called her husband Aiden? Not that the reason mattered. Once he awoke, their captor would discover he wasna the man he believed. God help them then.

A second man dismounted and joined the first. He pressed a cloth against the cut in Bróccín's head. "'Tis a nasty gash." His gaze went to her with suspicion. "What happened?"

"We were crossing the river and I fell in," she explained, deciding on half-truths until they could escape. "He dove in to save me, but the strong current swept us downstream. A short distance from here, he hit a rock."

"Who you are?" the man she deduced was their leader asked. At her silence, Sir Quentin stood. "I told you, you willna be harmed. On that you have my word."

Unsure what to say, but for an unexplainable reason believing him, she nodded. "His wife."

Astonishment, and something more—humor, perhaps—widened his eyes, and he burst out in laughter.

The surrounding men joined him in his merriment.

She glared at their leader. "I dinna lie."

"Lass," Sir Quentin said, the humor fading, "Sir Aiden MacConnell"— he nodded to the others—"as my men and I, have fought together for many years. Well we know who he is. Though I find myself *extremely* curious to discover why you would claim such when I know for a fact that he isna married."

Coldness rippled through her. They knew Bróccín? Impossible. Whoever the man called Aiden was, his looks must favor her husband's. Nor would she admit more.'Twould bode ill if they learned Balfour was a powerful noble within Lord Comyn's ranks.

At her silence, Sir Quentin exhaled a frustrated sigh. "Until Aiden awakens and explains who you are, you will remain with us."

She swallowed hard.

"I am Sir Quentin," the leader continued, "and these are my men: Sir Torrance, Sir Vide, and Sir David who is holding you."

Gwendolyn gave a curt nod.

"And you are...?" the daunting man asked.

"Sarah," she lied. Without their knowing her or of Bróccín's nobility, when they slipped away, 'twould aid in their escape.

"Sir David will release you," Sir Quentin said, "but first you must swear that you willna try to run." At her hesitation, his thick brows lowered.

Eyeing Sir Torrance carefully tending Bróccín, she gave a slow exhale. "I—"

The soft thud of hooves sounded a moment before a man with a shock of red hair and ice-blue eyes rode into the clearing.

Relief swept her. Sir Cailin, one of the two men who had arrived with Bróccín at Latharn Castle! She looked behind him, expecting to see Sir Rónán and others loyal to Comyn in his wake, men who would save them.

He rode alone, cantering toward the men without fear.

As if he belonged.

Fear edged through her, but she damned the doubts. He was loyal to Bróccín, his fealty was given to Lord Comyn, and—

Cailin's gaze shifted to her, and his eyes widened with shock. He drew his mount to a halt. "Lady Gwendolyn?"

Panic rioted inside. Why had he revealed her real name?

Quentin frowned. "You know her?"

"Aye." Regret flashed in Cailin's eyes. "I am sorry, my lady."

"Sorry?" she asked, further confused by his apology. Why would he... Fury flowed through her as she understood. She glared at the traitor, wishing she had her blade to cut out his black heart. She tried to throw herself forward.

Strong arms tightened around her, preventing her from moving.

"For what," she spat, needing to hear confirmation of his deception, "that you betrayed your friend? Bróccín trusted you and you repaid him by conspiring with the enemy?"

"You are wrong." Cailin muttered a curse. "Lady Gwendolyn, never were you to be involved."

"But I am," she seethed, damning him with her every breath, "and I deserve an explanation."

"You do." Cailin glanced at the first knight. "What has she been told?"

Quentin frowned. "Naught except Aiden's name and that we are loyal to the Bruce. Why?"

On a rough sigh, Cailin rubbed the back of his neck. "Why indeed?"

She scowled at the man she'd believed was her husband's friend, one she, too, had liked.

"His name isna Bróccín," Cailin continued, his voice softening, "but Aiden MacConnell."

Her whole life stilled. "You lie!"

Expression solemn, Cailin shook his head. "Nay."

Pain slashed her heart as the pieces emerged, painting the brutal picture of the truth. She glared down at the man who was her husband. She had wondered about the dichotomy of his character, of how he seemed to be two men at once.

Fury built, roared within her until she trembled with outrage. "And h-he is loyal to the Bruce?"

"Aye."

Like an anvil to her chest, the remembrance of how she and Bróccín had kissed, of how he'd touched her, and how she'd begged him to take her to bed crushed her until she struggled to breathe.

Bróccín?

Nay, Aiden.

A stranger, a man she did not know.

"We were never married?" she hissed, struggling against the ultimate lie, that he'd allowed her to care, and how she'd foolishly given him her trust.

Expression grim, Cailin slowly shook his head. "Nay, my lady, 'twas all a ruse."

Chapter 12

Fury slammed through Gwendolyn, blurring her every thought until rage took on its own life. The entire situation; her betrothed's arrival, their rushed wedding, all based on lies.

Bróccín—

Nay, Aiden.

Had lied.

Had used her for...

Her outrage shoved up another notch against her ultimate humiliation. She was unsure of his exact motives. She had suspicions, but given the way he had helped to destroy the hard-won fragments of the life she'd forged since her father's death, she deserved to know the specific reason.

She scowled at Cailin, a man she'd foolishly believed she could trust, though he had been naught but part of the deception. "Why were you in Latharn Castle," she demanded, "and my marriage to Aiden allowed?"

"An explanation that," Sir Quentin interrupted, "however interested I am to hear, will have to wait. Aiden's injury needs tending, and with Comyn's men about, we must return to camp posthaste."

Eyes dark with concern, Cailin scoured the landscape, nodded.

Fists clenched, she glared at every man. "I hope Comyn's men find us. 'Twould give me immense pleasure to watch them cut out your wretched hearts."

With a sharp tug, Sir David secured a cloth over her mouth and then bound her hands before her waist with rope. He swung into his saddle and hauled her before him.

Seething, Gwendolyn remained silent. Let the fools believe that trussing her up and surrounding her with a contingent of knights would squelch any thoughts of rebellion. 'Twould give her the advantage when she made her move to escape.

She narrowed her gaze as they bound Aiden's gash, then lifted him to lean against Cailin on his mount.

Cailin shot her a frustrated glance. "You will be given dry garb once we reach camp."

With a cool look, she angled her jaw. Like Aiden and Rónán, he'd deceived her. But however inexcusable, Aiden's sin was worse. With his vows uttered to God, he'd crossed a sacred boundary and allowed her, along with those who'd witnessed the event, to believe they were wed. Having given his pledge using Bróccín's name nullified their wedding, their bond of marriage naught but a myth.

She stifled the ache that ripped through her soul.

Mouth tight, Cailin waved the men forward, then kicked his steed into a canter.

Sir David's grip on her firm, he nudged his mount forward.

Twigs snapped beneath the horse's hooves as the men riding in company enveloped her within their protective circle as they rode through the forest.

Each knoll they crested she covertly scoured the surroundings, noted the distance of the stream to the north, the mountains, and other details that would aid her once she was free.

With stealth, Gwendolyn brushed her hand against the dagger that lay hidden beneath her clothing. How much farther until they reached King Robert's camp? She had to escape before then.

A man's shout sounded nearby.

"'Tis Comyn's men," Sir Cailin hissed to the others. "Follow me." He cut hard toward a dense stand of fir.

Through the branches, she glimpsed several of her liege lord's knights in the distance. Her heart slammed in her chest. They were leaving! Using her shoulder, she pushed her gag down.

Sir David grabbed her arm. "Cease!"

She started to twist away, caught sight of the warriors disappearing in the distance. Gwendolyn sagged. Even if she called out now, at this distance, Comyn's men would never hear her. For any chance to escape before they reached the Bruce's camp, she couldn't raise her captors' suspicions further.

The rich scent of pine, the scrape of needled limbs, and the soft thud of hooves filled the air as their steeds pushed between the thick boughs.

Shielded within the dense cover, Sir Cailin waved the men to halt. Face taut, he guided his mount over. "Had you succeeded in alerting Comyn's men," he said, his words ice, "for their gallantry in trying to rescue you, they would have died."

The arrogant toad! "Seasoned knights or not, with you and your warriors outnumbered more than three to one, my liege lord's men would have defeated you with ease."

"I willna discuss the incompetence of Lord Comyn's forces," Cailin said, his voice raw with frustration. "You have naught to fear. I swear to you, you willna be harmed."

She scoffed. "After the lies you have fed me, I should trust you?"

Cailin scowled. "Believe what you will." He nodded to Sir David.

Her captor secured the cloth over her mouth.

However curious, she smothered the temptation to glance toward Aiden. After his carefully crafted lies, he did not deserve her concern.

With a nod, Cailin reined his mount forward; his men followed.

Wind slid through the trees as they wove their way through the dense boughs. Halfway down the incline, they broke free of the shielding limbs. Sir David's hold loosened.

Cailin's mount ahead of them stumbled, and then found firm footing. "'Tis slick with moss," he called to his men.

As her captor's horse stepped onto the soft ground, his mount faltered. Gwendolyn fell forward and caught the steed's mane.

Bent low and blocked from her captor's view, she withdrew her dagger, hid the weapon within the outer folds of her clothing. Silently cheering her success, she sagged back, as if she had succumbed to fatigue.

"Steady, lad," Sir David said to his mount, and then guided him onto firmer ground, while the other riders surrounding them separated to avoid the slippery terrain.

Thankful for the knight's diverted attention, her movements awkward with her hands bound, she carefully positioned the blade, edge up, beneath the knot securing the ties. With each of the horse's steps, the rocking motion brought the rope against the dagger's edge.

The twisted hemp scraped.

She held her breath, waited for her captor to try to seize her weapon.

The warrior continued guiding his destrier through the weave of trees.

Confident the thud of hooves on the rock and moss smothered the steel severing woven hemp, she pressed the rope harder against the dagger.

Several strands frayed.

The tightness on her wrists eased.

A hawk screeched, its wingspan daunting as its majestic shadow rippled across the canopy of leaves overhead.

The ground angled down, and a gust of wind laden with summer heat, the scent of earth, and fir filled the air. Patches of moss littered the slope, increasing until, near the bottom, the spongy growth covered every rock until 'twas hard to distinguish where the stones ended and the grass began. The faint rush of water sounded ahead.

They were riding back toward the river. Why? There could be only one reason. They must be nearing the Bruce's camp.

Fighting a wave of panic, Gwendolyn pressed the rope harder against the blade's edge. After several more slides, the tie fell apart.

Heart pounding, she shoved the binding beneath her clothing, ignored the tingles at her wrists, and kept her hands out of his sight. When they rode near a thicket, she discreetly dropped the bindings.

Gwendolyn secured her blade. Fighting back exhaustion, she scoured the land, searching for anything that could aid her escape.

"Sir Quentin," Sir Cailin called. "Blood has started to seep from Aiden's wound. We will halt in the firs ahead so I can stop the flow."

Still bleeding. Irritated at herself that after his deception she'd still care, Gwendolyn smothered the thought of all he had done to keep her and her people safe. He deserved naught but her condemnation.

Beyond the rich green swath of grass, the churn of the water increased.

She clasped her dagger tight.

Sir David's horse pushed into the thick stand of fir, separating them from the other riders.

Needled branches enveloped them, and she fisted her free hand in the horse's mane.

A large bough loomed ahead.

Pulse racing, Gwendolyn leaned forward, as if ducking below the limb. Once enshrouded within the dense green, she dove toward the moss and needled ground.

With a curse, Sir David caught the edge of her gown. "Halt!"

She jerked back, slammed against his mount's shoulder. Teeth clenched, she twisted, slashed her blade.

Fabric tore.

Gwendolyn tumbled back, landing hard. Ignoring the burst of pain, she scrambled beneath the dense cover and out the other side.

"She has escaped," her captor roared from behind her.

Pine boughs scraped her face as she pushed to her feet, ran. Muttered curses and the muted thud of hooves sounded behind her as she raced toward the rush of water, her muscles screaming with each step.

"I will catch her," Sir David shouted.

Pain cut through her chest and leaves slapped against her as she sprinted toward the water.

Hooves flashed at her side.

She veered around a rock.

Three steps until the bank.

Two.

Highland-fed water spewed around her as she stepped into the rush. She gulped a breath, dove.

Water erupted beside her. The warrior's hand grabbed her shoulder and then pulled her up. Before she could whirl and fight, Sir David had torn her blade free. He cast the dagger into the river.

His brows were slammed into a fierce frown as he wheeled her to face him. "Dinna move." After a brisk search for any other weapons, he carried her to shore, withdrew another thick hemp tie, and this time secured her hands behind her back.

Gasping for breath, she narrowed her gaze. "If you believe this will stop me from escaping, you are wrong."

Sir David lifted her until she was nose-to-nose to him. "And would you be able to use a weapon given another chance?" he demanded. "Feel a blade slice through flesh and watch the life fade from a man's eyes, knowing you could kill someone who may have a family, people who care?"

"For my people, I will do what I must," she snapped, but she could not deny that his words resonated. Fortunately, she hadn't had to make such a decision yet.

With a grunt, as if she were not more than an irritating midge, the warrior tugged her toward his mount, swung up, and then dragged her before him.

"You did not replace the gag. Are you not worried that I will scream?" she challenged.

"There is nay reason," Sir David said with irritating calm. "The Bruce's camp is over the ridge."

Her heart sank, but she remained silent, refused to show fear.

Her captor kicked his mount forward. Moments later, they rode into the swath of pines.

At the scrape of limbs, she saw Aiden's gaze lift and meet hers as Cailin secured his wound.

Emotions and exhaustion warred within, weighted beneath the dreams his betrayal had crushed. She had believed in him, worse, had allowed herself to hope, to fall into the delusion that one day he would come to love her.

The bastard.

Gwendolyn lunged toward him.

Sir David's arm jerked her back.

She glared at Aiden. "I despise you!"

Grief darkened Aiden's gaze, and he winced as he shook his head. "I never meant to hurt you."

Hurt? Too trivial a word to describe the pain tearing through her heart, the devastation of every foolish dream she'd allowed herself to hold dear.

Muddy water plopped onto her sodden clothes as she gulped a breath of pine-rich air, then another, damning how her body had begun to shake. She'd trusted him, believed he'd cared for her, when every step of the way, with his every kiss, with his every intimate touch, he had lied.

She lifted her jaw. "Nay doubt 'twas a boon to watch your enemy's fields' burn. How you must have inwardly rejoiced that we made your mission so much easier."

"Gwendolyn—"

"How dare you speak to me with such familiarity!" she attacked, the memories of his mouth upon hers, of how he had touched her, brought her pleasure, too vivid.

Aiden gave a frustrated sigh. "Once we reach camp, we will talk."

"Save your words for someone who might believe you," she growled. "You have earned naught but my contempt."

A frown deepened Cailin's brow as he finished securing another strip of cloth around Aiden's wound. He glanced toward the man holding her in the saddle. "David, before we go, ensure Lady Gwendolyn has nay other weapons hidden."

"I disarmed her when I caught her." The knight's gaze narrowed on her. "Nor will I underestimate her again."

Pride flickered in Aiden's eyes, faltered to sadness. "A warning I would have given you had I been awake."

"One," Cailin said, "I should have passed to Sir David upon her capture."

She scowled, far from impressed by either man's praise. "A caution men rarely consider when dealing with women."

With a grunt, Cailin mounted his horse.

Aiden clasped his friend's hand and then swung up behind him. He glanced toward her.

Gwendolyn turned away.

Sir David guided his mount into the midst of the knights.

'Twas clear he wouldna risk allowing her any further chance to escape. As they rode over the moss and brush-tangled land, the churn of water grew. A shiver rattled through her as the worry she had fought to keep at bay surged inside.

What would King Robert do when he learned of her capture? Would he order her to a nunnery? Without a holding or coin, would Scotland's monarch abandon her to fend for herself? Or, considering her loyalty to Comyn, would he have her killed?

Please God, let the Bruce think she was worthless to his cause and cast her out. Alone, she could make her way to her liege lord. Given her faithfulness to him over the years, and after her having married the noble he'd ordered...

Her bravado wilted.

Nay, she hadn't married Bróccín MacRaith, Earl of Balfour. Her oath was naught but impious utterings against the sacrament of marriage. No marriage had taken place.

Gwendolyn concentrated on her immediate goal. Somehow, she would sneak past their defenses. More important, regardless the challenges ahead, she would find a way to reclaim Latharn Castle.

* * * *

Men's murmurs from outside the tent mixed with the distant clash of blades of warriors training as Aiden, standing beside his Templar brothers, stared at the Bruce. The king's words moments before left him stunned.

Though he'd considered a Templar connection to Latharn Castle, to find it true was incredible. Nor was that the only news of great import.

Aiden caught Cailin's worried glance before shifting his gaze to the king. "Her father was loyal to you, Sire?" he asked, still working past the shock of the disclosure."

"Aye," the Bruce replied.

"Your Grace," Aiden said, damning the hurt the news would bring her, "Lady Gwendolyn isna aware of her father's fealty to you."

"Due to the Earl of Hadington's role as a spy against Lord Comyn, her father believed 'twas best to keep his daughter ignorant of that fact. After I had united Scotland and once Latharn Castle was safe, he had planned to inform her. Except"—the king's eyes darkened with anger—"he died."

Confused, Aiden frowned. "'Tis not uncommon for men to die in battle, Your Grace."

"If the Earl of Hadington had been killed during combat," the Bruce said, his voice hard, "I would agree!"

Aiden stilled at the revelation, the ramifications immense. "Sire, Lady Gwendolyn was informed her father was killed during a skirmish."

The king grunted. "A lie fed to her by Comyn. Her father died at Comyn's castle. I suspect the Earl of Hadington's loyalty to me was discovered and he was murdered."

God's sword, the news of her liege lord's betrayal would devastate Gwendolyn.

"With the Earl of Hadington's death, after I had subdued Comyn, I had planned to seize Latharn Castle. Except—" The king poured a glass of wine, swirled the ruby liquid in the cup, and then lifted his gaze to Aiden. "I received news Comyn was sending the Earl of Balfour to wed Lady Gwendolyn. With the earl's fierce reputation and strong alliance with Comyn, a union I couldna allow."

"The reason why you chose Cailin, Rónán, and me to assess the castle," Aiden said.

"Aye." The king took a sip of wine. "With the strategic stronghold shielding Templar secrets, I couldna risk anyone but those of the Brotherhood assessing the fortress. Like Avalon Castle, now overseen by Stephan MacQuistan, Earl of Dunsmore, Latharn Castle is one of the few fortresses in Scotland that are critical to the Templars."

Aiden remained silent.

The king took another sip, then set aside his goblet. "Before the Grand Master was arrested, he sent a secret runner with a holy relic to the Earl of Hadington to hide until I could reach the noble. Once I had defeated Comyn, I planned on having the artifact moved to Avalon Castle to be stored with the rest of the Templar valuables. God help us if the Earl of Balfour discovered the treasure belonging to the Brotherhood in the secret chamber."

Curiosity teased Aiden as to exactly what was hidden, but he discarded the thought. The Templars guarded many important treasures. Now, as before, they must ensure whatever the Grand Master had concealed beneath the fortress was kept safe.

"Which brings us back to Latharn Castle." The Bruce nodded to Aiden. "You will lead the assaulting force. Once taken, find the Earl of Hadington's secret ledger. 'Twill hold details of where the hidden tunnels and chambers are located. I will send the Earl of Broc to move the treasure with the other holy relics beneath Avalon."

Aiden nodded. "Aye, Your Grace."

The king leaned back in his chair. "Lady Gwendolyn may know of the ledger's location, which would save you great frustration."

"With her closeness to her father, and with the confidence with which she ran the stronghold," Aiden said, "I suspect she does."

"Information we must discover." The Bruce frowned. "Though I doubt, with her learning of your deception, a fact she would be willing to share with you."

"Though furious and stubborn," Aiden said, refusing to give up hope she would talk to him. Forgiving him was another matter. "She is rational, Sire. I am confident we can come to an agreement in which she will reveal the hidden ledger's location."

King Robert rubbed his jaw. "You speak highly of a woman who at this moment would rather see your head on a pike."

"I speak naught but the truth," Aiden said, damning that, against his intent, she had become important to him. "Lady Gwendolyn is strong-willed and speaks her mind. The lass is passionate about those she cares for, braver than most, and…"

He stilled beneath the intrigued glitter in the king's eyes. Blast it, well he knew of the ruler's affinity for independent women, though his point wasna to express his own interest. His sovereign needed to understand the damage served to her virtuous way of life. "She is innocent of all but trying to defend her home. I ask that you offer her your protection."

The Bruce stared at him a long moment, then dropped his hand to his side. "I will consider your request. Return to your tent. Once I have decided what to do with the lass, I will send for her."

"I thank you, Your Grace." Confident King Robert would ensure Gwendolyn was kept safe, Aiden gave a low bow and then strode out. He pushed away the sense of loss at never seeing her again. 'Twas for the best. Regardless of his feelings for her, she had no place in his life.

In his tent, Aiden paced. Blast it, soon the Bruce would send for Lady Gwendolyn. Despite his assurances to the king, he wanted to speak to her before that meeting. To say what, he wasn't sure. Yet leaving her to the Bruce's decision felt paltry, given all she had experienced and how he had hurt her.

Wincing at his throbbing head, he stood, glanced at Cailin. "I must talk to Gwendolyn."

His friend stepped before him. "I dinna think 'tis a wise decision, my friend."

"Move away."

A muscle worked in Cailin's jaw. "And what will you say to her that will make anything better? 'If the priest hadna been called away that fateful night, I would never have wed you?'"

"'Tis the truth," Aiden snapped, damning the words, sounding pathetic even to him. On a heavy sigh, he rubbed the back of his neck, thankful for the dry clothes, feeling warm for the first time since he had jumped into the river. "I need to try."

"God's teeth," Cailin charged, "think! What will talking to her change? Will it lessen her anger? Make the false wedding not exist?"

Fists clenched, he glared at his friend, the weight of his lies a stain upon his soul. However intimate, at least he hadn't taken the unconscionable step of consummating their farce of a marriage; for that he never could have forgiven himself.

On a rough breath, Aiden shook his head. "Your questions are ones I have asked myself. Yet I need to try."

"You care for her," his friend said, his voice softening, "but the last thing I want to see is for you to make things worse. For you both."

"Ironic, is it not? Over the years, the life of a Templar fulfilled me, a life I was willing to die for. Never did I imagine a time would come when I would find a woman who would make me care. Now," Aiden rasped, his throat tight, "I doubt if I will ever forget her."

"Mayhap if you speak with King Robert about seeking her hand, he will—"

"The war to reclaim Scotland is far from over. Nor do I have anything to offer her."

Cailin frowned. "You are the Earl of Lenox."

"Nay longer," Aiden snapped, cursing the reminder. "After my family died, I returned to Thorburn Castle to find my home seized by the English. Any claim to the stronghold, or my nobility, is long since lost." The throbbing in his head grew. "I can offer Gwendolyn naught but the title of wife to a landless knight." He gave a bitter laugh. "Regardless, after what has transpired, even if I held the rank of duke, she would never welcome me into her life."

Sympathy darkened his friend's gaze. "But you dinna know for sure."

"Her eyes," he whispered, aching at the memory. "God help me, the hurt, the anger. After my betrayal, I deserved both. Though I dinna expect her to forgive me, I must try to explain, and to prepare her for what may come. For her, 'tis far from over."

On an exasperated sigh, his friend glanced at his injury. "How fares your head?"

He skimmed his fingers gingerly across the gash Rónán had sewn. "'Twill heal."

Cailin grimaced. "I am still trying to accept the Templar ties to Latharn Castle."

"I as well. 'Twas astonishing to learn that, like Avalon Castle, Latharn Castle had been designed by the Brotherhood." Aiden paused. "You can imagine my surprise when Gwendolyn informed me of the tunnels and hidden chambers below, more so that her great-grandfather hadna designed but overseen the building of the refuge."

"I was shocked when the Bruce confirmed your suspicion," his friend agreed. He paused. "How will you convince Gwendolyn to tell you where the secret ledger is?"

"I will find a way." A dubious task, considering she despised him, but one that, for his king, he would achieve. Aiden glanced toward her tent, gave a deep sigh. "If I am to succeed on any front, I must speak with Gwendolyn before the king sends for her."

"Go," Cailin said. "I will let you know when the Bruce requests her presence."

"My thanks." Aiden stepped outside, the warmth of the late afternoon sun far from easing the heaviness in his heart.

Birds chirped in the trees, the murmurs of men filled the air, but he focused on her tent.

At his approach, the Knights Templar guarding the shelter nodded. "Aiden."

"Quentin, how does Lady Gwendolyn fare?"

His mouth tightened. "She has said naught."

Blast it. He wished he could turn back time to the day in the cave. If only for a while to savor the way she had watched him with desire, and how foolishly he had wanted more. Aiden pushed aside the canvas.

At the scrape of fabric, she turned. Gray eyes narrowed. "Leave me."

A cold welcome he'd anticipated. In a way, one he had almost hoped for. At least she wasna indifferent. He entered, let the flap fall into place, secluding them from the world.

She turned her back on him.

"I need to explain."

Silence.

Aiden stepped closer. "Cailin, Rónán, and I were sent to study Latharn Castle."

"To gather information?"

At least she'd replied. He would find solace in that. "Aye."

She whirled, her face flushed with anger. "'Tis why King Robert is here, is it not? You and the others were to report to him what you learned so he could devise an attack?"

"Aye. Latharn Castle was to be seized before Lord Comyn learned of the Bruce's intent."

"And what of me? Or," she demanded, "am I naught but chattel to be cast aside?"

"God's sword," he hissed, "you were never supposed to be involved!"

"Odd, given 'twas my home."

He muttered a curse, damned the entire situation. "King Robert will ensure you are well cared for."

"Will he? Oh, aye. I forget that I am to heed your words as you are a man whom I can trust. I assure you," she said, her voice ripe with sarcasm, "you bring me great comfort."

"Gwendolyn—"

She stormed over, thrust her finger against his chest. "How dare you come here, thinking I could care about anything you have to say? Aiden, is it? Or is that today's false name, to be replaced by another tomorrow?"

"You are angry—"

"Angry, nay, furious. You played the role of my husband, touched me, allowed me to..." Her entire body trembled with fury. "You are despicable!"

Aiden's gut tightened. He searched her face for a glimmer of softening, a chance that somewhere in this twisted mess she'd find a sliver of forgiveness.

Failed.

He swallowed hard, wishing he could undo what he had done but doubted a time would ever come when he could repair the damage he had caused her. "I regret the distress you have endured."

Her mouth tightened. "Is Bróccín dead?"

"He is. On my way to your castle, my men and I came across him, mortally wounded."

"So he didna betray Lord Comyn."

"Nay."

Her gaze shrewd, Gwendolyn studied him for a long moment, as if unsure of whether to accept his claim as true. "Why would he trust you with Lord Comyn's betrothal writ?"

"We were friends as children," Aiden admitted. "When I told Bróccín who I was, and believing me loyal to his liege lord, he gave me the writ. He explained the content, and requested I pass on his regrets for having failed you."

"Yet you chose to play the role of my betrothed."

"I did," he said, his voice hard, "nor will I apologize for my decision. We are at war. Gaining access to Latharn Castle, learning its defenses and other critical information would have allowed the Bruce to seize the stronghold with minimum loss of life on both sides."

She arched a sarcastic brow. "And marriage to me served King Robert best how?"

"Blast it, I never planned for the ceremony to take place. My men and I were to remain for a few days at most. Then the priest was summoned to Rome, and you revealed that by Comyn's dictate, we must marry before he departed." He paused. "Duty came first."

"And the reason you didna consummate our marriage?" she said, her voice ice. "I am the spoils of war, am I not?"

"Making you a pawn, physically or otherwise, was never my intent," Aiden said. "Yet by pretending to be your husband, and given access to the entire castle, including the ledgers, I could bring more information to our king. And then the English arrived and seized the stronghold."

Gray eyes darkened like an impending storm. "How inconvenient for you. Meanwhile, Latharn Castle is lost, and the farms my people have worked years to plant, along with the homes they labored to build, are destroyed."

Actions he regretted to this day. "I couldna allow the Duke of Northbyrn access to either. 'Tis prudent to remember that 'twas the English who betrayed the pact made with Lord Comyn. However much you despise me for destroying your tenants' property, denying those resources to the English troops serves Comyn as well as the Bruce."

Her eyes blazed, but he caught lines of fatigue on her face, her pale features evidence of their difficult travel.

A wave of tiredness swept over him, and Aiden gave a slow breath. "I dinna expect you to forgive me, but I needed to explain."

Like a regal queen, she angled her jaw. "If you are finished, you can leave."

At the coldness of her words, he stared at her, remembering their kiss, and how she'd fallen apart beneath his touch. He swallowed hard, their passion now seeming as if a memory. 'Twas clear at this moment he'd get no further with her, let alone convince her to divulge the location of the ledger.

Aware 'twas prudent to make a strategic retreat, Aiden stepped back. "If you have need of me, ask Sir Quentin. He will ensure I am reached."

"I willna."

With a muttered curse, he strode into the warmth of the fading sun, scanned the encampment. A soft summer breeze swept across his face as he noted cookpots hanging over fires, and the faint scent of venison and herbs filling the air.

He dragged in a deep breath. So upset he'd departed without talking to her about her meeting with King Robert as well as prepare her for what may come. Topics he would broach upon his return.

He nodded to Quentin, who stood nearby. "I shall fetch her a plate of food."

His friend grimaced. "The lass hasna touched the fare I placed inside earlier."

"I will ensure that she eats." How, he had no idea, but he'd think of something. He could finish their discussion then. Another round of their contentious repartee he did not look forward to. Yet, however unwise, he was drawn to her. An unfathomable situation.

He turned, noticed Cailin walking toward him, a frown wedged across his brow.

Aiden met him half way across the encampment. "What is wrong?"

"King Robert seeks Lady Gwendolyn's immediate presence, and has asked for your attendance as well."

Aiden stilled. "Why would our sovereign want to see us both?"

"I am unsure," his friend said. "His request surprised me."

Nor would Gwendolyn be pleased by the Bruce's command. An understatement. "My thanks." Dread sliding through his mind, he headed toward her tent.

At his approach, Sir Quentin lifted his brow.

"The king wishes me to escort Lady Gwendolyn to him."

With a nod, his friend stepped back. "Godspeed."

Aiden grunted. "I will need your prayers." He lifted the flap.

Her eyes met his, narrowed.

As if he was pleased with the situation? "King Robert has requested your presence. I will accompany you."

"I dinna need you there."

Aiden released a slow breath, damned the words he must share. "He asked to see us both. With his seeking my presence as well, I am thinking the reason canna be good."

Chapter 13

Eyes narrowed with fury, Gwendolyn swept past Aiden. Sunlight shimmered on her hair as she stormed across the encampment, the tumble of soft, golden waves at odds with the hard set of her face. He caught up to her, kept pace, ached to slip his hand around her elbow and pull her to a stop.

Need churned in his gut as he remembered his fingers sliding through the silky length, of the heat in her eyes as she'd turned to him, and of how, if only for a short while, she'd wanted him.

With each step she took, the burn of his deception ate through him, their passion-driven intimacy and her gasps of pleasure clear in his mind. God's teeth! He couldn't forgive himself for having allowed such; why should he expect her to?

"King Robert is a fair man," he said, hoping to ease her worry.

"He is my enemy, or have you forgotten?" she ground out, her pace lengthening.

Aiden widened his stride to keep at her side. "He is the rightful king to Scotland, and one who seeks to unite our country. Unlike Lord Comyn, who consorted with the English."

A gust rich with the scent of earth and a hint of pine tangled in her hair; she remained silent, her look fierce. Blast it! He halted before his sovereign's tent. "Inform King Robert that Sir Aiden and Lady Gwendolyn are here."

The sentry ducked inside. A moment later, he emerged and stepped to the side. "The king bids you to enter."

On edge, Aiden nodded. Had the Bruce selected a lord high within his ranks to wed her? He grimaced, too aware she would never comply with such a command, one he'd intended to prepare her for. Or at least try.

If given the opportunity, he'd offer for Gwendolyn's hand himself. A foolish thought. Aside from the fact that he was untitled, after his deception, she'd rather drive a dagger in his heart than agree to marry him. 'Twas best to pray that whatever fate the Bruce chose for the spirited lass was one that kept her safe.

* * * *

Smoke from the fires and a mixture of meats and vegetables lingered in the air as Gwendolyn stepped inside the king's tent.

The flicker of torchlight illuminated numerous chests stacked against one side. A portion of the other was shielded by a ruby drape of velvet, behind which she suspected lay a bed. A rug of deep gold embroidered with a lion rampant in red on each corner lay before the sturdy, unadorned wooden throne. Poised upon the seat, as handsome as he was powerful, Scotland's ruler watched her, his eyes sharp with intelligence.

She fought for calm as she halted before the king.

Power radiated from the monarch, a man confident in his command and determined to achieve his goal, regardless the cost.

Aiden stepped up to her side, bowed. "Sire."

The hint of nervousness in Aiden's voice had her glancing over. Taut lines marred his face, and his eyes, dark with worry, rested on the king. Had something occurred since he'd spoken with her?

On a shaky breath, she focused on the king, curtsied. "Your Grace."

"Lady Gwendolyn, 'tis with regret that we meet under such circumstances," the Bruce said, his voice grim. "Given the situation, 'twas unavoidable."

Unavoidable? Fury trampled the nerves in her mind, and she scowled. "Sending warriors to spy on my home in preparation for an attack is hardly unavoidable."

A fierce brow raised, then the ruler glanced toward Aiden. "Lady Gwendolyn isna a weak-willed lass."

"Nay, Your Grace," Aiden replied, his words tight. "As I mentioned, she speaks her mind."

A whisper of a smile touched the Bruce's mouth. "An admirable trait, is it not?"

"'Tis, Sire," Aiden replied.

"I am standing right here, Your Grace," she said, insulted that they talked about her as if she was not there.

The king's gaze narrowed on her, and the lightness of a moment before faded. "You are indeed." He stood, strode over.

Muscles rippled with his every step. The power exuded by this royal warrior was palpable, yet Gwendolyn found herself unafraid.

Accounts of his intelligence, determination, and forthright way of speaking were well known, traits that had caused King Edward I, and now his son, Edward of Caernarfon, immense misery. From their first meeting, 'twould seem the claims she'd heard about Scotland's sovereign were true.

A pace away, he paused, towered over her with a measuring look. "You are afraid of little?"

She held his gaze. Regardless of the escalating thud of her heart, she held his gaze. "I say what is on my mind."

An intrigued smile curved his mouth. "Indeed? I bid you, my lady, to share your thoughts. I find myself curious to hear them."

Aiden stiffened at her side, but Gwendolyn ignored him. Any influence he'd had in her life was past. Once she'd trusted him, no longer. As for repercussions for her words, the king could order her killed at any time. She had little to lose.

"I want Latharn Castle returned to me." She angled her jaw. "'Tis my birthright."

The king grimaced. "One seized by the English."

Heat swept her cheeks. "Through treachery."

"Deceit they are well familiar with. Nor," the Bruce said, loathing tainting his words, "was their duplicity uninvited. Edward of Caernarfon's forces sailed to Scotland in a plot conceived with Lord Comyn. He will learn, as I did years ago, that the Sassenach canna be trusted."

The king's use of the disparaging term for the English indeed fit their despicable acts. "Once my liege lord discovers their betrayal, he will ensure 'tis a decision they will regret."

"Lady Gwendolyn," the Bruce stated, "there is little he can do to avenge their treachery. Had Lord Comyn been able to raise sufficient troops, he wouldna have sought Edward of Caernarfon's support."

The enormity of his statement smothered any remaining belief and forced her to face the truth. Regardless whether Latharn Castle was held by the English or the Bruce, any hope of reclaiming her ancestral home was gone.

"With Comyn's weakening force," the Bruce continued, "and without England's support, in time, all of Scotland will be beneath my rule. Which, as its *king*, is my right."

Hurt, anger, the memory of how the Bruce had murdered his rival, the Lord of Badenoch, at the church of the Greyfriars to ensure he received the crown, erupted in her mind. Then faded as quickly at the way, over the past months, since the Bruce was crowned at Scone, he had begun to unite the clans. Against the odds, he had raised an army, a growing force now methodically storming the Highlands, devastating the opposition to claim a country that was indeed his.

She stiffened against a surge of anger, the frustration of her country torn. Gwendolyn shot a cool glance toward Aiden before facing the king. "Aye, Sire, 'tis your right."

"Yet," the king said, "I am not without sympathy for your cause. Well I understand your wanting to recoup a birthright wrongly seized."

"Indeed," she agreed. "Your grandfather, Robert Bruce of Annandale, claimant to the crown after King Alexander III's death, was denied the throne most believed was rightfully his."

Though in public many would fervently disagree, in private few doubted the facts. If King Edward I hadn't insinuated himself as an arbitrator in deciding the true claimant for the Scotland's crown in 1292, instead of John Balliol, Bruce of Annandale would have been crowned as Scotland's king. A title that eventually would have passed to his grandson.

For a long moment, the monarch studied her. With a sharp exhale, he strode to his wooden throne and sat. He stroked his jaw. "Rarely do I meet women of such strength, or one who dares push against my will."

At his soft tone, she stilled. What was she thinking to challenge the king? "Sire, I—"

"Though you overstep the boundaries of convention," he continued, "'tis from passion for your beliefs, a strength I admire." He lifted his goblet in a silent toast, took a sip, then lowered his chalice. "Lady Gwendolyn, I have decided to entertain your request to be mistress of Latharn Castle."

Disbelief swelled in her chest. Mary's will, he was returning her home!

The powerful ruler narrowed his eyes, his gaze piercing, and unease twisted in her gut. A strategist...of course he wouldn't return the significant stronghold without conditions. "What are your terms, Your Grace?"

He set aside the goblet and leaned forward, braced his elbows on the arms of his chair, and steepled his fingers.

Gwendolyn held her breath. 'Twas as if she stood upon a precipice, the Bruce offering the only hope of seeing her home restored.

"You must agree to two stipulations."

She swallowed hard. "They are...?"

"First, you must swear fealty to me."

Given the situation, an unavoidable request. However she despised the king's plotting to seize her castle, for her home, her people, she would support the Bruce.

In fairness, however much she loathed this turn of events, King Robert was a man who had fought many adversaries and had proven himself more than only a warrior to trust but a noble intent on uniting Scotland. Gwendolyn nodded. "I will, Sire."

At her side, Aiden's body relaxed.

The powerful king stood. "Kneel before me."

Legs trembling, a swath of blond hair slid over her face as she knelt, a curtain to shield her tears.

The slide of steel against leather filled the silence as he withdrew his sword.

Her breath eased in shallow gasps.

He stepped forward, lay the end of his blade upon her shoulder.

The cold steel weighed heavily upon her soul.

"Do you, Lady Gwendolyn, swear fealty to me, forsaking your allegiance to Lord Comyn?"

Gwendolyn damned Aiden as the faces of her tenants swam before her as she prepared to give a vow she thought she would never make. "I do, Sire." He touched the sword upon her other shoulder before removing the pressure of the forged steel, but not the weight of her regret.

He sheathed his weapon. "Stand."

Heart pounding, she pushed to her feet, met his gaze. "And the second condition?"

The king's eyes darkened, yet she could swear she saw the hint of a smile. "Sir Aiden gives you high praise, approval that has swayed my decision to allow you to return to your home."

Confusion rippled through her. Even after she had treated Aiden with such disdain, he'd commended her to his sovereign? She looked over, but the knight kept his gaze straight ahead. What had he told the king? The hunger she'd witnessed in Aiden's eyes that night beneath the falls stormed her mind, capturing her breath.

Smothering the unwanted thought, she shifted her gaze to the king. "How so, Your Grace?"

"Among other things, he explained how once your word is given, 'tis one I can trust."

She stiffened. Aiden had claimed he'd never meant to hurt her. Did his intervention with the royal prove his sincerity?

Regardless of his motive, his words had swayed King Robert. For that she would be thankful. "Aye, Sire. I am a woman of my word."

"In addition, Sir Aiden's insistence that Latharn Castle needs a formidable warrior who will keep the stronghold safe is a belief I share. Do you not agree?"

"I do, Sire."

A smile curved Robert Bruce's mouth. He nodded to Aiden. "For your loyalty, you will be charged with the duty of protecting the stronghold."

Eyes widening, Aiden's gaze fell on her before shifting to his king. "I am greatly honored, Sire, but mayhap Lady Gwendolyn's home would best be served by—"

"Someone with your expertise," the king finished. "We are at war. I need my best warriors well placed."

Aiden gave a low bow, straightened. "I swear to you that I will keep Latharn Castle safe."

Pain sliced through her chest. Loyalty to the damnable king was one thing. But this… Her outrage grew. No, 'twas asking too much!

"Your Grace," she forced out as she struggled for a way to sway the king, "Sir Aiden is but a knight. Given Latharn Castle's strategic location, the stronghold doesna need a castellan but a noble, a formidable leader with a large contingent to ensure the fortress is kept safe."

"Lady Gwendolyn," the king said with soft warning, "I admire your passion and your forthright manner, but I willna tolerate your advising me in my royal decisions."

Indeed, instead of allowing her to return to her home, he could have locked her in the dungeon or worse. "Forgive me, Sire."

"Sir Aiden is a man I deeply respect, one who has earned my complete trust," the Bruce said, his voice cool. "Latharn Castle is fortunate to have a warrior of such caliber to protect it."

"Forgive me, Your Grace, 'tis that I am confused," she said, fighting to keep her mounting frustration at bay. "Moments before, you said you would entertain my request to be the mistress of Latharn Castle. If given a large contingent to keep the fortress safe, I would have no need of him."

* * * *

Dread descended as Aiden awaited his king's reply. Aye, he'd recommended a strong force to protect Latharn Castle once seized, but never had he expected the Bruce to select him for the task.

King Robert stepped before Aiden. "You have served me faithfully since we met at Urquhart Castle almost a year ago, a time difficult for many."

Fighting back the wash of fury at how King Philip IV of France had betrayed the Knights Templar, Aiden focused on the Bruce, remembering his surprise to learn Scotland's king was a Knight Templar as well. "Aye, Your Grace," Aiden rasped. "I pray for those still beneath King Philip's harsh rule."

"As do I," the Bruce said, his voice weary, "but now isna the time to discuss a topic of such distress, but to right a wrong."

Aiden stilled. A wrong?

"Kneel before me."

Confused, Aiden complied.

The soft slide of steel against leather again sounded. As with Gwendolyn, his sovereign lay his sword upon Aiden's shoulder. "Be it known that from this day forward, I award you, Aiden MacConnell"— he moved the blade to his opposite shoulder—"the title of Earl of Lenox."

On a sharp breath, Aiden jerked up his head and met the king's proud gaze. "Earl of Lenox?"

The king arched a brow. "I am well aware of the details of your lost nobility. 'Tis your father's title I now bestow upon you. In addition, once Latharn Castle is seized, you will be awarded the previous noble's title, Earl of Hadington."

Gwendolyn gasped.

"And after Latharn Castle is seized," the Bruce continued, "you will lead a contingent to seize Thorburn Castle. Once captured, your home, lost to the English years ago, will again be yours. You will then be charged with keeping both strongholds safe, and as necessary, supporting my cause."

Aiden struggled to breathe against the enormity of this moment. After his family had died and he had returned home to find Thorburn Castle captured, never had he believed that one day he would reclaim his heritage.

"Lord Lenox," the king boomed, "rise."

Humbled, Aiden stood, bowed to the man who had resurrected his dream of reclaiming his home and, incredibly, returned his legacy. "My deepest thanks, Sire. I swear that I will serve you with the utmost faith."

With a satisfied nod, the king sheathed his sword. His gaze moved to Gwendolyn. "'Tis settled. You have stated your desire to be Latharn Castle's mistress, and to have the stronghold protected by a noble, a formidable warrior with a large contingent to ensure the fortress is kept safe. A request that will be fulfilled upon your marriage to Lord Lenox."

Marriage! Still reeling from the generous promise of a prize beyond which he had ever dreamed, the Bruce's words exploded in Aiden's mind.

He vaguely registered her sharp intake of breath.

'Twould seem that, like her, the king's decisions came with conditions.

Warmth slid through him at thoughts of her as his wife, of having a lass whom he admired, and a woman who made him want. A look at her crushed his foolish thoughts. The icy paleness of her face underscored her revulsion at the idea. How could she not feel otherwise after his deception?

Mayhap there was something he could say to spare her such a fate. "Sire, before—"

"I find the match between you and Lady Gwendolyn beneficial in many ways, Lord Lenox," the king stated, his shrewd gaze watchful, "do you not agree?"

Aiden searched for a reason to avoid the king's dictate to wed, his sovereign's earlier inquiries about the lass now making sense.

At the time, exhausted and injured, thankful to have arrived safely, and proud of Gwendolyn as he had stood before the king, he'd painted her as a woman of strength, fortitude, and determination. An admission given in the hope that instead of being treated with disregard as the enemy, she would be awarded protection.

God's sword, why hadn't he considered the real possibility of such a decision, more so with his friends' teasing? The Bruce's fascination with such women was well known. Weren't his friends, Stephan MacQuistan and Thomas MacKelloch, who were now married to equally spirited women, proof of such?

Though neither had asked for this marriage, and however much she detested him, if he refused to wed Gwendolyn, he couldn't be sure that whoever she did marry would treat her with the respect she deserved.

Though she loathed him, he still cared for her deeply. "I agree, Your Grace."

With a nod, the king faced her. "And do you, Lady Gwendolyn, consent to the match?"

A slow pounding filled Aiden's chest as her eyes darkened with distress, the dismay he'd caused. Bedamned, never had he meant to hurt her, to cast her into a life wed to a man she despised.

Her lower lip trembling, she lifted her jaw, her words a rough whisper. "I agree, Sire."

"Excellent. Now let us celebrate." The Bruce walked to the side table, refilled his goblet with wine, and poured two more. He handed one to each of them. "A toast to you, Lord Lenox, and to Lady Gwendolyn, for achieving your heart's desire." He raised his cup and drank deep.

Aiden downed the spiced wine, noted she took but a sip. Considering her upset, his elation at his liege lord's generosity faded.

For a second time they would wed, although this marriage would be real. She would have a husband to govern her people, her castle. Gwendolyn had fought for her independence, and he knew part of her would fight this union for that reason alone, not to mention the betrayal he'd served her.

His being away on campaign would allow each of them time to adjust to their marriage, distance she would welcome.

"Your Grace," the guard at the door said.

The king glanced up. "Aye."

"The priest has been sighted and will arrive shortly," the guard said.

Priest? Aiden's heart pounded. They couldn't wed now, they needed time to—

"Once the priest reaches my tent," King Robert said to the sentry, "ensure he is escorted inside."

"Aye, Sire." The guard bowed, and then departed.

"Y-Your Grace," Gwendolyn rasped. "Our wedding can be performed at Latharn Castle once 'tis seized."

The king's eyes narrowed. "Nay. The marriage will be done this day."

Chapter 14

Aiden damned the flare of anger in Gwendolyn's eyes, the disdainful resignation as well. Nonetheless, soon the deed would be done. How he and Gwendolyn fared after their marriage would be another matter.

Still, an urgent issue remained. "Your Grace, to prevent the English from gaining a foothold in the Highlands, 'tis imperative that we reclaim Latharn Castle posthaste."

The Bruce gave a solemn nod. "Once the marriage vows are said, meet with your men and devise a strategy."

Eyes blazing, Gwendolyn took a step forward. "Sire, I must be included in the plotting. 'Tis my home, one I intend to fight for."

Aiden faced his king. "Nay! I have familiarized myself with the stronghold; 'tis unnecessary for Lady Gwendolyn to return. I willna allow her to be placed in danger."

She rounded on him. "A concern you didna raise while we burned the homes and fields of *my* people."

"However regrettable the damage," Aiden said between clenched teeth, "'twas an action necessary to remove resources the English could use."

She scoffed. "And what of my skills with a knife or as an archer? Are they nay longer of value?"

Blast it! "I didna have the luxury to keep you safe before. Now I do. You will stay here with my king," he stated. "I know the location of the secret entry. There is little more you could offer."

"You know of only one." Fierce eyes held his as if on a dare. "But you are ignorant of the others. Passageways I know like the back of my hand and, if necessary, could navigate in the dark."

"Details," Aiden said with cold precision, "the hidden ledger will reveal."

She gave a cold laugh. "If you believe you could find my father's journal without my assistance, you are a fool."

"Enough," the Bruce bellowed.

Furious he'd allowed her to draw out his anger before his king, Aiden bowed to his sovereign.

"Knowledge of the castle's secret passageways is imperative to ensure the mission's success." Palms flat on the arms of the chair, the Bruce leaned forward. "As we dinna have the secret journal, and given Lady Gwendolyn's skill with weapons and knowledge of the stronghold, she shall be involved in the planning and will accompany you to the castle."

Triumph flared in her eyes.

"But"—the king's gaze leveled on her—"once you have revealed the location of the other tunnels, for your own safety, you will remain hidden during the attack. And, after Latharn is recaptured, you will turn over your father's ledger to Lord Lenox."

Jaw tight, she nodded. "I agree, Sire."

The tent flap opened. The outline of a lean man donned in a vestment shadowed the entry. He stepped inside, bowed. "Your Grace."

"Father Morref." The Bruce stood. "I appreciate your haste."

"'Tis my pleasure, Sire." He nodded toward Aiden and then Gwendolyn. "When I received the king's writ earlier this day regarding one of his noble's betrothal, I was honored to be asked to perform the sacrament of marriage."

Betrothal? Aiden shot his sovereign a cool look, understanding the satisfied gleam in the royal's eyes. After he'd briefed King Robert this morning, 'twould seem the Bruce had decided their fate. The ploy of moments to gain both their agreements to wed was naught but a formality. From the ire in Gwendolyn's eyes, a fact she realized as well.

"Your name?" the cleric asked.

"Aiden MacConnell, Earl of Lenox." Emotion stormed him as he stated his father's title, a designation now his. The moment felt like a dream, except the priest's presence left Aiden dredged in reality.

Father Morref's gaze shifted to her. "And yours, lass?"

For a long moment she remained silent, and then she lifted her chin. "Lady Gwendolyn Murphy."

The Bruce withdrew a ruby pouch from within his garb, walked over, and placed the sack in Aiden's palm.

Aiden unwrapped the velvet folds, stilled. Inside lay a small gold band, the delicate circle forged with a Celtic weave embracing a large emerald along with several smaller rubies. On a sharp breath, he met the king's gaze. "I thank you, Sire."

With a nod, the king stepped back.

The priest slid his finger beneath the silk ribbon marking a page and opened the Bible. "Lord Lenox, please move closer to your betrothed."

Aiden glanced over.

Face ashen, she stared straight ahead.

A sense of doom settled over him as he stepped to her side. The priest's words blurred in his mind, echoing those he'd heard at Latharn Castle. When asked, he, as Gwendolyn, gave the appropriate response.

The priest lay her icy fingers on Aiden's palm. "The ring."

On an unsteady breath, Aiden slid the ornate ring in place.

The priest smiled and made the sign of the cross. "I now pronounce you man and wife."

A satisfied smile curved the king's lips. "I congratulate you both."

"I thank you, Sire," Aiden replied, the weight of the responsibilities ahead fisted in his chest. Their marriage was but the first of many challenges ahead. After their castles were reclaimed, another, greater battle stood between them, this one personal.

Gwendolyn curtsied, her movements wooden. "I thank you, Your Grace."

Warmth shimmered in the priest's eyes as he stowed the Bible beneath his vestments. "I wish you both every blessing." With a bow to the king, he departed. As he exited, for a moment the camp beyond came into view; knights sparring, pots hanging over cookfires, and warriors tending to their weapons as if this were an ordinary day when 'twas anything but.

"Lord Lennox," the Bruce said, reclaiming Aiden's gaze. "Once you, Lady Gwendolyn, and your men have devised a plan of attack, report to me. I will address any concerns."

"Aye, Sire. Given the urgency of the situation, we depart at first light."

The Bruce nodded. "A decision I anticipated. I sent instructions earlier to my master-at-arms to ensure the men are ready."

Aiden bowed. "I thank you, Sire." After Gwendolyn curtsied, he took her arm.

"Lady Gwendolyn."

At the king's voice, she paused, and Aiden turned at her side.

"Your Grace?" she asked, her voice thick with emotion.

He withdrew a deep purple velvet bag, sealed by a gold filigree cord, a carved Celtic cross on each end. "'Tis from your father."

What little color that had returned to her face fled. "My father?" Her eyes clouded with confusion. "What has my father to do with this?"

"He was loyal to my cause," the king replied, his voice solemn.

Disbelief filled her eyes, and she glanced at Aiden before facing the royal. "L-loyal to you?"

Robert Bruce walked to her, placed the bag in her palm, then curled his fingers atop hers. "When your father was dying, he arranged to have this sent to me. In the writ he wrote, *'Give this to my daughter. When the time comes, she will know what to do.'*"

Her mouth opened and then closed, her cheeks tinged with red. "He never told me," she whispered, her words thick with hurt. "Why?"

The king's sage eyes held hers. "Given the unrest in Scotland since King Alexander's death, of your father's numerous travels, and how he often left you at Latharn Castle alone, he felt 'twas best."

Gwendolyn's throat worked. "H-how long had he been loyal to you?"

"Years," he replied without apology.

"Years?" The brittle word collapsed into a strangled whisper. She stiffened. "I see." She gave a cold laugh. "And I was fool enough to believe he loved and trusted me."

"You are wrong," the king said, his words soft. "You were everything to him."

Outrage flashed in her eyes. "If I mattered, if he had trusted me, he would have informed me of his alliance with you. 'Twould seem, as with you, I am naught but chattel." Her hand crushed the velvet. "I thank you, Sire, for restoring my home." After another deep curtsy, head held high, she strode out.

God's teeth! Aiden glanced at the king.

The Bruce's brow lifted. "She is your greatest challenge, Lord Lennox. Dinna fail her."

Challenge? An understatement. "Aye, Sire." He bowed, then hurried out.

Late afternoon sunlight beat down upon him as he caught up to her as she entered the path into the woods, frustration rushing his words. "We must come to an agreement to make our marriage work."

She shot him a scalding glance before hurrying down the slope. "With your having been granted both castles, I find little left to discuss. You have what you want."

"Blast it—"

Eyes narrowed, Gwendolyn whirled at the bottom of the incline. "Did you know of my father's loyalty to the Bruce?"

He sighed. "I learned of it this morning."

"And like the king, found such critical information unnecessary to share. 'Tis what men do, is it not? Decide what to tell or keep from women." She glared at the crushed velvet clenched in her palm. With a hiss of disgust, she hurled it into the woods. The sack landed within the ferns with a soft thud.

"Gwendolyn—"

She stepped back. "Leave me."

How he wanted to respect her request. "Do you not wish to help plan the assault?"

Gray eyes narrowed. "I will be there."

With their future sealed beneath a marital vow, 'twas imperative to find a compromise, a way to work together. He smothered the words. There would be time to talk later. "I have an errand I must attend to. Once I am finished, I will escort you to the meeting."

Cool eyes held his, and then, with a curt nod, she left.

Scowling at her departing figure, Aiden rubbed the back of his neck. *That went bloody well.* He glanced toward the ferns, then pushed aside the leafy stems until he spied the glint of the gold filigree cord. He retrieved the sack.

However upset, once she calmed she might want her father's gift. Securing the pouch within his garb, he headed toward where his men were caring for their weapons.

* * * *

"Married?" Cailin asked.

Aiden lifted his dagger from the whetstone, noted the amused expressions that crossed his men's faces. "'Twould seem when I lauded Lady Gwendolyn's attributes to the king earlier this day, I sealed my own fate. Unknown to me, once I departed, King Robert sent for a priest."

In brief, Aiden explained how the Bruce had evoked their agreements to wed a short while before the priest's arrival.

"You know how the Bruce admires strong, intelligent women," Cailin said.

Aiden wiped his blade, remembering the fate of his Templar brothers, Stephan MacQuistan and Thomas MacKelloch, too well.

"Though not your choice," Rónán said, "she isna a stranger."

As the men chuckled, Aiden scowled at them. "Never did I wish for Lady Gwendolyn to be entangled in this blasted mess."

"Mayhap," Cailin agreed, but at least you care for her."

At the truth in his friend's words, Aiden paused, unsure how much to admit. "Aye, she has become important to me, but the way I deceived her, she is furious with me. Nor was she pleased to learn of her father's loyalty to King Robert."

Quentin grimaced. "What will you do now?"

Other than sharing a bed? God's sword, now wasna the time for thoughts of her body naked beneath his, assuming he could ever breach her icy defenses.

"What I intend to do is to think of the mission, as will all of you," Aiden stated. "The king has instructed me to lead a contingent to recapture both Latharn and Thorburn Castles, and has ordered us to design the attack. One I will brief him upon this night."

His friends nodded.

"But," Aiden drawled, aware his men wouldna be pleased, "a plan he insists Lady Gwendolyn help us create, along with allowing her to travel with us to the stronghold."

Rónán's brows narrowed. "The king granted her permission to be part of the assault?"

"Nay, she will remain hidden during the attack," Aiden explained. "In return, she agreed that, once the stronghold is seized, she will give me her father's hidden ledger."

"Which solves our having to find the Templar journal." Cailin grimaced. "Given the king's allowing Lady Katherine to sail with Stephan when we attacked Avalon Castle last year, you shouldn't be surprised by his decision this day."

At his friend's reminder, Aiden grimaced. "Indeed." Nor could he change the way of things now. "I will get Lady Gwendolyn and meet you at our tent."

* * * *

Chest tight, standing at the edge of the forest, Gwendolyn slowly exhaled. With the plans for the upcoming attack to reclaim her home made and the king informed, she'd needed time alone. She stared at her wedding ring, the cold weight resting on her finger with macabre finality. A glint of the setting sun reflected off the emerald and rubies, as if mocking her plight. Numb, she ached to rip off the ornate band and cast it deep into the woods.

Except, unlike the gift from her father, disposing of the ring would change naught. She'd given her vow and was wed to a man she couldn't trust.

Footsteps upon grass had her hand clasping her dagger as she turned. Aiden came into view and she released her blade.

He halted before her, his expression tense. "Walk with me."

The sincerity of his words made her hesitate, then, at last, nod her agreement. Despite how betrayed she felt, she remembered their many days of being hunted, how her welfare had been his first priority. Out of respect for that, she would at least listen to what he had to say.

In silence, he led her away from where the knights practiced near an open field, the scrape of blades a violent setting against the soft breeze rustling through the leaves. In the forest, he followed a well-trod path moving well away from camp.

Disquiet rippled inside as she glanced around the sweep of trees and clumps of brush and ferns. "Are you not worried that Lord Comyn's men may be near?"

"If any of the guards see danger, they will sound the alarm. And with the number of troops filling the king's encampment, I doubt Lord Comyn's men are foolish enough to take such a risk."

She prayed so.

A gust of wind sent the leaves overhead into a frantic dance. The breeze settled, and shimmers of fading sunlight sprinkled the path ahead, like fairy dust tossed.

No, 'twas naught magical about this day.

The gurgle of water sounded. Through the breaks in the trees she made out the stream meandering below.

The path angled down.

At the bottom, Aiden halted on a flat rock covered in moss, the churn of water tumbling past.

The subtle scent of ferns, the fragrance of pine, and the tang of moisture filled the air as she halted paces away, the weight of the gold band on her finger like a chain upon her heart.

Brow furrowed, Aiden glanced at her. "I wish to reiterate my regret. You didna ask for any of this, a fact I well understand."

His sympathy far from eased her anger. "The king bestowing upon you my castle along with your ancestral home, once both are recaptured, along with your father's title and mine, is quite a boon."

A muscle worked in his jaw. "Never did I intend for us to wed or seek your home or your father's title."

From his surprise as the king had announced his intention, that she believed.

"Neither," he said, his voice dry, "did your challenging the Bruce to reclaim Latharn Castle help your cause."

"Challenging?" The flare of anger was sharp and quick. "'Tis my legacy. Nor did I expect him to make the condition for my return that we marry. Condition." She scoffed. "An ultimatum."

"One you could have refused."

"And if I had, I would have lost any claim to my home."

Green eyes darkened, but he remained silent.

Frustrated, she turned, watched a leaf caught within the churn as it floundered down the rock-laden current.

A chill rippled through Gwendolyn, and she rubbed her arms. "Now what?" With her fealty sworn to King Robert, they shared the same loyalty. One her father had given to the Bruce years before, a fact he'd kept hidden.

On a rough sigh, Aiden picked up a flat rock. With a flick of his wrist, he skimmed the thin wedge over the surface of a nearby pool, where twigs spun lazily in the breeze. Droplets splashed into the air as the stone skipped across the surface several times before sinking into the depths.

He glanced at her, his gaze solemn. "We are wed. However unwanted by either of us, 'tis a situation we can make work to favor what we each desire."

Far from convinced, she arched a doubtful brow. "How so?"

"Once Latharn Castle is recaptured, you will remain there. I will leave behind a force large enough to ensure it remains protected. The rest of the men and I will depart to reclaim Thorburn Castle. Once seized, I will rejoin the Bruce."

It sounded so simple, yet life had taught her to trust little. And this was war… Regardless of how furious she was at him, concern edged through her at the possibility of his never coming back.

Mouth tight, he selected another rock, flipped it in his palm. "If ever you need anything, you have only to call upon me."

"But you will visit?" she asked with caution, assuring herself that she was pleased by his generous offer, yet for an unexplainable reason, emptiness clattered inside.

"Not unless you send for me. Or, if I receive news that the situation warrants such." He paused. "From this day forward, I will be your husband in name only. You shall have the freedom you desire, or as much as I can give you."

Heart pounding, she swallowed hard, the unexpected emptiness within swelling to a fierce ache. "You would sacrifice an heir?" she breathed.

His fingers tightened around the stone. "Unless you wish otherwise. Nor is my lineage the only ancestry affected," he said, his words tight. "Upon our deaths, both our lands and titles will be seized by Scotland's king to bestow upon another." He hurled the rock into the middle of the stream. It landed with a loud splash. "The choice of how we proceed is up to you."

How could he place this upon her without notice, then expect her to decide? "Why are you proposing this?"

For a long moment he held her gaze, the sadness within easy to read. "I offer naught but to return a portion of your old life. As I stated earlier, never were you to be involved or hurt."

"Yet there were intimacies," she said, furious he would treat their moments in the cave with such disregard when, during that time, a transformation of what she'd felt for him had occurred. "We were together, some nights more than others."

"In the cave," he said, his voice tight, "if I hadna pushed you away, we would have made love. My touching you was wrong; making love to you considering the circumstance would have been unforgivable."

Heat stroked her face, adding to her bedevilment. And now, a king's dictate had tossed his life, like hers, into chaos.

Guilt at his unselfishness collided with lingering hurt.

After they had wed, he could have brought her to his tent and taken her. Instead, he'd left her untouched.

The words of agreement to his bargain lingered on her tongue.

As if sensing her confusion, Aiden nodded. "You have time to decide. Once Latharn Castle is seized, I will ask you again. I brought you here so we could have privacy for me to explain my intention."

Her pulse racing, she stared at him as the rumble of water echoed in the fading light. "Why are you doing this?"

"I explained."

"You did, but 'tis odd that at a time when women are rarely given any choice, you would sacrifice not only the intimacy of marriage, but a castle, along with any chance for an heir."

A muscle worked in his jaw. "I am a man of honor."

Indeed, he had more integrity than any man she'd ever met. So why did she not accept his offer? 'Twas not as if she wanted this marriage, or that he held a place within her heart. Still, she hesitated. Though his decency was a strong reason for his proposal, something did not make sense.

"Aye, you are a man of honor," she agreed, "but there is more behind your offer than mere duty to your king."

Green eyes narrowed, assuring her that she had the right of it.

For a moment, Gwendolyn thought he would walk away. When Aiden continued to stare at her, she stepped closer. "Whatever that reason is, 'tis causing you great distress."

Body tense, he turned away.

Undeterred, Gwendolyn stepped beside him, waited.

The rumble of water sliding past filled the silence as the waning light sifted through the leaves, laying a mottled pattern across his broad shoulders.

Despite all that had happened between them, she couldn't resist the genuine concern that something had left him in such anguish. She lay her hand upon his arm. "Let me help you."

Aiden's throat worked as his fingers unfurled, his hands lying limp at his sides. "Naught can be done. The time to repair the horrendous injustice has long since passed."

Mary's will, what had happened to have caused him such despair? "Why not?"

"Because a life I and many others loved, one chosen to serve *Him*, has been lost."

Air rushed out in a gasp as the pieces fell into place, explained his chivalry, why he had fought to keep his distance from her, and his offer of moments before. Yet his actions did not explain the heat of his kiss. Or did it?

"I-I am so sorry," she breathed.

"You have done naught wrong," he growled.

"But I have, I pushed you... Then, I didna know." She shook her head. "Forgive me."

"For what?"

Gwendolyn stared at him, swallowed hard. "I didna know you had intended to become a priest."

Chapter 15

The scent of water and moss filled the air as Aiden blinked in confusion at Gwendolyn standing before him a pace away. Disgusted with himself for doing such a poor job of explaining, he shook his head. "I am not wanting to become a priest."

She frowned. "But you said a life to serve *Him* had been lost."

God's sword, how had his explanation become so tangled? She deserved the truth of his past. At least, what he could share. "I will tell you, but first you must swear to tell nay one."

Worry flickered in her gaze. "What have you done?"

"Swear it."

She hesitated. "I swear I will say naught."

"I am a Knight Templar. Or was."

Her lips parted on a soft gasp. "But a Knight Templar canna marry, or…" Gwendolyn's face paled. "'Tis because of the arrests in France last fall, is it not?"

Heartache balled in Aiden's chest as he faced the water sliding beneath the fading rays of light, the shimmers like golden tears. "King Philip's betrayal destroyed an honorable way of life for the Brotherhood. Devout warriors who had sworn to do naught but protect."

"I am so sorry," she breathed. "When I heard news of the charges, and given King Philip's craving for power, I refused to believe them."

Gray eyes held his for a long moment, the sadness, the grief within touching his soul.

"But," she continued, "the French king's perfidy does not explain why you are in Scotland."

He gestured toward a large moss-covered stone. "Sit, please."

After a slight hesitation, she complied.

He settled at her side, angled his body to face hers. Against the gurgle of the stream and the sway of leaves, he explained how, after the Grand Master had received warning of King Philip's intention to charge the Templars with heresy, Jacques de Molay had set into motion a plan to secretly dissolve the order, an arrangement crafted many years before in the event of such a threat.

"'Tis understandable that the Grand Master had devised such a scheme, but it does not explain why you are in Scotland." Gwendolyn's hand trembled as she withdrew a leaf caught within a snarl of ivy, released it into the soft breeze.

The aged brown sheath floated in an awkward tumble, landed within the current, and then turned in helpless disarray down the slow-moving stream.

Lines marred her brow as she met his gaze. "You are not here alone, are you?"

"Nay. Before the arrests began, beneath the cover of darkness, the Templar fleet fled La Rochelle to preserve the treasures held within the Paris temple. Several ships sailed to Scotland, the remainder to Portugal."

"Thank God you and so many others were able to escape. With the Brotherhood warned of King Philip's intent, why couldna all of the Templars leave?"

Aiden fought against the despair at those who'd suffered, the overwhelming grief that'd haunted him since that fateful night.

"I, along with others who were chosen to flee," he rasped, "were sickened that we couldna forewarn men we had fought alongside over the years." He swallowed hard. "The Grand Master explained to those loyal to King Philip, the Brotherhood's daily routine must appear unchanged. Any slip, any hint that we had discovered the sovereign's plan could cost not only the loss of many more Templar lives but the sacred treasures we swore to protect."

"I am so sorry." She lay her trembling hand upon his. "I canna imagine the hurt you and your men suffered."

For a long moment he stared at her fingers, moved by her act of compassion. How long had he held in his grief, never sharing the hurt or daring to release the sorrow he had been convinced once unleashed would overwhelm him?

Yet, for the first time since King Philip's betrayal, he found himself needing to share, or mayhap he had found someone important enough in his life to whom he could expose his sorrow.

Foolish thoughts. Theirs was a union based on lies. Though she offered sympathy, 'twas due to her gentle heart. Still, Aiden coveted her kindness, and a part of him wished they could indeed have forever.

"We still grieve," he admitted, "a fact that I doubt will ever change."

"Understandably." After a gentle squeeze, she withdrew her hand.

Aiden yearned to entwine his fingers with hers, to forge a permanent bond. In the end, he remained silent, stowing his dangerous thoughts. Once Latharn Castle was seized, he'd vowed to Gwendolyn he would be gone from her life.

"There isna a Templar seaport in Scotland, so why were any ships sent here?"

"King Robert's religious exclusion and the Scottish clergy's refusal to acknowledge his excommunication allowed the Bruce to offer all within the Brotherhood entry into his realm with impunity."

She tossed another dried leaf into the current, watched as it drifted in an awkward path to follow the last. She turned. "Did the Bruce know your ships were on their way?"

"Nay. When we arrived at Urquhart Castle, Stephan MacQuistan, the Templar in charge, presented the king a writ from the Grand Master."

She gave a slow nod. "With King Robert recently crowned and struggling with the challenges to unite Scotland, 'tis understandable he welcomed an elite fighting force to bolster his ranks."

"Under other circumstances I would agree," Aiden said, the amazement of the news still leaving him humbled, "but Robert Bruce is more than Scotland's king. He, too, is a Knight Templar."

* * * *

Gwendolyn's eyes widened as more pieces fell into place. The tie to the Brotherhood explained the king's inherent trust in Aiden, the reason he'd reinstated his familial holdings, along with his father's title, and why he'd chosen this fearless knight to reclaim and protect her home.

Except it did not answer one important question. "Why would King Robert require that we wed?"

"Upon the dissolution of the Knights Templar, the Grand Master bid those who had escaped to blend into the culture and, in time, marry."

"Which makes sense but doesna explain why the Bruce would insist on our union."

Face taut, Aiden dug his boot into the mossy bank. "The king has an inclination to pair women of wit and strength with men he respects."

She arched a brow. "An inclination?"

A wry smile touched Aiden's mouth. "Ours isna the first Templar union King Robert has arranged to some degree."

"What do you mean?" she asked, more confused.

"Stephan MacQuistan, my close friend, was the first to fall within the king's marital mischief. Months later, Thomas MacKelloch, though not ordered to wed, because of the king's meddling, ended up doing so. 'Twould seem," he said, his voice dry, "that you and I are the latest in His Grace's endeavors."

The sheer absurdity of such a claim had a smile tugging at her mouth. He was teasing her. Yet the grim acceptance in his eyes underscored his belief.

"You are telling me that the Bruce," she said, trying to understand such an absurd notion, "a powerful ruler intent on uniting Scotland, a warrior known for his ferocity in battle, and a highly skilled tactician, has a fondness for arranging marriages?"

"'Twould seem, as proven by my friends' fates and ours," Aiden said, "one of his preferred diversions."

"I see." But she did not. None of this made any sense, but what had since she'd met this valiant knight?

In fact, most warriors bestowed a castle and a wife would have accepted both without regard to her outrage. But Aiden sought to repair the wrongs dealt her and had offered her Latharn Castle once seized.

Though he was attracted to her, and regardless whether the Brotherhood had been secretly dissolved, he'd made it clear 'twas a way of life he intended to pursue.

With Aiden grieving the deaths of many of his comrades, hadn't he suffered enough? And yet, before 'twas over, because of the French sovereign's false charges, many more brave men would die.

Against the rumble of water, a bird's distant call echoed through the forest, faded.

For a moment, she studied the canopy of leaves where sprinkles of fading sunlight fragmented through the dense swath of green to dust the forest floor. 'Twas a setting carefree in its existence, a time to enjoy the warmth tumbling within the breeze before the chill of fall tinged the air.

But everything had changed.

Any lingering anger toward Aiden faded. God in heaven, how could she condemn his loyalty to the Bruce or the Brotherhood when he, as she, was caught within circumstances beyond his control?

Her chest tightened at the heartache he'd endured. Aiden was a good man. Throughout their time together, he'd been fair and had treated her with high regard. Nor could she dismiss her pull to him, one that however upset, and regardless of how much she'd fought to squelch, hadn't waned.

Yet his goals in life excluded her, a point proven by his willingness to sacrifice ever having an heir.

After all he'd suffered and lost, if he wanted to live the Templar way of life, however much she wished otherwise, 'twas a choice she would respect.

"Now what?" she whispered, saddened that within days he would be gone.

"Do you agree with my proposal?" Solemn green eyes darkened. "To live apart. Separate lives. Forgoing an heir?"

Throat tight, worried he'd see the distress in her eyes, she stared into the forest. "Aye."

"Once Latharn Castle is seized," he said, his voice empty of the passion of moments before, "with my need to capture Thorburn Castle, and then support our king in his battles, none will question my departure. Once I am gone, you, as I, will live the life you have chosen."

On a hard swallow, she nodded, skimming her fingers across the cool moss, struggling against the sense of emptiness at thoughts of his leaving. A reckless notion. Never had he intended to be part of her life. As a man, he may want and care about her, but with his loyalty to the Brotherhood, 'twas a life he would never allow himself to consider.

She glanced over. "You miss being a Knight Templar?" Gwendolyn asked despite herself.

"Very much. Almost a year has passed since the arrests began. Yet I still canna wrap my thoughts around the fact that the Brotherhood is nay more than a shell of its greatness."

At the anguish within his words, guilt swept her that she'd hesitated to free him from a bond he did not wish for. "What of your father's title, granted to you by the king?"

"In truth, 'tis still as if a dream. Never did I believe an opportunity to reclaim my legacy would exist." He shrugged. "Regardless, nobility changes little."

"I would think your reestablished birthright, along with your family's stronghold, would change everything."

Solemn eyes lifted to hers. "Nay. Once Thorburn Castle is reclaimed, I will leave sufficient guard to ensure its protection, then I will return to fight alongside our king until Scotland is united."

The cool resolve to fulfill his duty was firm, but where was the laughter, the tenderness, those moments that had gone beyond duty and created a life?

Like those she and her father had enjoyed. She smothered her deep yearning for Aiden and faced the truth. The closeness she'd believed they had had was a myth. Only her feelings had deepened during their time together, not his.

"Your loyalty to the Bruce is admirable, like my father's," she said, unhappiness sliding into her voice.

A frown curved Aiden's mouth. "Your father kept you ignorant of his fealty to the Bruce to protect you."

"He should have trusted me! I am not a simpering lass."

"He should have." Aiden paused. "Gwendolyn, there is one more thing I must tell you."

Anger slammed through her. "There is naught more I need to know."

He caught her arm as she tried to stand and pulled her back down. She tried to tug free; he held firm.

"'Tis about your father," he said, his words solemn. "He didna die in battle."

"W-what?" she gasped, trying to wrap her mind around his claim.

His hold gentled. "He died in Lord Comyn's castle. King Robert believes your father's loyalty to him was discovered and he was murdered."

Horror filled her, merging with outrage. She gulped a deep breath, then another. "The bastard! I trusted him, gave him my complete loyalty, when all along he deceived me."

"He will pay for his treachery," Aiden hissed.

Angry tears slid down her cheek, and he drew her against him. "Never will I forgive Comyn."

"Nor I."

He stroked her hair as she leaned against him. "'Twould seem my father knew Comyn wasna a man to trust. I only wish," she said, the hurt at her father easing, "that he had told me."

"Your father did what he believed best."

Gwendolyn drew in a deep sigh. "I know, but 'tis not easy to accept." She shook her head. "As if life gives us easy choices."

Aiden pressed a kiss upon her brow, and her heart ached as she remembered their earlier discussion of his leaving, his departure to give her the life he believed she wanted. Except she did not want him to go, but to remain with her.

On an unsteady breath, she sat back. "After King Robert has united Scotland, will you return to Thorburn Castle?"

For a moment his eyes softened with yearning, then grew cool. "'Tis foolish to think of the future. With each battle, I understand a chance exists 'twill be my last."

"You canna die," she gasped.

Mouth tight, he shrugged. "The day will come."

"How can you speak of your death with such indifference?" she demanded.

"I have witnessed the loss of too many warriors in battle to not have accepted such a fate," he replied with stoic calm. "Life promises naught but change. 'Tis up to each of us to make the most of each day, not carve out thoughts of a future that may never come."

Her emotions raw, Gwendolyn pushed to her feet, furious he could discuss his mortality with such ease when she struggled to think of him no longer in her life. Over the days they'd shared, he had become important to her, more than she'd ever believed possible. Her anger built. Did she matter so little to him that he would sacrifice an heir, walk away, and never see her again?

"How are you making the most of each day when you think only of war?" she lashed out.

With slow intent, he stood, his gaze cool. "My duty doesna change the opportunities presented to me," he said, his voice even, "such as being able to give you the gift of your home and the life you choose."

His selflessness left her floundering. Never had she met such an honorable man. "And what of your happiness?"

"My happiness?"

The genuine surprise in his eyes, as if he'd never considered such, deepened her sadness. "Aye. Once Scotland is united, and if you have evaded death, what will you do then?"

He shrugged. "If that time comes, I will return to my ancestral home."

"That is all?" she asked, unsure if she was more annoyed at herself for persisting with this discussion, or at him for taking everything in stride, as if he hadna offered to forsake any chance of having an heir. Did he not understand what he was giving up? A home, a family, a...

Shaken by the feelings he ignited, the dreams he stirred, Gwendolyn glanced at the darkening sky, a hint of stars flickering in the wash of purple and fading streaks of gold. She stepped back. "'Tis late."

"'Tis." For a long moment, he held his gaze, then stowed the desire he evoked deep within.

This was what she wanted, her life, as his, to go their separate ways. If for a while she had believed more existed between them, she had been wrong, understandably so. Distraught over her father's death, after meeting a man of such caliber and believing he was her husband, she'd sought his compassion.

Gwendolyn made to step past him, paused. His scent of man and earth teased her, reminded her of how it'd felt to be in his arms, of how he'd left her trembling beneath his touch. "Aiden…"

His eyes were shuttered, and he moved out of reach.

Tears burned her eyes at his withdrawal, more so after he'd held her, offered compassion moments before. Not trusting herself to speak, she strode past, but a part of her yearned for what they'd lost.

Lost?

Nay, little about their relationship was that simple. The only thing she knew was that Aiden was indeed an honorable man. Ultimately, he'd chosen to continue his duty as a Templar over being her husband in life and love.

She wiped away the tears, then hurried through the forest, more than ready to return to Latharn Castle, surrounded by people she loved, those who cared for her. Aye, numerous challenges awaited her in rebuilding her home. The demands would keep her busy, erase thoughts of Aiden. Over time, her feelings for him would fade.

* * * *

Illuminated within the torchlit camp, Aiden muttered a curse as he watched Gwendolyn disappear inside her tent.

Cailin sauntered up to him. "The lass looks sad."

"It has been a long day," Aiden said, more than ready to place the upheaval of the last few hours behind him. "I told her the truth about her father's death, nor has she calmed since we spoke our vows."

His friend gave a slow nod. "Lord Comyn has earned a dangerous enemy in deceiving her. As for your marriage, in time, she will accept the union."

"Nay," Aiden said, struggling to hide the misery letting her go had caused. 'Twas the right choice. Though she had become important to him… Important, nay. She'd become as necessary as his next breath, but he found solace that in the end she'd find peace. "Once Latharn Castle is seized, I will move on."

His friend smiled. "I did not mean after this battle, but once Scotland is united."

A muscle worked in Aiden's jaw. "I will not live with her."

Surprise flickered in the Templar's eyes. "But you are wed."

"A union neither of us wanted."

"Mayhap, but I see the way you watch the lass," Cailin said. "You care for her. Though she will not admit it, I believe her feelings for you have also deepened."

However much he wanted to believe his friend, Aiden grunted. "Gwendolyn has made it abundantly clear that she never wanted to marry."

"God's blade, if we had never intervened, what do you think would have happened when the Bruce's troops seized Latharn Castle?" Cailin demanded. "Do you think her life wouldna have changed then?"

"Aye, but we never would have met, and her life's path is for King Robert to decide."

"A decision," Cailin said with emphasis, "the king has already made. One I thought you were pleased with."

Anger blazed inside Aiden, and he damned the hurt, as if a part of him wasn't being torn apart. "Dinna you understand? How much I care for her matters little. She has lost enough. Nor will I cause her further distress." A fact he must remember. "Once Latharn Castle is reclaimed, she will have her home and a proper guard. 'Twas all she ever wanted."

"And what of you?" his friend demanded. "With the dissolution of the Brotherhood, the life we loved, the calling we have lived for, is gone."

He scowled at the fierce pang the reminder brought, no doubt deliberate. "Our duty remains. The Templar treasures must be protected."

"An assignment that belongs to Stephan MacQuistan."

Indeed. A man he respected, and one who was like a brother to him. "Neither can I forget my vow to serve the Bruce."

"Aiden," Cailin said, frustration edging his voice, "one day Scotland will be united and the fighting will cease. What will you do then?"

"Return to Thorburn Castle."

"Blast it, you know I am speaking about your marriage with Gwendolyn, yet you are making me pull any details from you like teeth."

Aiden rubbed the back of his neck as he stared blindly at the warriors within the torchlight preparing equipment across the camp for the morning's departure. "As much as I wish otherwise—" He dropped his hand. "I will respect Gwendolyn's wishes and stay away."

"With how much you care for the lass, if you do, you are a fool!"

"I would think," Aiden said, his words soft with warning, "as a Knight Templar, you would understand."

His friend's eyes narrowed. "Understand what, your sacrifice of ever being happy?"

"Blast it—"

"You have a wife, one who regardless of what you believe, of the words she offers, wants you," Cailin stated. "You have allowed pride to dictate your decision, and refuse to give the feelings that exist between you a chance."

"I never should have involved Gwendolyn in this twisted mess!"

"You did naught but your duty. Your decisions were made for the good of our sovereign." Cailin paused. "However unplanned your meeting with the lass, 'twould seem in the end a union that will do more than serve the king's needs, but 'tis a marriage in which you can find happiness."

Aiden hesitated, remembering their talk and her questions about his life after. No, 'twas foolish to hope she would entertain thoughts of him in the years ahead. "I will restore what she has lost," he said, clinging to that logic. "Her home, one without me."

His friend grunted with disgust. "But you care for her?"

"Cailin, 'tis not—"

"Admit it!"

Aiden fought to smother the surge of emotion. Failed. Hurt stormed him to think of never seeing her again. He'd believed himself detached from Gwendolyn enough that he could walk away, yet now he realized the truth.

He loved her.

God's sword. After losing his family during his youth, his years as a Templar had provided a life where naught but friendships were forged, serving Him and protecting Christians traveling through the Holy Land, he'd found a woman who had broken through all defenses.

"I do care for her. She is unlike any woman I have ever met. In truth, I was attracted to her from the start. Except," he said on a rough swallow, "my feelings will not change my decision. I have given her my word, one that I will not break."

Disgust flared in Cailin's eyes. "Does she know about your youth?"

"Leave it!" Aiden said between clenched teeth.

"Why do you refuse to allow her close? Is it because you are afraid she will care, or..." The Templar's eyes widened. "God's blade, you love her."

Fisting his hands at his sides, Aiden stared at the forest, the shadows of the night clinging to the branches like the emptiness in his heart. "How I feel about Gwendolyn changes naught."

"It changes everything."

"Do you think I dinna understand the devastation of losing your family," Aiden rasped, "of waking each morning wondering why you lived when those you loved lay dead? Blast it, she has lost her mother and now her father. In her time of desperation, I understand her need to find something that matters, when grief is so raw that you wish to curl up and die."

His friend grunted. "So you will sacrifice a chance of a future with her because you worry that if she loves you and you die, 'twill hurt her further?"

"She is to never know how I feel! I promised her she would have her home." He unclenched his hands, dragged a deep breath, then another, forcing himself to calm. "I will savor the few days we have left, then 'tis done."

Silence fell between them filled with the murmurs of men securing weapons, talking with others as they worked, melding with the soft whispers of the night.

"Because we are friends, I will say this," Cailin said. "If you walk away from this woman without telling her how you feel, you are making the biggest mistake of your life."

Aiden glared at his friend. "Mayhap, but 'tis my mistake to make."

Chapter 16

Hours later, through the open tent flap, Gwendolyn scanned the wash of stars flickering in the night, the soft breeze infused with the scent of smoke drifting past. Sadness built inside as she glanced at the moon lingering overhead. A silvery wash spilled across the treetops to underscore her misery.

The pad of steps grew louder.

She turned. Outlined by torchlight, Aiden and Cailin walked toward the tent. In the short time she had known Aiden, she'd come to recognize the way he walked and found pride in his being a man who stood behind his word regardless the cost. Gwendolyn smothered the ball of regret at the thought of not bearing his child.

On a sigh, she narrowed her gaze as the men moved closer. At the entry, they halted.

"I will see you at first light. I urge you to reconsider what we have discussed." With a nod, Cailin departed.

Caught within the pale light, Aiden ducked and entered.

She stiffened as he moved past and made a pallet a distance from hers. She should have expected him this night. Though they had made agreements for the future, to those within the camp they were married. Neither did she miss the irony that 'twas their wedding night.

Again.

'Twice she'd married him, and 'twould seem the second oath would forevermore bind her to Aiden.

Shadows smothered his face. Unable to read his expression, she remained silent.

Blankets shifted as he settled. "Are you asleep?"

"Nay. I was thinking of the conversation with King Robert, you, and your men regarding how to capture my home," she said, giving up the hope of seeing his muscled form in the darkness. "The plan is impressive. Never would I have thought of setting the ships ablaze, severing the mooring lines, and allowing the vessels to drift, then collide into one another."

"'Twill destroy a good portion, if not all of the English fleet, plus provide a much-needed distraction." Covers rustled as he shifted. "When the English bolt from the castle to try to salvage their ships, the Bruce's main force will seal off any avenue of escape and attack. A moonless night will serve us well, sea fog even more so."

"With the moon waning," Gwendolyn said, unsettled by thoughts of the upcoming battle, "by the time we arrive 'twill be little more than a sliver when we attack. As for the sea fog, 'tis another matter."

"I understand your reason for wanting to accompany us," he said, "but I again ask that you disclose where the hidden passageways are, along with the location of your father's secret ledger, and remain in King Robert's camp."

Though soft, she heard the worry in his voice. "I will go. I have done, and will continue to do, whatever I see fit to tend to my people's well-being and restore my home."

He gave a frustrated growl.

Let him be angry. After the events of this day, there was enough for them both. She turned on her side.

Through the opening in the tent, a falling star streaked across the sky, faded.

Gwendolyn closed her eyes to make a wish, then stilled. As if such existed. 'Twas naught but the dreams of a young girl, a time long past. However ill achieved, soon she would regain her home.

Unbidden, a child's face whose laughter filled her heart shimmered to mind, a handsome lad with Aiden's eyes. Regret twisted inside at what would never be.

She should be happy. She'd agreed to her husband's offer and her future was set.

"Then accompany my force when we prepare for the attack," he growled at last, "but remember your promise to remain within the secret tunnel until I send word that Latharn Castle is seized."

Her hands tightened on her covers. "The only reason I conceded not to fight was your reasoning that if I were captured, I could ruin everything."

"I have little doubt you would be a fierce opponent," he said, his words tight. "'Tis the horrors of battle I wish to spare you."

On edge, Gwendolyn tucked her blanket around her waist, sat up, and rubbed her arms. "I wish the fighting was over."

"As do I. I am weary of battle, of the dying, of seeing the devastation brought by war." Blankets shifted. "Nor did I wish to spend the evening talking of such horror."

A feeling she shared. Silence fell between them, punctuated by a hoot of an owl and the tremble of leaves in the forest.

"Are you tired?" Aiden asked.

"Nay," she admitted. "I am too restless to sleep."

He stood. "Come."

Curious, she pushed aside the covers. Her eyes accustomed to the night, she followed.

Silvery light flickered over the land like wishes cast, the gentle breeze filled with a hint of flowers, and the coolness of the night.

At the trees near the edge of the encampment, she hesitated.

Aiden took her hand, tugged her forward. "Dinna worry, we will be safe. "Several hundred more warriors loyal to the Bruce arrived this day. To ensure the enemy doesna infiltrate the camp, King Robert has increased our guard around the perimeter."

"When did they come?" she asked, surprised she had missed the influx of such a large contingent.

"While we were discussing the plans for the attack with the king." Aiden stepped off the path, weaving through the dense woodland without hesitation.

Moments later, the thick foliage broke away.

She gasped at the sharp drop off from the stone ledge paces away.

His grip on her hand tightened. "You are safe. Here, sit." Aiden drew her beside him on the smooth rock. "Look up."

Framed within the night, stars filled the sky in a magnificent array. Their glitter melded with the waning moon's light spilling upon the land, exposing the wall of the cliffs and the endless miles of forest below.

Aiden gestured to the left. "See the milky swath of light smeared across the sky? 'Tis said the path is created from the sparks cast off the blades of warriors locked in mortal combat."

As surprised as moved by his story, a smile touched her lips. "You are crafting a tale."

"Mayhap," he said, laughter touching his voice. "Do you have a better reason why the stars are set together in such a pattern?"

"Nay. Nor do I think you brought me here to discuss such mysteries," she said, appreciating the way the light spilled along the cliff side and the forest below. "Regardless of the reason, 'tis beautiful."

"I thought you might enjoy this view. 'Tis a favorite of mine."

Secretly delighted, she teased, "What if I was afraid of being so high?"

The warmth of his chuckle slid through her like a caress. "Lass, I doubt you would be afraid of anything so simple."

"But I could have been."

His thumb caressed the top of her hand.

Awareness shot through her, and her breath caught in her throat as he turned to face her, his eyes dark with need.

He leaned closer, his mouth a breath from hers, and a sense of something important filled her, of a moment, a wisp of time that somehow could, if she allowed it, change everything.

"Do you ever wish for what you have nay right to ask for?" he breathed, the sadness in his voice breaking her heart.

Aye, of how much I want you, she silently replied.

As if coming out of a trance, Aiden stiffened, withdrew his hand.

Missing his touch, bereft even though she knew 'twas foolish to toy with the unattainable, Gwendolyn searched for something to return the moment to safer ground. "Does anything worry you?"

"I refuse to answer that and look weak in your eyes."

"I doubt there is such a possibility," she said, finding the statement true.

For a long moment he stared at her, and she caught the edge of sadness in his gaze. "You speak highly of me when we have known each other for but a short while."

"Mayhap," she agreed, "but during that brief time, I have discovered you are a man of your word, one who cares."

"'Tis great praise indeed."

"Praise you have earned. Even when I didna know your true name, your deeds exposed you as a knight of high regard."

Quiet fell between them, broken by the soft sounds of the night, and she enjoyed the peace his company brought her. A serenity that, once he departed for Thorburn Castle, she would miss.

Leather scuffed rock as he stepped back. "'Tis late. We must return to camp if we are to rest at all."

As if with thoughts of him stirring in her mind she could rest? Not wanting to end this time between them, but doubting 'twas wise to remain, she nodded.

* * * *

Several days later, as the sun slowly edged toward the horizon, Gwendolyn sat near a break in the dense brush, stared at her home in the distance.

Hundreds of tents littered the roll of land, livestock grazed in several places, and near the castle, a trebuchet was being built.

At the sounds of steps, she glanced up.

Sir Cailin moved up the incline toward her.

She arched a brow, refusing to allow Aiden's friend to see her disappointment. Since the morning they'd departed for Latharn Castle, Aiden had kept his distance.

As the Templar neared the top of the embankment, Cailin crouched to keep behind the thicket, and then moved to where she sat. "You dinna mind company?"

"Nay." She glanced toward the stronghold. "Though far from reclaimed, 'tis good to see my home."

He settled on a nearby rock, gestured toward the mist-laden coast. "We are fortunate sea fog has begun to form. By dawn it should be thick enough to slice."

"How did Aiden know the mist would appear?"

Cailin glanced at the clear sky, then to where the dense blanket of white hung over the water a distance out to sea. "The conditions are right."

"How do you know that?"

"From our time at sea. If you sail enough, you notice a connection with wind, air, the sun's heat or lack of it, and the resultant weather."

"I canna begin to imagine all you and the others have learned over your years as Templars."

"'Tis difficult to think the life we love is over."

At the roughness of his voice, she shook her head. "I am sorry."

"As am I. One day King Philip will regret his treachery to the Brotherhood."

"He will," Gwendolyn whispered, as would Comyn. She shoved aside thoughts of the noble, savored the gentle breeze sliding past edged with the scent of the sea. "When will Aiden begin the assault?"

"At the hour of the wolf."

"A Templar phrase?" she asked with a smile.

"Nay. This expression was coined long before the formation of the Brotherhood. It means the hour before dawn."

Her smile faded. "I have sailed with my father over the years but never heard that phrase."

"Because 'tis a term familiar to warriors."

"I see." An icy prickle swept up her spine as she glanced toward the fortress. "I fear many will die." Including Aiden. A tremor slid through her. No, he must live!

"Shielded by fog, we shall be able to position ourselves to gain the advantage," Cailin explained. "During the attack, the loss of life will be minimal and, more importantly, belong to the English."

"I wish 'twas over," she breathed.

He grunted. "'Twill be soon enough."

Torches flickered on the distant wall walk, and she faced the warrior, his eyes watching her in the fading light. "I doubt you have come to speak of tactics."

He removed his water pouch, offered her a drink.

"Nay."

After several sips, Cailin secured the top, stowed the sewn leather. "You care for Aiden."

She smothered the surge of emotion. In her heart, she had reconciled herself to letting him live the life he desired. "He and I have come to an arrangement."

"Arrangement," he scoffed. "'Tis a situation neither of you want. Once Latharn Castle is seized, 'tis a mistake if you let him walk away."

"He has told you the details of our arrangement?"

Cailin gave a curt nod.

Hurt he'd shared their private agreement, she stiffened. "Why?"

"In truth, I badgered him because he is my friend."

Far from understanding, Gwendolyn frowned. "Then why are you not raising your concerns to him?"

He grunted. "I assure you, I tried. He refuses to listen."

"And what makes you think talking with me will change anything?"

Blue eyes riveted on her. "If I didna believe you cared for Aiden, I assure you, I wouldna be here." He raised his hand as she made to speak. "He is more stubborn than most."

That she could attest to.

"Tell me, has he spoken with you since we left King Robert's camp?"

An ache squeezed her chest. "Nay."

"Nay doubt because he believes 'tis for the best." He released a frustrated sigh, then stared at her for a long moment. "I am here to help you win Aiden. Do you want him?"

Heart pounding, she fought for calm, unsure what to say, or if she should admit her feelings for Aiden. She gave a shaky nod. "Aye."

"Ask him about his past."

Gwendolyn frowned. "As a Templar?"

"Nay, about his family."

So caught up in the mayhem since Aiden's arrival, the English seizing the castle, and their escape, she hadn't inquired about his youth. "What about them?"

"'Tis his story to share, but one you need to know before he departs."

A tremor ripped through her, and coldness wrapped around her heart. "Why are you telling me this?"

"Because you are important to him, more than he will admit."

She stilled. "Why would you say that?"

"Because I see the way you stare at him when you believe others are not looking." He paused. "And the way he watches you."

She forced herself to smile, to ignore the slash of hurt. "You are mistaken. I am naught but a duty. A point he has made *very* clear."

A muscle worked in Cailin's jaw. "You are wrong."

Hope ignited, but she smothered the feeling. But the mystery of Aiden's past left her curious. What could have occurred to make Cailin believe 'twould change what was between her and Aiden?

"If he cares for me," Gwendolyn said, "why has he kept his distance since we departed King Robert's camp?"

"Because he promised to give you your life back."

She frowned. "That doesna make sense. Aiden explained that the Brotherhood was everything to him, a life he will never relinquish for anyone, including me."

"If you want him," he said, his voice cool, "ask him about his family. I pray he tells you, helps you understand all he has overcome, the demons he battles to this day, the torment that began before he joined the Brotherhood." He stood. "I have said enough." With a curt nod, he walked away.

Confused, she watched him head down the steep slope. She scanned the bank in search of Aiden. In the distance, he stood alongside another man in deep discussion.

What had happened in his youth that had caused him such torment? If she learned what had happened, would things indeed change between them, as Cailin believed?

Did she want them to?

With a sigh, she glanced toward the castle, the home she loved, and for the first time, seeing the stronghold evoked a sense of emptiness.

Chapter 17

The deep purples of night, devoid of any hint of the oncoming day, infused the heavens, the sliver of moon but a faint whisper in the sky. From the ridge, Aiden peered between the bushes, pleased the sea fog, illuminated by the soft brush of starlight, had begun moving inland.

He smiled as the dense layer of white edged up the shore, engulfed all within its path until naught was visible except the torchlight upon the wall walk.

Time was on his side. He would wait a few more hours to allow the fog to creep farther onshore before he moved his men into position.

At the clatter of rock to his right, Aiden clasped his blade and peered through the fog. "Who is there?"

"'Tis Gwendolyn."

His body tightened at the throaty slide of her voice. She materialized from the mist, a maiden who drove him mad with desire. His hand relaxed as a new battle built inside. Sheathing his weapon, he fought to smother the ache in his heart at her nearness.

A warm rush filled him as she moved closer.

"Why are you here without a guard?" he snapped as he scoured their surroundings. Distance between them 'twas for the best for her, if not for his own renegade heart. More time together would do naught but strengthen a bond he'd sworn to sever.

"I needed to speak with you."

He glanced toward her, and the shot of desire almost drove him to his knees. "Though I believe the English are ignorant of our presence, 'tis dangerous to be away from camp."

"I am not foolish enough to be unarmed." The slight waver in her voice betrayed her confident stance, and Gwendolyn started to step back.

"Tell me," Aiden said, damning his growing weakness for her.

"You have avoided me since we departed the king's camp. Why?"

Pain slashed his gut, and he cursed her question, that he'd made her doubt herself in any manner. For her strength, wit, and fierce determination, she deserved naught but respect. "Given our unwanted marriage, I thought you would find my staying away a welcome reprieve."

The taut lines of her face softened. "Had I despised you, aye. But I dinna."

Panic prickled over his skin. What was she saying? Once the Bruce had claimed Scotland, did she want him to return to Latharn Castle? Nay, 'twas naught but his own yearning.

Aiden cleared his throat, wanting to pull her into his arms and, if only for a moment, feel her mouth against his. "I am relieved you dinna hate me."

"However angry I was with you, I never could. Throughout our time together you have always acted loyally, have done your best to protect me."

Too aware of her, of her taste, of how her body felt against his, he exhaled. "We should return to camp."

"Tell me about your family?"

Heart pounding, he froze. "What?"

"I was thinking of how little I know of you."

His chest tightened beneath thoughts of his family torn from his life, of his guilt for having survived. With cool precision, Aiden removed her hand, not wanting to discuss this time in his life with her. "My past matters little."

"It matters to me," she said, the sincerity of her words wrapping around his anguished memories with a strangling hold. "You know about me, my father, my brief marriage. Yet I know naught about you except for your being a Templar."

His denial to tell her anything about his youth was ingrained, but against all logic he found the thought of sharing his past with her important.

A cool gust of wind laden with the salty tang of the sea whipped past. Leaves rattled in the shrubs, then stilled.

"During my twelfth summer, my family and I were returning to Scotland after a visit to France. En route, a violent storm destroyed the ship."

"What happened?" she asked, her voice raw with dread.

A shudder swept him, then another, as his mind lurched back to the screams, the explosions of thunder, and the towering waves battering the bow with merciless force. "Storm-fed winds destroyed the sails, leaving the ship helpless in the tempest's fury. My father ordered us to remain below, but with the foolish confidence of a lad, I climbed above deck. The cog plunged into the next trough, and a wall of water crashed over the bow, tearing crates free and ripping me off the ladder and over the side."

"Oh, God!" she gasped.

"Tossed about within the rough seas, by sheer luck I caught the edge of a plank. In the..." His voice began to break, and he looked away, swallowed hard. "In the darkness I clung to the wood, prayed for help, for any sign of life. Hours passed, and with each one, hope that somehow the ship had survived, that my family still lived, faded. Exhausted, numb from the cold, I lost consciousness."

Her hand lay on his arm, but, raw with emotion, he did not turn to her. With the grief of his youth exposed and struggling for control, he refused to risk the desire to take her into his arms and accept the comfort offered when it could lead to naught.

"Your family?" she breathed.

He swallowed hard. "I was the only one aboard who survived. Naught was retrieved of the ship except for fragments of wood strewn along the shore, one plank bearing the vessel's name.

"I am so sorry."

Aiden gave into his growing need to touch her and linked his fingers with hers. Another breeze swept past, thick with the scent of the sea. "'Twas a long time ago."

"It was, but I understand the hurt."

She did, and however dangerous, the tension knotted in his chest eased with the telling.

"I am confused," she said.

He rubbed his thumb over her silky skin. "About what?"

"Why would the Bruce bestow your father's title and castle upon you when they were already yours to claim?"

"Because," he whispered, the fury he'd buried all these years raging through his words, "once I was rescued and returned to Thorburn Castle, 'twas to discover the English had seized my home."

Her fingers tightened on his. "Mary's will, what did you do?"

Shame filled him, and he withdrew his hand. "Terrified, alone, and unsure of how to proceed, I fled. In the end, I was taken in by the Knights Templar." He stared into the star-filled night sky. "In their teachings, I found a sense of peace, although the anger and grief refused to be silenced. I poured myself into training, used each crusade to hone my skills. Though my goal was to protect the Christians traveling to the Holy Land, 'twas mired in my need for revenge."

* * * *

The horror of what Aiden had endured left Gwendolyn aching for him, and for the guilt he struggled to hide. "Anyone who had shared your experience would crave vengeance. That you rose above your grief, your fury, says much about you."

He whirled, his eyes narrowing. "Dinna paint me a hero."

How could she do otherwise? He had overcome insurmountable odds and had not only lived but had become a fierce warrior, a leader of men many admired, including her.

"With my vow given to the Templars, never did I expect to reclaim my heritage. If given the opportunity," he continued, "I would sacrifice my birthright to save the Brotherhood tortured and killed beneath King Philip's treacherous hand." He abruptly turned and with long, ground-eating strides, headed toward camp.

Grief swept her at all he had endured, and she caught up to him and fell into step at his side.

At their tent, he halted. "Try to sleep."

Gwendolyn moved before him, overwhelmed by all he had made her feel. "What of you?"

"I will make a pallet outside." He stepped back. "Sleep 'til I wake you. In a few hours, once my men are in position, you will be escorted to the secret tunnel." With a curt nod, he walked away.

An ache twisted in her heart as Gwendolyn watched him go, understanding Cailin's reason for her to learn of Aiden's past, to see all he had endured. He was a man who had lost his family, a tragedy that had dictated his actions since.

And as for her...

The urge to call out to him, to beg Aiden to stay with her this night, wavered on her lips. She caught the flap of the tent, torn as to what to do.

His stride steady, his muscled outline faded in the night.

Gwendolyn's fingers tightened on the fabric as she wondered if letting him go was indeed a mistake. On a shaky breath, she stepped inside the tent, settled on her pallet. There would be time after the battle to speak with her husband, to decide what she truly wanted, though warmth at thoughts of Aiden left nay doubt what she would choose.

* * * *

Enshrouded by dense fog Aiden crept forward, his every step on the sand, along with the handful of his men who followed, amplified. The deep rumble of the swells rolling up the beach echoed into the night, the raw smell of salt and night a potent mix. Sound carried a great distance in the mist, the reason he'd instructed his men to remain silent until he gave the order to attack.

Through the first layer of white, he made out the faint glimmer of stars, the claws of night upon the land firm within its grasp.

Glutted with pompous superiority, the English would believe themselves safe from an attack, more so at night. An arrogance they would rue.

A short while later, with his men hidden below the cliffs, Aiden turned to where Gwendolyn had stopped paces away with the two guards he'd assigned to her. His heart ached at her fierce beauty, and he cursed that once the castle was secured, he must let her go.

She held his gaze, her mouth tight, her eyes filled with determination.

"After you are within the tunnel, stay there until you are told the fighting is over," Aiden whispered. "Once I receive word you are inside, my men and I will row out and set fire to their ships. When they are ablaze and the English surge from the castle to save their fleet, my force will attack." He paused. "Do you have any questions?"

"Nay." Gwendolyn stepped before him, her face white within the silvery smears of light. "I thank you for all you have done."

He fisted his hand, not wanting her thanks, but her. A desire, given his vow, that would never be. "Latharn Castle is far from ours."

Her eyes darkened with pride. "But 'twill be. Because of you." She pressed a soft kiss on his mouth. "Know that I will pray for you." Her voice broke on the last words.

Aiden caught her shoulders. "I will come back to you. That I swear!" Her soft gasp made him realize his error. Blast it, never was she to know how much she meant to him. His heart breaking, he gave her a gentle shove. "Go."

"Godspeed." The soft crunch of leather on the sand filled the silence as she and her guard crept down the beach.

Aiden watched her go, damned each step that took her farther away from him. He'd fought in many battles, but the stakes hadn't been so high.

Nor had he been in love.

A soft cry of a hawk echoed in the night.

The sign. Aiden turned to Cailin. "Take charge of the remaining men. Keep hidden until the ships are ablaze and the English storm from the castle. Once they are too far from the stronghold to retreat, attack."

"Aye," Cailin replied.

Aiden glanced toward the fortress. "Is Rónán in place?"

His friend nodded. "He, along with twenty men, are hidden near the stronghold. Once we have cut off the English, they will slip inside and seize the castle."

"Excellent." Aiden turned, then hesitated. "My friend, we have been through much. If anything should happen to me, ensure Gwendolyn is taken care of."

Somber eyes held his. "I swear it."

"I thank you. And now," Aiden said, focusing on their mission, "I think 'tis time to teach these English bastards a lesson!"

"Aye," Cailin agreed, "'tis indeed."

Waves rolled up the shore as Aiden led the few men he'd selected to the wooden boats pulled onto the sand. Once the crafts were shoved into the surf, they rowed toward the moored cogs.

Halfway there, as he dipped his oars into an oncoming swell, the edge of the tidal current caught him. Muscles bunched, Aiden rowed beyond the dangerous pull of water, aware that the intense flow could drag an unsuspecting man a great distance out to sea.

A short while later, he halted near the anchor of the farthest craft, severed the mooring. Freed, the ship drifted toward the main fleet. Aiden climbed aboard, then slayed the guard, the resistance from the Englishman pathetic. After binding several lengths of wood, he soaked them in oil and set them ablaze.

Thick black smoke billowed above the flames, the stench of the burning rags filling the air as Aiden climbed down the ladder, the putrid bundle firm in his grip.

At the bottom, he glanced around the crates for signs of another guard. Seeing none, he lit fires around the hull.

The roaring flames built and spread around him. A sharp snap sounded to his side, then a hiss. Wood groaned beneath collapsing wood, and he whirled.

God's sword, whatever cargo they carried was fueling the blaze, the ship going up faster than expected. He drew back to heave the torch onto the crates near the end of the hull.

A blur appeared before him a moment before he caught the glint of steel.

Aiden blocked the swing with the torch, withdrew his sword with his free hand.

"Ye bastard!" his attacker shouted.

Forged steel sank into the flaming wood, driving Aiden back. Sweat streaming down his face, heat building with each breath, he swung.

The assailant screamed as Aiden's blade drove a huge gash along his side. Fury and pain marred the man's face. With a curse, he lunged.

Aiden shoved his dagger deep into the warrior's chest, but, still in motion, the attacker's body collided with his. Arms flailing, Aiden stumbled back, tripping on several collapsed timbers. He grabbed for a nearby post, missed, slammed against the planks below.

Pain exploded in his head. Against the roar of the growing flames and the cloying smoke, he gasped for breath.

Blackness threatened.

Heat an inferno around him, he forced himself to sit. He heaved his enemy's body away and shoved to his feet. Flames consumed most of the interior hull and soot-drenched smoke billowed through the hatch he had climbed down only moments before.

Head throbbing, Aiden wrapped his hands around the woven hemp, cursed with each effort as he pulled himself onto the dock.

Fire blocked his path to the severed mooring.

At the screams of men and the clash of swords, he glanced to the shore. Outlined within a haze of murky white, a violent battle came into view.

Bedamned, he had to reach his men! Teeth clenched against the pain, Aiden slashed a nearby coil of rope, secured one end to the rail, tossed the rest over the side. He swung his leg over the polished wood, paused.

The boat had broken loose and was drifting away.

Wood groaned below, and a blast of heat slapped him.

He turned.

Flames surrounded him.

Bedamned, once he reached the sea, he'd have to swim. With a tug to ensure the knot was secure, he began his descent.

Halfway, the line dropped further.

With a curse, Aiden glanced up.

Fire danced along the top of the hemp. A twisted piece frayed. Smoke belched, and flames consumed the loosened line.

The rope groaned.

Snapped.

Aiden fell.

* * * *

The faint roar of battle and the screams of pain echoed down the tunnel. Gwendolyn's fingers on her dagger tightened.

"Steady, lass," a deep male voice said.

She glanced toward Sir Vide. "I should be fighting alongside Aiden's men to reclaim my home."

"Aiden wants you safe."

She scoffed. "Safe doing naught." She glanced toward the exit. Sunlight streamed inside, assuring her hours had passed. Frustrated, she paced. She should have insisted she be allowed to fight.

"Lady Gwendolyn?"

Rónán's distant call had her whirling. Heart pounding, she watched as the honorable knight came into view, realized that now, naught but the rumble of waves filled the air. Hope ignited. "Is the battle over?"

Smears of blood on his mail, the knight halted before her. "Aye," Rónán said, grim satisfaction on his face. "Latharn Castle is secure."

She steadied herself as relief threatened to buckle her knees. "Thank God."

"My lady." Sir Vide gestured toward the blackened portion of the tunnel. "Does this passageway lead inside the stronghold?"

"Aye, it comes out at the stables."

"I ask you to go inside the keep and remain there until we have cleared away the dead." The Templar grimaced. "'Tis not a sight I, or any of the warriors, would wish to see."

"I thank you, but good men have risked their lives to reclaim my home. I willna shame them by cringing in a corner whilst I hide from the realities of war."

Respect flickered in the knight's gaze. "Aye, my lady."

Sand crunched beneath her slippers as she hurried past the knights to the seaward exit, needing to see Aiden. To thank him, she assured herself, but with her castle seized, his leaving weighed heavy upon her mind.

At the entrance, Gwendolyn paused.

An icy shiver swept her at the bodies of the English strewn over the shore, the spill of blood staining the outgoing swells and smearing the sweep of the beach she so loved.

Rónán's gentle hand touched her shoulder. "My lady, return to the castle through the tunnel."

She stepped free. "Nay." Head held high, she walked toward where the men loyal to King Robert were standing on the beach, staring at the billowing smoke from the Englishmen's cogs. Aiden and his men had sunk their fleet.

Anxious to see him, she scoured the shore as she made her way toward Cailin. Where was Aiden?

At her approach, Cailin turned.

The grief in his eyes stole her breath, and time slowed to one breath. Heart pounding, refusing to acknowledge his silent revelation, she searched the men working around them, spotted those who had been chosen to row out and set the ships ablaze.

Everyone except Aiden.

Nay, he'd returned and had joined his men in the castle. Fisting her hands against the rush of fear, she faced Cailin. "Aiden?"

Face ashen, the Templar gestured toward a nearby boat scarred with blackened wood. "We found the craft he took down the shore and brought it back."

The fragile control of her emotions broke. "W-where is he?"

Cailin's somber eyes held hers. "He didna return."

"Nay," she said as her legs weakened and fear stole every shred of composure.

"We have scoured the shore," the knight rasped, "nor has anyone seen him."

She gasped for air, once then again. No, he couldna be dead! Grief swamped her, and she tried to breathe, but the world became a mist around her. Her body swayed, and hands caught her as she fell.

Chapter 18

Heart aching, Gwendolyn stood on the shore. Through blurry eyes she took in the damaged ships, their splintered and charred boards littering the beach from the attack three days past. Sadness gripped her soul at the vivid display of the horrors of war.

Aye, they'd recaptured Latharn Castle. But the price had been too high.

Fresh tears burned her eyes as she scoured the swells for any sign of life, any movement, any flicker of hope that Aiden lived.

"Lass," Cailin said, his voice raw with fatigue and grief, "three days have passed. You have searched day and night with little sleep."

She fisted her hands. "As have you all."

"You are tired and all but weaving on your feet. Return to the castle. If only for a while, try to rest."

Anger flared within the heartache. "I refuse to give up. Aiden is still alive."

"I pray 'tis so, but we have searched the beach for miles, rowed through the wood-filled swells and found nay sign."

"I would know if he was dead!" Gwendolyn refused to meet Cailin's gaze, to see the pity in his eyes, and the regret. She ignored the doubts threatening to smother her, clung to her heart's belief.

An incoming wave surged up the beach, its tip curling, then spilling on the sand with a deep rumble. The foamy edge carried endless fragments of blackened wood, numerous broken crates, and other items from the ships yet to be recovered. Wreckage scraped within the surf as the wave receded as another swell rolled ashore.

In the distance, Gwendolyn caught sight of a swath of forest green cloth with Celtic designs woven at the edge.

Recognition slammed through her. "God, nay!" Gwendolyn bolted.

"Lass?"

Water splashed as she ran through the incoming wave. Waist high, the current pulled at her legs.

She trudged deeper.

On a sob, she jerked the tattered swatch from the tangled heap of floating debris. Her hand fisted around the soggy cloth and her eyes filled with tears. She gulped a deep breath, then another.

Cailin came to her side. "What in the..." His face paled. "God's blade," he rasped, "'tis a piece of Aiden's tunic."

Coldness sliced through her. Like a fool, she had convinced herself she wanted a life alone, that she could walk away from all Aiden made her feel.

Yet as she stared down at the delicate weave of gold crafted into a Celtic cross, her heart splintered into a thousand pieces. Without wanting to, she had fallen in love with him.

A sob burst free, then another, as she clutched the cloth to her chest. Her shoulders quaked beneath her grief, beneath the weight of so many words left unsaid.

Cailin drew her against his chest. "Let yourself go, lass. You have held your heartache in too long."

At his tender entreaty, she caved beneath a hurt so raw her knees threatened to give way. "I never told him that I loved him."

"Aye, lass...he knew."

"You are so very wrong. H-he only knew of my anger."

Silence thickened as one moment rolled into two, and still the knight held her. Even as she cried out her denial and cursed the battle that had twisted her world into despair, Aiden's friend lent her strength, held her up, his wise whispered words guiding her back to the much-need footing of sanity.

Piece by piece, she gathered her composure, and on a rough exhale, she stepped away.

Tears rolling down her cheeks, she stared at the incoming wave, sparkling beneath the morning sun as if mocking her anguish. "Nay, Cailin," she whispered, "I refuse to believe he is gone. He is strong. A leader of men. A warrior unlike any other I have ever known." She turned and peered into the large knight's caring eyes. "He is still out there," she said, her voice cracking beneath a surge of hope. "And if it takes 'til my last drawn breath, I will find him."

"Lass—"

Cailin caught her arm.

The damp piece of Aiden's tunic clenched in her hand, she pulled free. "I am riding south. Nay doubt, like he did in his youth, Aiden was able to float on a piece of the damaged ship." She suppressed the swell of tears. "The current has taken him farther down the shore than we believed. He must be there." She narrowed her eyes. "You can accompany me, but I warn you, you willna stop me." She sloshed through the surf toward where her mount waited.

The men on the beach working to clear the rubble glanced up as she stormed past. Their looks of pity only strengthened her resolve. They may believe their brave leader was dead, but until she saw proof, she would keep searching.

As she swung onto her mount, the soft clop of hooves upon sand sounded behind her. She glanced up.

Mouth grim, Cailin drew alongside, gave a curt nod. "Let us go."

Aye, let them find the man she loved.

* * * *

Hands clamped around the broken slats of wood he clung to, Aiden forced his eyes open. Sunlight shimmered off the choppy surface, at odds with the wind-fed swells he'd battled at sea.

The distance cliffs grew closer.

Joy surged through him and he began kicking harder. God's sword, how far had he traveled? After watching the sunrise for the past three days, as he had floated in the open ocean, his every attempt against the strong current ending in utter failure, there was no telling. Over the last few hours, with the wind shift, he had begun to make progress toward shore.

He glanced at the strip of his tattered tunic, which sealed a large gash in his arm, thankful he had stopped bleeding. Yet with sun-blistered skin and dizziness, and desperate for water, if he did not reach shore soon... he stifled a shudder. No, he would make it, if only to find Gwendolyn.

What a fool to think he could walk away and never see her again. 'Twas thoughts of her beautiful face, her spirit, and her giving nature that had kept him alive. He must find her and tell her the truth.

His broken raft lifted above the incoming swell. He kicked with the wave. He moved ahead but an arm's length. Bedamned, at this rate 'twould be another day before he made it ashore.

Dragging his body higher on the blackened slats, Aiden scanned the storm-littered coast in search of movement. As if after three days his men would continue their search for him. During the first two days, sea swells had robbed him of seeing land, and the moonless nights had drenched him in darkness.

Regardless, he had mapped the stars overhead, knew he drifted southward. But how far? Another shudder wracked his body. With his strength depleting, he must make land soon. Like a beacon of hope, Gwendolyn's smile shimmered bright in his mind.

By God, he'd reach her!

Muscles screaming, Aiden shoved himself into the water, clung to the edge of the tattered board. Using his good arm and ignoring the pain, he kicked in unison; with each stroke he paddled toward the strip of sand below the cliffs.

His vision dimmed. He gritted his teeth, swam harder.

A light breeze built, tossing waves against him as he edged forward.

Arms aching, as he reached out he realized the current had caught him. Euphoria fell away as he drifted toward where the rocks along the coast cut into the incoming surf.

Heart pounding, he rose with the next swell, kicking hard.

His fragmented craft edged closer.

Fighting exhaustion, Aiden doubled his efforts. Inch by precious inch, he neared the coast away from the dangerous rocks.

At last his boot scraped against the sandy bottom. Aiden collapsed against the charred frame while the incoming wave shoved him higher up the beach. When the surf slid back, he rolled free from the battered wood, then braced his legs against the withdrawing rush.

The next wave rushed ashore. Aiden shoved to his feet, staggered up the slope. Another surge of white water littered with sand slammed against him and threw him off balance. He thrust his boots into the sand and trembled beneath the powerful rush.

As the churning water ebbed around him, he stumbled onshore, then collapsed to his knees.

Throat raw, dragging in gulps of air, Aiden searched the dips in the land, breaks in the rock for any water left from a recent storm.

Waves rumbled behind him, and the foam-edged surf slid halfway up his body.

Gwendolyn with her whispered words, her laughter, and her beautiful curves. She reached out for him, beckoning him forward, encouraging him to endure and stay focused.

Muscles screaming, he crawled toward her as she stood beside seaweed entangled with sun-dried grass. But she moved back toward the shady overhang of trees. He followed, wincing against the sun-warmed sand, and the sharp, hot stabs of rock upon his knees and fingers.

Cool shadows engulfed his body as the wind rattled branches overhead, but he could no longer find her. Frantic, he searched, but his body began to tremble.

Unable to fight the inrushing surge of darkness, on a groan, he collapsed, succumbed to the whirl of blackness.

* * * *

After rounding the curving shore, Gwendolyn drew her mount to a halt. The cloth from Aiden's tunic firm in her hand, she searched the coast.
Naught.

Cailin's horse at her side snorted. "'Tis growing late, lass. We must turn back before it grows too dark."

She glanced skyward, stunned to find the sun on the horizon, and streaks of purples and oranges filling the sky. "Nay. We have at least another hour before nightfall. As long as I can see, I am searching." Gwendolyn kicked her mount into a canter.

At the next bend, she heard Cailin curse before he shot in front of her and caught her steed's halter, stopping her advance.

"What are you doing?" she snapped. "Move aside!"

He gestured to the cliffs. "'Tis the English!"

She glanced up, saw a group of knights riding east. Thank God they hadn't seen them.

"Come!" The Templar led her deep into the shadows. "We must stay here until we are sure they have gone."

"I thought the duke's men were captured or dead?"

Cailin grimaced. "As did I."

"Where do you think they are heading?"

"To Lord Comyn."

Her cheeks burned at the mere thought of the bastards. "After their duplicity, do they believe he would help them?"

"They are taking a risk," Cailin said, "but after they didna find you during the search, mayhap they think you are dead and Comyn is ignorant of their nefarious intent."

"Mary's will. And with my not having warned Comyn, he will believe their lie." A new fear shot through her. "Do you think Comyn will try to reclaim the castle?"

Cailin shook his head. "Nay. The English will warn him about the battle, more that their force is all but depleted."

On a hard swallow, Gwendolyn glanced toward the sky. Clouds had gathered, smothering the sun. She followed the feeble rays of light that spilled across the ocean to where water lay stranded in smooth crevices of rock. The fading hues glinted in the depression. Proof of another day lost, another day Aiden hadna returned.

She hugged the tattered cloth against her chest, and tears welled. He felt so close to her. "Lass, we must return."

Cailin's voice, rough with understanding, reminded her that 'twas not only her who was filled with dread at thoughts that Aiden had died, but all the others who called him friend.

She gave a shaky nod.

The knight reined his mount forward.

With her heart breaking, she scanned the coast one last time.

Empty waves rolled ashore as if to mock her.

She stared at the ragged cloth, at the brutal reminder of Aiden's fate. Her throat thick with emotion, she lifted her reins.

Stilled.

In the distance, caught in the fading wisps of light, a lone figure staggered up the beach.

Her heart wrenched. She gasped. Had she dreamed him into being?

Cailin whirled his mount to her side. "What is wrong?"

Hand trembling, she pointed down the shore. "'Tis…Aiden!"

The warrior caught her mount's reins as she started forward. The horse snorted, and he held tight. "Whoever it is, he is too far away to be sure. It could be the enemy. Stay here."

"Nay." She tugged her horse sideways, ripping the leathers from his hold. "'Tis him!" Gwendolyn kicked her mount into a gallop.

"Lass! Come back!"

Cailin's words faded beneath the salty breeze as she urged her steed faster.

On his next step, the lone figure staggered, then sprawled to the sand.

He was hurt! A pace away, Gwendolyn drew her mount to a halt, jumped to the ground. Tears rolling down her cheeks, she knelt beside his still form.

Cailin dismounted, moved to the opposite side. He caught Aiden's shoulder. Together they turned him over.

Aiden groaned.

A wave rumbled ashore behind them as she caressed his face. "Aiden."

On a soft moan, his lids lifted. A frown worked across his brow, then his eyes closed.

"'Tis Gwendolyn," she urged, tears spilling down her cheeks, "wake up."

The Templar frowned. "We will carry him back to camp."

Aiden's lids again lifted, then his eyes widened in dazed disbelief. "Gwendolyn?"

The rawness of his words, the reddened skin on his body from the days at sea attested to his weakened state, but he was alive. "Aye," she whispered as joy poured through her, "I am here."

Cailin helped him to sit and then pressed the water pouch to Aiden's lips. "Drink."

After several slow sips, Aiden pushed the pouch away. Tender eyes shifted to her. His hand shaking, a weak smile creased his face as he pressed the palm against her cheek. "Y-you saved me. Brought m-me ashore."

She wiped away her tears. "I knew you were alive."

"Indeed," Cailin agreed, his voice rough. "She refused to stay at the castle." He secured the container, stood. "I will retrieve the horses." He walked away.

"I was so frightened," she admitted. "I thought—"

Aiden drew her against him. "I would never leave you." He cupped her face, his glance so fierce she trembled beneath the intensity. "I vowed that once we reclaimed Latharn Castle I would leave and never return. Never in my life have I broken my word." He gave a shaky breath. "Until now. I love you, Gwendolyn, and canna let you go. You are all I have thought of these past three days."

Happiness exploded inside her and fresh tears spilled down her face. "You love me?"

"I do," he rasped, "and if it takes forever, I will win your heart."

Tenderness tightened in her chest, entwined with her love for this man. "You willna have to. After you didna return, I realized I canna imagine a life without you. I love you, Aiden, and need you with my every breath."

His mouth crushed over hers, and she welcomed the heat, the need only he inspired. Too soon, he broke the kiss and drew her into his arms.

A horse whinnied, and she smiled, never so happy in her life. "Can you ride?"

Warmth glittered in his eyes. "Aye. H-help me up."

She slipped her arm around him, assisting him into a stand, and moments later, Cailin settled Aiden atop her horse. With a wide grin, she climbed up behind him.

"Let us ride," she said, her arms sliding around his waist as she reached for the reins. "'Tis time to go home."

Chapter 19

At the beach below the castle, Aiden lifted one of the last damaged planks from the sand and tossed it into the fire. He appreciated the stretch and strain on his muscles, proof that, after, a fortnight he had completely healed from his ordeal at sea.

A gust whipped across the incoming waves, casting sprays of white into the air. He inhaled the aromatic scent of the sea and smiled.

Life.

Such a fleeting gift, one he'd pondered little until the battle of Latharn Castle and his brush with death.

Emotion swelled inside as he glanced at his wife, working at his side. The time spent overseeing repairs had allowed him to heal, but also to be with her, to learn more about the woman he'd wed.

A distant rumble of thunder resonated from the west.

"A storm is brewing," Gwendolyn warned.

He frowned at the dark clouds in the distance. "'Twill be a while before the rain arrives." Completeness swelled inside Aiden as he took in the stronghold. The most important repairs to the castle had been seen to. Still, 'twould take several months before everything was complete. "I depart in the morning, comforted in knowing the knights I leave behind will keep you safe."

Her lower lip trembled as she cast a shard of wood into the fire. "I dinna want you to go. Nay tomorrow, next week. Ever."

Desperation rose like bile in his throat, and for the first time in his life he damned his leaving. Being apart from this incredible woman, even for a short while, seemed tantamount to forever.

On a hard swallow, he faced her. "I will be away a few months at most."

"But you canna be sure."

"Nay." On a silent curse, Aiden drank the ladle of water she offered, refilled it, and then handed her the scoop.

From the tower, a guard called out, "The king's banner waves in the distance!"

Aiden scanned the slope leading to the castle where, weeks before, he, Cailin, and Rónán had ridden, caught the flicker of the king's standard waving in the afternoon breeze. He frowned.

Gwendolyn dropped the ladle into the bucket as she peered up the incline. "I thought you were expecting the Earl of Dunsmore to transport an artifact of importance for the Bruce, but not until you had returned."

"Aye." A holy artifact, one of great importance to the Templars that, regardless of their endless searches in Latharn's tunnels, they hadn't found. News he dreaded sharing with his king.

Their gazes met and worried eyes held his.

Aiden drew her to him. "I dinna know why he has arrived early, more so accompanied by the king. Regardless the reason, 'tis one we shall soon learn."

"I will ensure preparations are made for their stay and meet you in the bailey before they arrive."

He lifted her hand, pressed a kiss upon her palm. "Until then."

A blush swept her cheeks. "I willna be long." She hurried away.

He watched her go, admiring her lithe form, matching the grace of her character. Blast it. Fully healed, he'd planned on spending this last night with Gwendolyn alone, but 'twould seem the hours ahead would be engaged in conversation with the Bruce concerning the next attack. He strode toward the castle.

* * * *

Horns blared.

Creaks from the portcullis opening echoed through the castle as he halted at the center of the bailey.

The scrape of the door sounded. Then Gwendolyn rushed toward him. Breaths coming fast, she halted at his side, nodded. "Everything is ready."

Horns again sounded from the wall walk as King Robert rode into the courtyard. His crown glinted in the afternoon sun, his yellow tunic embroidered with a deep red lion rampant atop his mail, the same color and design of his steed's caparison.

"The nobleman at the king's side is Stephan MacQuistan," Aiden said.

"The Templar who seized Avalon Castle and wed Lady Katherine?"

"Aye." On a nervous breath, shoulders back, she turned to the king as he halted before them.

Aiden couldn't have been prouder of his wife. He gave a deep bow. "We welcome you to Latharn Castle, Sire."

Gwendolyn curtsied. "Welcome to our home, Your Grace."

The Bruce and the earl dismounted, and a lad hurried forward to lead their destriers away. "Rise," the king said.

"Lady Gwendolyn," Aiden said, "may I introduce you to Stephan MacQuistan, the Earl of Dunsmore, and my friend."

"My lord," she said.

Stephan bowed. "'Tis a pleasure to meet you, my lady. I have"—he shot an amused glance toward the king before nodding to her—"heard much about you. In the future, I look forward to your meeting my wife. 'Twould seem you and Lady Katherine have much in common."

A smile curved her lips. "I look forward to that moment."

"One nay doubt she will enjoy as well." The earl turned to the king.

The Bruce turned to Aiden. "We had hoped to find you still here."

"Your Grace, my men and I are prepared to sail on the morning tide," Aiden said. He shot a curious glance at Stephan.

His friend remained silent.

"Lead us to somewhere you, Lady Gwendolyn, the Earl of Dunsmore, and I can speak in private," the king stated, his words solemn.

"Aye, Sire." Aiden started toward the keep, not missing the concern on Gwendolyn's face. Moments later, he opened the door to the solar. Sunlight streamed through the stained-glass windows, spilling swaths of blues, reds, and purples within the chamber. Once he'd ushered the small group inside, Aiden closed the door.

The king halted at the center of the room, folded his arms across his chest. "Due to the great value of the holy relic hidden below Latharn Castle, I decided to join Lord Dunsmore as he transported the artifact to Avalon Castle."

Aiden cursed the answer he must give his king. He glanced at his wife, then back to the sovereign. "Sire, we found nay mention of the receipt of the holy relic from the Grand Master in the secret ledger. We have searched every tunnel and found naught but supplies."

"If there is another chamber hidden below, Your Grace," Gwendolyn added, nervousness sliding through her voice, "'tis one my father never disclosed."

Aiden gave her hand a quick, supportive squeeze, then let go. "With your permission, Sire, I shall continue the search until 'tis found. Then, when I do, I shall personally deliver the artifact to Avalon Castle." Body taut, he awaited his sovereign's ire for having failed.

"'Tis here." A grim yet confident smile touched the king's mouth. "The writ I received from your father stated he had sent you a message with the location and instructions regarding it. Clearly, his missive never arrived."

She shook her head. "Nay, Sire. I received naught."

"Regardless," the king said, "I know where the artifact is hidden."

"If you knew," she said, confusion in her voice, "why did you not tell Aiden long ago, when you gave him the task?"

A frown touched the sovereign's brow. "I didna know then. A sennight after you departed, the monk who gave your father the last rites arrived at my camp. He explained that before your father died, when he hadn't heard from you and, concerned the missive he had sent to you somehow had been lost, he revealed the location of the secret vault to him and asked that the information be delivered to me." King Robert paused. "Given my travels during my campaign to claim Scotland, a quest that has taken the monk several months to achieve." He paused. "Lady Gwendolyn, bring me the gold key with the Templar Cross."

She frowned. "Key? I... There isna such, Your Grace."

The king grimaced. "I see you havena opened the pouch sealed with a gold filigree cord I gave you after you wed. Bring it to me now."

Frantic eyes moved to Aiden before shifting to the monarch. "I—"

"Sire, Lady Gwendolyn had me place the key in a safe place. I will be but a moment." Aiden winked at her as he strode off.

She watched him in disbelief. Incredible to think that after all their efforts over the past weeks, there was another secret to be found.

A short while later, he reentered the solar, the satchel in his hand.

"Give it to Lady Gwendolyn," the king instructed.

Her fingers trembled as she accepted the velvet sack, then loosened the ornate cord. She withdrew, and then unrolled, a delicate swath of copper silk. Amazement widened her eyes as she lifted the key. Within the stream of sunlight, an emerald centered at the apex lay a glittering prism across her hand. "'Tis beautiful," she breathed.

"Aye," the king said with pride. "More important, it unlocks a secret, the identity none but the Templars can ever know of. Come; I will show you where the vault is hidden. Once we have removed the holy relic, Lord Dunsmore and I will depart."

* * * *

As the setting sun lingered on the horizon, pride surged through Aiden as he watched the king, Lord Dunsmore, and their contingent ride east along the shore.

As they rounded the bend, the faint whinnies of horses carried on the breeze as the army faded from view, and his gaze dropped to their tracks etched in the sand. With each new wave that smoothed the beach, their passage disappeared.

Memories of the gold-plated chest they'd removed from the secret hiding place rolled through his mind, still overwhelmed by the moment he'd first seen the gilded trunk. One described in the Book of Exodus as containing the Tablets of Stone on which the Ten Commandments were written.

The awe on Gwendolyn's face, and the king's, and Stephan's, had matched his own. With care, they had secured the sacred container within a larger, plain chest, and then the king and Stephan had departed with the treasure.

"I still canna believe the key to unlock the secret vault was in the velvet sack," Gwendolyn said, her voice filled with wonder. "To think, I tossed away such a treasure because of my foolish anger. Thank God you retrieved my father's gift."

Aiden smiled and entwined his fingers with hers. "You were angry. I had planned to return the king's gift to you, but between battle preparations, my recovery, and the castle repairs, the pouch was forgotten."

Pewter-gray eyes warmed. "I thank you for being so thoughtful. I am blessed to have such a husband."

He kissed each fingertip, then her palm. "'Tis I who is blessed. I love you, Gwendolyn. You are a wonderful woman, one of strength and wit, with a kind heart." Aiden drew her against him, tipped up her chin. "Months ago, at the wedding of Thomas MacKelloch, a Templar and a close friend, I insisted a woman and a family are not my desire. That I preferred the life of a warrior."

A smile teased her mouth. "And now?"

His heart swelled as he drew her against him. "Now I think differently." He crushed his lips upon hers before easing his mouth away and nipping along the soft curve of her jaw. Her soft gasps heated his blood as their gazes met. "It took me too long to acknowledge I had fallen in love, but now I canna exist without you."

A blush slid up Gwendolyn's cheeks. "I have a confession to make as well."

He arched a brow. "And that would be?" Intrigued, doubting his life would ever be boring with her at his side.

"My showing you is best." In the fading daylight, she took his hand and led him to where a sun-bleached limb lay half-buried on the shore. Eyes sparkling with mischief, she gestured to the rough charcoal outline of a man, a chunk torn free from the crudely shaded heart.

"You did this?" he asked. After witnessing her spirit since they had met, he far from found himself surprised.

"Aye. On the morning of your arrival at Latharn Castle, furious that I had to wed to keep my liege lord's guard at the stronghold, I drew this. As I drove my dagger into the blackened heart, I told Sir Pieres that I needed nay husband."

Aiden chuckled. "I am lucky to have survived."

"Your saving Kellan and her colt helped to begin to win my heart," she said with a smile. "I was prepared to dislike you. In truth, I half-loathed you before we met."

"That was unfair."

Her smile faded and her eyes darkened with need. "It was. As angry as I was, fairness wasna in my heart to give. Then I met you."

A simple look and he wanted her. With Gwendolyn 'twould always be so. He caught her mouth in another heated kiss, lingered. "I assure you, when I rode into your castle on that fateful day, never did I expect to stay, more so to find a woman I would respect, let alone love. And I found both." Drawing her to his side, he glanced along the shore. "'Tis beautiful."

Warmth touched her gaze. "'Tis my special place, one I wanted to share with you."

He inhaled, the salty tang in the air, along with the soft cadence of the waves, spilling ashore like a balm to the soul. "Though stunning, I find myself wanting to be alone in the privacy of our chamber with my wife." Aiden caught her mouth in a tender kiss. The spear of need was immediate, and he savored the desire, the building of heat.

She arched against him, took, demanded, her every move stealing his breath.

Blood racing hot, Aiden broke away, skimmed kisses down the silken column of her neck. "Come to bed with me, Gwendolyn. I canna wait any longer."

Eyes dark with hunger held his. "Have you healed enough?"

In answer, he scooped her into his arms and strode toward their home. Gwendolyn laughed, the sweetest sound to Aiden's ears.

A short while later he secured the door behind him. Candlelight filled the chamber, illuminating her within the golden light as he lowered Gwendolyn to her feet.

On a soft gasp, she slowly turned, staring at the numerous baskets of flowers, the delicacies filling a platter: several wedges of cheese, cured meats, and pastries garnished with honey and slices of golden baked apples. In a basket to one side lay several bottles of wine. A well-planned banquet that made her eyes pool with joy and her mouth water.

"Where did all this come from?" she asked as she stared up at him with tenderness.

"I asked the cook and a maid to prepare everything while we said farewell to King Robert." He moved his hands down the arms of her cream silk gown. "I wanted to surprise you."

Her eyes grew misty. "You have."

Humbled by this woman, one who had destroyed the walls guarding his heart, he drew her closer. "Every time I look at you, you steal my breath. I canna believe you are mine." A flush swept her cheeks, and he liked having put it there. "More so after having seen the figure with the charcoal heart slashed out."

Gwendolyn laughed, a rich, happy sound. "There is that."

His heart full, Aiden claimed her mouth in a deep kiss, lingered, thankful to have found her, more that they would be together for the rest of their lives.

Emotion raw in his chest, he swept her into his arms, strode toward the bed. Gray eyes darkened with desire as he settled his body intimately over hers. Braced on his forearms, Aiden stared down at her, never before feeling this blessed, this complete.

He rolled onto his back, took her with him, until she straddled him.

"What are you doing?" she gasped.

"This." Within the golden wisps of light, he skimmed his fingers along the curve of her neck, sliding lower to loosen the ties of her clothing. With reverence, he peeled away the gown, exposed the soft swell of her breasts. He swallowed hard, lifted his gaze to hers. "You steal my breath, Gwendolyn." Hands trembling, he cupped her soft curve, raised up to taste.

At her moan, at how her body trembled beneath his touch, he slowed, took his time, his hands caressing, stroking, wanting to discover her body's every secret.

As he moved his hands to cup her hips, like a temptress, she began to rock against his hard length with slow, mind-destroying strokes.

At the wicked smile in her eyes, Aiden realized she knew exactly what she was doing to him. "Lass," he groaned, "you are driving me mad."

"Nay," she said with a smoky laugh. "This"—her hand loosened his garb, she freed him, and then lowered until her soft breath spilled over his hard length. Her eyes locked on his—"is what I do if I want to drive you mad." Her tongue flicked over his sensitive tip.

Sensation exploded, and his body trembled as her mouth continued its wondrous foray. He gasped for air. "Lass, I dinna think—"

"'Tis what I planned." Gwendolyn slid her lips over his full length, her tongue doing magical things as her mouth possessed him, went deeper.

With a groan, Aiden caught her hair, torn between giving her free rein and taking charge. Or, with her expertly licking him, sucking his hardness as her fingers joined in their sensual assault, did he have a chance of such.

Gwendolyn's throaty purr assured him she enjoyed this sensual command. The swirl of sensation grew, built. On edge, Aiden rolled her over, pinned her beneath his body, and gritted his teeth against a wave of heat threatening to shatter his control.

"I thought you liked that?" she asked with feigned innocence.

Liked that? An understatement. It had taken the last fragment of his will not to allow her to finish. "Aye," he rasped, "too much. A moment more and…"

She chuckled.

The lass was enjoying herself, not that he didn't appreciate her skill. Aye, later he would allow her to touch him as she chose, and would well enjoy her clever hands. For now… "We will see who is laughing."

After discarding the remainder of his garb, he took his time exposing her to his view, touching her, enjoying the way her body arched, how her fingers skimmed over his flesh. Their breaths merged, entwined, and he savored her each gasp, delighted in learning what pleased her, astounded by the sensations her touch ignited.

Aiden linked his fingers with hers as he poised himself at her slick entrance, lifted her hands over her head. "I love you, Gwendolyn."

* * * *

Gwendolyn's heart pounded as Aiden stared down at her, humbled she'd found a man of such compassion, a stalwart warrior who had won her heart. "I love you, Aiden," she replied on a whisper.

Heat filled his eyes as he moved his lips over hers, and she took, gave, savored the slide of their bodies, and his whispered words as his mouth worshiped her skin. Candlelight flickered against the walls in a sultry sway as she enjoyed his touch, explored his hard curves.

Sighs melded into gasps, the magnitude of what he could make her feel, of what he had given her leaving her humbled. Never had she believed she could care for a man with such intensity, much less love him and want him with her forever.

Until Aiden, she had never truly understood how a man could transform her life, not only bringing her hope but heart-felt happiness.

Gwendolyn welcomed him into her slick warmth. Ecstasy filled her as she met his every thrust, wanting him, wanting their children, and wanting their life together. Pressure built, and an explosion of intense pleasure blurred her thoughts. Then she was floating, caught in a whirlwind, slowly drifting back.

Aiden's cry of release joined hers, then he rolled to his side and cradled her against his chest.

Breath coming fast, her body glistening within the glow of firelight, she snuggled against him, never so happy in her life. Emotion swelled in her throat, and she damned the morning, but hours away.

Brows narrowed, he lifted her chin. "What is wrong?"

Emotion clogging her throat, she damned the passage of time, wished they could remain here forever. "I dinna want you to go."

Fierce eyes held hers. "Neither do I want to leave you, but I will return, that I swear."

Pushing back the tears, refusing to mar the beauty of this night with sadness, Gwendolyn lay her hand on her stomach, prayed they had created life. "Mayhap I am carrying our child."

His eyes softened with emotion. With reverence, he threaded his fingers through hers. "I pray so; 'twould be the greatest gift," Aiden said as he rolled her onto her back with a teasing smile, "nor am I a man who leaves naught to chance." Catching her mouth in a fierce kiss, he again drove deep inside her.

Epilogue

Encircled within Aiden's arms, Gwendolyn leaned against his chest. She looked down upon their sons, asleep in their crib, thankful for Aiden's return. Tears burned her eyes at the precious memory of him holding Hughe and Ihon in his arms, and of the astonishment and love on his war-hardened face. 'Twas a memory she would cherish forever.

Pride filled Aiden's eyes. "They are handsome lads."

"Like their father."

He turned her in his arms and lifted a brow. "Indeed?"

"Very much so." She exhaled with a contented sigh. "After you seized Thorburn Castle, King Robert was generous to allow you to return instead of continuing with his men."

Aiden grunted. "A decision based on need. With Latharn Castle recaptured and news of Lord Comyn's need to keep a firm presence in the Highlands, our sovereign wants to ensure the Templar stronghold remains safe."

"Regardless the reason, I am thankful you are here," she said. "It seemed like forever until you returned."

"Each day I was gone, I missed you desperately." He cupped her chin. "Gwendolyn, I love you; forever you will have my heart."

"I love you as well," she whispered.

Pride filled his gaze. "I am still astonished that we have two sons."

She arched a playful brow. "Did I not tell you twins have been known in my family?"

"Something you omitted. But"—he tilted her head and claimed her mouth, slow, with possession until she shuddered against him—"I believe they need sisters."

Heat searing her, she pressed her body against his. "Do you, now?"

"I do." Aiden lifted her in his arms and strode toward their bedchamber. "And I am a man who finishes what he starts."

Gwendolyn's laughter filled the room as he lay her on their bed, loving his playfulness, the inherent gentleness, the warrior who from the first had swept her off her feet. "I am counting on that, my lord."

Acknowledgments

My deepest appreciation to Dick and Ann Brandt for sharing how, during World War II, if a soldier already had someone to write to, they would pass a letter requesting to be a pen pal to someone without one. This intriguing fact was my inspiration for Aiden and Gwendolyn's story.

My sincere thanks to Cameron John Morrison, Kathryn Warner, and Jody Allen for answering numerous questions about medieval Scotland and England. I would also like to thank The National Trust for Scotland, which acts as guardian of Scotland's magnificent heritage of architectural, scenic, and historic treasures. In addition, I am thankful for the immense support from my husband, parents, family, and friends. My deepest wish is that everyone is as blessed when they pursue their dreams.

My sincere thanks to my editor, Esi Sogah; my agent, Holly Root; production editor Rebecca Cremonese; copy editor Randy Ladenheim-Gil; and my critique partners, Cindy Nord and Michelle Hancock, for helping Aiden and Gwendolyn's story come to life. A huge thanks to the Roving Lunatics (Mary Beth Shortt and Sandra Hughes), Nancy Bessler, and The Wild Writers for their friendship and support over the years!

*A very special thanks to Sulay Hernandez for believing in me from the start.

Meet the Author

A retired Navy Chief, AGC (AW), Diana Cosby is an international bestselling author of Scottish medieval romantic suspense. Diana has spoken at the Library of Congress, appeared at Lady Jane's Salon NYC, in *Woman's Day*, on *Texoma Living! Magazine*, *USA Today*'s romance blog, "Happily Ever After," and MSN.com.

After retiring from the navy, Diana dove into her passion—writing romance novels. With thirty-four moves behind her, she was anxious to create characters who reflected the amazing cultures and people she's met throughout the world. Diana looks forward to the years ahead of writing and meeting the amazing people who will share this journey.

Diana Cosby, International Bestselling Author
www.dianacosby.com

Forbidden Alliance

Keep reading for a sneak peek at the next romance in the Forbidden series
Coming soon from Diana Cosby and Lyrical Books!

Chapter 1

Snow pelted Elspet McReynolds as she clutched her dagger, her gaze riveted on the two roughly dressed men paces away.

"Hand over the sack!" the stocky one demanded, a jagged scar across his cheek.

His partner with a scraggly beard narrowed his eyes.

Heart pounding, she tightened her grip. God in heaven, how had her simple plan gone so horribly wrong? She'd despised robbing these strangers, a contemptable action forced by the Earl of Dalkirk's treachery.

Horrific images of the day before stormed her mind. The grizzly death of her mother and step-father, her step-brother Blar's screams as he was dragged away by the murdering bastard's men, and how the earl had hauled her to his chamber.

Nausea welled in her gut at memories of her vicious fight for freedom. How dare the arrogant bastard believe that she would ever willingly share his bed. Had the noble not deflected her dagger, she would have driven the *sgian dubh* deep into his vile heart. She found grim satisfaction that her blade had left a long gash across his cheek.

With the noble howling in pain and demanding that she be captured and killed, she'd fled Tiran Castle. However much she yearned to leave Dalkirk land, she couldn't leave her step-brother to die in the earl's dungeon.

Terrified for Blar's life, she'd begged her family's longtime friends to help her discover if he was alive. They'd agreed. But once they'd thought her asleep, she'd overheard them planning to turn her in to gain favor in the earl's eyes.

Devastated by their betrayal, she'd slipped from their home.

Earlier today she'd found a castle guard who'd sworn that her stepbrother still lived. For a pound he'd agreed to help Blar escape. This, on her mind when she'd stumbled across their camp in the woods and had seen both strangers at the river, propelled her to foolishly try and rob them.

A brief search had revealed where the travelers kept their coin. Except, before she could slip away, they'd spotted her and given chase.

Body trembling, she glared at the angry faces of the furious men, damned she hadn't stolen one of their horses and ridden away. With the earl calling for her death, she had naught to lose.

Another snow-drenched gust whipped past blinding her from her ill-chosen victims. Too aware of the steep slope behind her, the harsh landscape typical of the Highlands, she edged to her left. If only she could reach the trees a short sprint away she might lose them in the dense woods.

The man with the scraggly beard stepped closer. "Hand it over!"

Her blade trembled in her hand. She must find a way to distract them. "Stay back."

"Nay one steals from me!" Teeth barred, the scarred man moved to the side and cornered her against the dangerous incline.

Fear a bitter slide in her throat, the icy ground crunched beneath Elspet as she edged back. "I am sorry. I needed but a few coins, I—"

The scarred man lunged.

With a scream she slashed her blade.

A thin line of blood streaked his chin. "You bloody bitch!" With a snarl, he caught her arms. After twisting both behind her back, he seized the bag of coins.

Panicking, she struggled to break free. "You have your money, release me!"

With a grunt, the thickset man stowed the leather sack. "Nay, lass, you have earned naught but punishment for your thievery." He wrenched open her cape. "Penance," he said as his eyes darkened, "I shall enjoy delivering."

His friend gave a cruel laugh. "A comely wench indeed."

"Nay!" Fresh terror building in her chest, and she drove her foot against her captor's thigh.

With a curse, the stocky man fisted his hand, swung.

Pain exploded in Elspet's head, and she collapsed onto the snow-covered ground.

* * * *

At a woman's scream, Sir Cailin MacHugh reined his war horse to a stop. Gaze narrowed, he scanned the area.

Another shriek rang out.

Jaw tight, he whirled his destrier toward the sound, and kicked him into a gallop.

Through the break in the trees ahead, a burly man stood over a slender woman garbed in a torn, pale green gown. At his side leered a man with a scraggly beard, as raggedly dressed as the first.

Fury exploded in Cailin's mind at memories of a woman he'd cared for deeply who had sought his protection after she'd been badly beaten. As he'd held her bruised and bloody body in his arms, prayed for her to live, she'd drawn her last breath. From that moment he'd sworn that never again would he allow a man to harm a lass.

Jaw set, he leaned low and urged his horse faster.

The attacker hauled her up, drew his fist back to land another blow.

Blade drawn, with a roar, Cailin jumped his steed over a fallen log and into the clearing. "Release her!"

Her attacker whirled. Outraged eyes shifted to fear as they locked on his broadsword. "You bloody want her," he snarled, "here!" He shoved the lass down the steep incline. "Run!"

Brush snapped as both men bolted to their horses and galloped away.

Instinct urged Cailin to give chase; lost against his need to protect. He kicked his mount to the edge.

Like a broken doll, fingers splayed against the snow-covered ground, the woman lay at the bottom of the hill.

An icy burst of wind howled past as he dismounted, then hurried down the slope.

Half-frozen rocks loosened, clattered ahead of him.

With a curse, he shifted to the right to avoid any falling debris hitting the unconscious woman.

Finally at the bottom, he knelt by her side. Chestnut brown hair dusted with the fall of snow framed her angelic face. A gash creased her right brow, and a bruise darkened her cheek, both in stark contrast to her pale skin.

With a prayer she was alive, Cailin gently touched her shoulder. Once, twice. "Lass."

Eyes the color of water drenched moss flickered open and focused on him. Their depth, intensity, stole his breath.

On a gasp she rolled away and then stumbled to her feet. Favoring her ankle, she backed up.

Cailin slowly stood. "Dinna be afraid," he said, keeping his voice gentle. "I am here to help you."

A shiver wracked her body, then another. With a grimace of pain, she tugged her cape together, then glanced upwards toward the knoll where one of the attackers had seized her moments before. Her gaze narrowed on him. "Wh-who are you?"

"Sir Cailin." Though years had passed since he'd ridden on Dalkirk land, he couldn't risk her recognizing his surname and warning his uncle, let alone the rest of the earl's reprobates, of his return. "And your name?"

The beautiful woman hesitated, her eyes dark with distrust. "Kenzie."

By her proper speech and the quality of her ruined gown, he suspected she was a woman of noble birth. The lass's reason for keeping her status a secret could be endless and as worthy as his own. With the brief time they would remain together, nor would he seek an answer.

"Does your family live nearby?" he asked.

She angled her chin. "Does yours?"

Blast it. Was her family of nobility within Dalkirk or had they given the earl their fealty?

"Do you know the men who attacked me?" she asked, suspicion raw in her words.

He shook his head. The combination of her physical struggle and swelling jaw made his gut twist. By God he'd catch the scoundrels. He gestured to her leg. "'Twas a nasty fall. You are injured."

Face taut, she shrugged. "Only bruised."

He grunted. "That I doubt. Let me carry you. You are favoring your ankle, you canna climb back up on your own."

Defiance blazed in her eyes. "I can make it without your help."

Regardless of the pain, if he let her, no doubt she'd try. "Aye, but 'tis rest and a warm fire you would be needing, not climbing up the brae, and," Cailin said with emphasis, "in pain."

In a calmer setting he would have lingered in speculation at her bold manner. Except with her injury, the snow falling at an increasing rate, and the howl of bitter wind, they needed to find shelter.

Scraping her teeth over her lower lip, she scoured the surroundings then stilled

He followed her gaze.

A step to his left, half buried in snow, lay her *sgian dubh*, a smear of blood across the blade.

Before she could move, he retrieved the knife and wiped it clean. Handle facing her, he offered her the dagger.

Eyes wary, she accepted her weapon. "Why are you helping me?"

"You were in danger."

Kenzie sheathed her blade. "As simple as that?"

He held out his hand. "Aye. We must go before the weather makes travel impossible."

After a brief hesitation, during which her gaze seemed to pierce his and evaluate his trustworthiness, she placed her hand upon his open palm.

At the silkiness of her skin against his, Cailin smothered the flare of awareness. Irritated by the desire she stirred, he lifted her in his arms.

Snow crunched as he carried her up the steep, icy incline. He tried to ignore how good she felt against him, failed. At the top of the cliff, more than ready to put distance between them, he gently set her on her feet.

Cheeks flushed, she nodded and moved back, clearly trying to shield that her leg still caused her pain. "I thank you, Sir Cailin. I owe you much. I—" Her face paled as she twisted around with a gasp. "My horse!"

Blast it, the thieves had circled back and taken her steed. "Do you know their names?"

She shook her head. "I have never seen them before today."

No doubt the robbers had believed her a lady, and easy prey. "Why are you riding without proper guard?"

* * * *

Dismayed by the turn of events, Elspet studied the handsome knight. Dark red hair framed blue eyes that no doubt had made many a woman want. His muscle hewn body and confident stance, that of a man used to taking charge.

Was this warrior one of the Earl of Dalkirk's men out searching for her? She struggled for an explanation that would satisfy the formidable knight so she could slip away before he recognized her.

"I was en route to my aunt's home in the Western Highlands when thieves attacked my guard. He was…" She drew in a ragged breath, allowed the terror since she'd fled Tiran Castle to fill her words. "H-he died. I escaped, or believed I had. Except the men caught up to me and…" Her breath hitched. "Thank God you arrived."

Somber eyes held hers. "They willna touch you again," he said, his voice somber. "That I swear."

A sense of rightness emitted from this man, a strength, integrity that left her feeling vulnerable and exposed. Shaken, Elspet dragged in a steadying breath. "How I wish you could promise such."

Intense blue eyes held hers. "I mean what I say."

However foolish, more so after her neighbor's betrayal hours ago and with him possibly one of the earl's men, she believed him. "Never have I seen you before."

The daunting knight's eyes grew unreadable. "I am but traveling through."

Tension in her body eased. Thank God, he was not in service to the noble. "You are a stranger to Dalkirk lands," she said. "What you witnessed today was but a pittance of the lawlessness the earl allows his men."

Surprise flickered in Cailin's eyes. "Your attackers are men within his guard?"

She hesitated. Regardless if he was an outsider and ignorant that the earl had ordered his knights to catch and kill her, 'twas wisest to take care with what she shared. Another shiver swept her. "Ignore my ramblings, 'tis exhaustion feeding my words."

A frown creased his brow. After a moment, he nodded. "'Tis time to leave."

"Where are you going?"

"*We*," he said with emphasis, "are riding to an inn up ahead where I have a room for tonight. You will have a meal, and a place to rest while your injury mends."

One she'd passed earlier this day. Though far enough away from where anyone would recognize her, without coin or time, a tavern she'd avoided. Neither did she wish to go with him.

She shook her head. "I canna—"

"While we sup," he continued, "we will discuss arrangements for you to reach your destination."

"You would escort me to my aunt's?"

"Nay. As you are without sufficient funds, I will arrange for a coach."

"I..." Elspet smothered another surge of guilt. "Your generosity is appreciated, but I refuse to disrupt your travels further. If you would kindly spare a pound, which will cover fare, meals, and lodgings for the remainder of my trip, I willna delay you further," she said with a demure look. "Money I assure you, once I know where you are headed, that I will repay."

He paused. "I dinna carry such a large amount when I travel."

She smothered a burst of panic. What was she going to do? However much she dreaded the thought, only one choice remained. She must rob another unsuspecting traveler, then make haste to reach the guard who'd promised to free Blar.

"I understand and appreciate your kindness," she forced out, "but I nay longer need your assistance."

A red brow lifted in stunned disbelief. "You want me to leave you here injured and without a mount or protection?"

Straightening her shoulders, she limped back a step. "Aye. If I find the need to rest, as you said, there is an inn nearby."

He frowned. "With how the storm is worsening, *we* will be fortunate to reach the tavern by horse much less on foot. Or, in your case, hobble. Nor, by your admission, do you have fare to pay for a room."

Blast it. She scowled at the thick flakes tumbling past, damned the throb in her ankle. All she needed was the coin, not more time spent with this alluring stranger. The delay may cost her stepbrother his life.

An errant ray of light broke through the clouds and shimmered off the knight's broadsword.

Elspet stilled. Atop a leather grip, an intricately carved gold crest lay etched within the pommel. She'd believed him but a knight, except a warrior could far from afford such a superior weapon, garb of such quality, or a destrier of such caliber.

Unease rippled through her. God in heaven, was he nobility? If so, why had he not proclaimed his title? Regardless, a sword of this quality would bring more than enough to pay the guard.

She lifted her gaze to his. As much as dishonesty went against her grain, especially when it was directed towards this courageous man who had rescued her, to save Blar, she had no choice but to steal his weapon. "I agree."

A dry smile touched his mouth. "I thank you, my lady, for allowing me to offer escort."

She didn't correct him. Let him think she was of noble birth, 'twould make it more difficult when he tried to find her.

The warrior swung into his saddle. With ease he lifted her before him.

Elspet tried to ignore the hard ripple of his muscle against her body, his warmth, the strength of his arms as they circled around her to lift the reins or how, for this moment, she felt safe. Given her predicament, she had no business noticing anything about this handsome knight.

Cailin draped his cloak around her. "I will protect you," he said as if sensing her need for reassurance, then he kicked his steed into a gallop.

Protect her? If he knew the truth of what she had planned this night, he would have abandoned her to the fate of the men.

* * * *

A short while later, settled in their room at the inn, the savory scent of food filled the air, and firelight from the hearth filled the chamber with a soft golden light and warmth. Elspet scowled at how the swelling in her ankle had grown steadily worse.

"I fear my aunt will be worried when I do not arrive," she said.

Cailin tore off a piece of bread, dipped it in the hearty stew, popped it in his mouth, then swallowed. "Given the ferocity of the storm, she will understand."

As she ate her portion of the fare, she scanned their tiny room. Aside from the hearth, a bed with extra blankets folded atop stood in the corner, and nearby sat a small table holding a pitcher of water.

However sparse the furnishings, Cailin's presence seemed to fill the chamber, a potent reminder of her predicament. "'Tis unseemly for us to share this chamber."

"Under normal circumstance I would agree." He took a sip of ale. "We were fortunate that I had already paid for a room. Given the steady flow of travelers seeking shelter since our arrival, by now even the stable is filled."

Indeed. With the throng of people below, they were fortunate to have acquired a meal and drink.

He refilled his goblet. "You will sleep in the bed. I will make a pallet beside the hearth."

And once he was asleep, she would leave, except... Another wave of guilt swept Elspet as she glanced toward the finely crafted broadsword hanging near the door. If only he'd had the coin to loan her, then she wouldn't need to resort to thievery.

While he continued to eat, she fingered the sack of powdered valerian root hidden deep in her gown pocket. A healthy dose would make him sleep.

However much she regretted taking his weapon, for a powerful man of wealth, procuring another would be naught but an inconvenience. More important, on the morrow she'd meet with Wautier Brecnagh, a merchant known for purchasing stolen goods. She prayed he'd give her enough to pay the guard to save Blar's life.

At least once she departed, they'd never see the other again. Given the stakes, neither could she afford to care what this handsome warrior would think of her.

Elspet rubbed her arms. "'Tis cold."

Eyes dark with concern swept over her. "Exhausted and injured, you might be coming down with a chill." Cailin crossed to the hearth.

On a trembling breath, she withdrew the valerian root. After a quick glance to ensure he hadn't turned back, she sifted a liberal amount into his ale, stirred.

Logs clunked in the hearth, and her fingers jerked. A swath of powder spilled on the table. Nay! She swept away the residue, secured the sack, and then stowed the herb.

Sparks swirled within the churn of smoke as he laid several more smaller pieces of wood into the flames. Brushing the dirt from his hands, he stood. "That should keep us warm for the night." He walked over, settled in the chair, and lifted his mug. Cailin's brow furrowed.

Her heart pounded. God in heaven, had she missed some of the powder? "Do you have a large family?" she blurted out, desperate to distract him.

Weary blue eyes shifted to her. "If I reply, will you be answering my questions about yourself as well?"

Tension eased within her. He suspected naught. "Nay."

With a grunt, he lifted his cup in a mock toast, downed the brew, then hissed. "God's blade, they must have scraped the dredges of the barrel for this rot."

She forced a smile. "As you said, we were fortunate that any food or drink remained."

"Nay doubt until the storm they had planned on dumping the foul brew." With a grimace he shoved aside the goblet then stood. "Go to sleep.

"I thank you." Mindful of her throbbing ankle, Elspet limped to the bed, and then slipped beneath the covers. Feigning sleep, she watched for signs of the herb taking effect.

At the hearth he made a pallet. Instead of lying down he knelt, and then made the sign of the cross.

Soft whispers of the Lord's Prayer reached her, each word thick with grief, each verse as if dredged from his soul. Once Cailin finished, he began again.

Mesmerized by the intensity, the passion of each word, she couldn't look away. What had happened to cause him such angst? A part of her tried to ignore the anguish in his voice, but another longed to offer him succor.

Elspet's heart ached. His faith was a potent reminder of how days before her belief in *Him* had been as strong. Except, after what she'd witnessed yesterday, she could no longer fathom believing in a God who put people through such horror.

After whispering several more paternosters, he again made the sign of the cross, and then sat back.

On a yawn, the warrior glanced toward her.

Through her lashes, she watched him.

For a long moment, he studied her.

And why wouldn't he be curious? She'd revealed naught about her past, and during their brief discussion of her travel, she'd remained vague. Neither had she pressed him for information.

However ill-timed and destined to be short lived, she found herself drawn to this handsome warrior. Foolish indeed when soon she would leave.

He started to turn away, and half-tipped over. On a muttered curse, he righted himself.

"Cailin?"

His lids raised, and she caught the slight dazed look. She gave a relieved exhale. The valerian root was beginning to work.

"Aye?" he replied.

"I want to thank you for rescuing me this day."

"'Twas naught."

"I disagree. Many would have ridden past without a care."

"That, I f-find," he slurred, "hard to believe."

"I would have agreed," Elspet said, "but since Gaufrid MacHugh, Earl of Dalkirk, took control of Tiran Castle years ago, everything has changed."

He sat, braced himself against the wall, his face pale at the effort. "Explain?"

What could it hurt? He was unlikely to remember this conversation. "He is a cruel man. All within Dalkirk fear him."

"As you?"

Tears threatened as horrific memories of yesterday rolled through her. "Nay. I despise him."

"Why?"

Far from pleased by the shift in the conversation, she looked away.

"Kenzie?"

Tears burned her eyes and Elspet damned that he'd ask or care. The crackle of flames echoed within the chamber, melded with a faint yell and laughter from below as if the night was normal.

A soft thud had her turning.

Eyes closed, Cailin lay on the floor, his red hair lay flopped against his cheek. On his next breath, a soft snore fell from his mouth.

Anxious for this moment to arrive, now regret weighed heavy upon her. Though she'd known the knight for mere hours, he seemed good, decent, and kind.

Refusing to let her conscience outweigh what she must do, Elspet pushed from the bed and hobbled over as quietly as she could. She allowed herself the luxury of skimming her finger along the hard line of his jaw, then sliding the pad of her thumb along his firm mouth.

In sleep his expression had softened as if a gentle man, except she saw the faint scar on his cheek, and another across the side of his neck that disappeared beneath his garb.

He was a man of war, one who would not tolerate being crossed. When he awoke he'd be furious.

A fact that couldn't be helped.

With a deep exhale, Elspet pulled a blanket up to his chest, then moved across the chamber and withdrew his broadsword from the scabbard. The weight of the weapon surprised her, but her gaze shifted to the gold crest etched within the pommel, then to the intricate carvings on the guard.

After securing the weapon beneath her cape, she opened the door. Throat tight she glanced back. "I am sorry, Cailin." Elspet stepped into the hallway, and quietly closed the door in her wake.

* * * *

Through the fog of sleep, Cailin forced his lids open, peered out. He cursed the pounding in his skull, the dizziness blurring his thoughts, and the awful taste in his mouth. Blast it, where was he, and why did he feel as if he'd drank too much?

Foggy memories of the men assaulting Kenzie rushed through his mind, of his saving her, and then their trek through the blizzard to the inn.

He sat. Pain spiked through his head. With a slow sweep, he scanned the unfamiliar chamber. Coals glowed in the hearth, the sheets on the bed lay turned back, a slight impression of where she'd slept remained, but the lass was gone. He rubbed his brow. Mayhap she'd gone downstairs for food. Foolish when the inn was filled and without his protection.

Cailin shoved to his feet, damned another blast of pain. He started to turn, stilled.

His scabbard was empty.

Unease prickled up his spine. Had she taken his weapon to fend off any threats? He grunted. As if with her ankle injured she could swing the sword with any force. Blast it, why hadn't she woken him?

Muttering a curse, he turned, paused at the smear of powder on the floor beside where he'd sat for supper. His mind churned with several reasons for the residue.

None good.

Wanting to be wrong, Cailin stalked over, swiped his finger through the powder, sniffed.

Valerian root!

He glared at the closed door. Nay, he hadn't slept, nor were his aliments the result of too much ale. Kenzie had drugged him, and then stolen his broadsword. His anger surged. Blast it, the lass was in league with the men whom he'd found her with yesterday. They hadn't been robbing her, 'twas naught but a bloody ploy for her to fleece him!

Fury seething through his veins, against the splintering pain in his head, Cailin jerked on his cape, gathered the few belongings he'd brought, then stormed from the chamber.

Aye, he'd find her.

God help her when he did.

Forbidden Legacy

A betrothal neither wants . . . a passion neither can resist.

When the English murder Lady Katherine Calbraith's family, she refuses their demands to wed an English noble to retain her home. Avalon Castle is her birthright, one she's determined to keep. After Katherine's daring escape, she's stunned when Scotland's king agrees to allow her to return to Avalon, but under the protection of Sir Stephan MacQuistan . . . as the knight's wife. To reclaim her heritage, Katherine agrees. She accepts her married fate, certain that regardless of the caliber of the man, Stephan may earn her trust, but he'll never win her love.

One of the Knights Templar, Stephan desires no bride, only vengeance for a family lost and a legacy stolen. A profound twist of fate tears apart the Brotherhood he loves, but offers him an opportunity to reclaim his legacy—Avalon Castle. Except to procure his childhood home along with a place to store Templar treasures, he must wed the unsuspecting daughter of the man who killed his family. To settle old scores, Stephan agrees, aware Katherine is merely a means to an end.

The passion that arises between them is as dangerous as it is unexpected. When mortal enemies find themselves locked in love's embrace, Stephan and Katherine must reconsider their mission and everything they once thought to be true . . .

Forbidden Knight

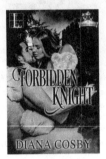

Deep within Scotland, a healer and a warrior join forces to protect Scotland's future . . .

There is an intruder in the woods near King Robert Bruce's camp, but when Sir Thomas MacKelloch comes face-to-face with the interloper, he is shocked to discover his assailant is a woman. The fair lady is skilled with a bow and arrow and defiant in her responses. The wary Knight Templar dare not allow her beauty to lower his guard. Irritated by his attraction, he hauls her before his sovereign to expose her nefarious intent.

Outraged Sir Thomas dismissed her claim, Mistress Alesone MacNiven awaits the shock on the arrogant knight's face when he learns that she has told the truth. But it is she who is shocked, and then horrified, as it is revealed that her father, the king's mortal enemy, has betrothed her to a powerful noble, a deal that could jeopardize the king's efforts to unite Scotland. Robert Bruce orders Sir Thomas to escort Alesone to safety. As they embark on a harrowing journey through the Highlands, Alesone tries to ignore her attraction to the intimidating warrior, but as she burns beneath Thomas's kiss she realizes this fearless knight could steal her heart.

An Oath Taken

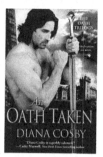

As the new castellan, Sir Nicholas Beringar has the daunting task of rebuilding Ravenmoor Castle on the Scottish border and gaining the trust of the locals—one of whom wastes no time in trying to rob him. Instead of punishing the boy, Nicholas decides to make him his squire. Little does he know the thieving young lad is really . . .a lady.

Lady Elizabet Armstrong had donned a disguise in an attempt to free her brother from Ravenmoor's dungeons. Although intimidated by the confident Englishman with his well-honed muscles and beguiling eyes, she cannot refuse his offer.

Nicholas senses that his new squire is not what he seems. His gentle attempts to break through the boy's defenses leave Elizabet powerless to stem the desire that engulfs her. And when the truth is exposed, she'll have to trust in Nicholas's honor to help her people—and surrender to his touch . . .

An Oath Broken

Lady Sarra Bellacote would sooner marry a boar than a countryman of the bloodthirsty brutes who killed her parents. And yet, despite—or perhaps because of—her valuable holdings, she is being dragged to Scotland to be wed against her will. To complicate the desperate situation, the knight hired to do the dragging is dark, wild, irresistible. And he, too, is intolerably Scottish.

Giric Armstrong, Earl of Terrick, takes no pleasure in escorting a feisty English lass to her betrothed. But he needs the coin to rebuild his castle, and his tenants need to eat. Yet the trip will not be the simple matter he imagined. For Lady Sarra isn't the only one determined to see her engagement fail. Men with darker motives want to stop the wedding—even if they must kill the bride in the process.

Now, in close quarters with this beautiful English heiress, Terrick must fight his mounting desire, and somehow keep Sarra alive long enough to lose her forever to another man . . .

An Oath Sworn

The bastard daughter of the French king, Marie Alesia Serouge has just one chance at freedom when she escapes her captor in the Scottish highlands. A mere pawn in a scheme to destroy relations between France and Scotland, Marie must reach her father and reveal the Englishman's treacherous plot. But she can't abandon the wounded warrior she stumbles upon—and she can't deny that his fierce masculinity, Scottish or not, stirs something wild inside her.

Colyne MacKerran is on a mission for his king, and he's well aware that spies are lying in wait for him everywhere. Wounded en route, he escapes his attackers and is aided by an alluring Frenchwoman...whose explanation for her presence in the Highlands rings false. Even if she saved his life, he cannot trust her with his secrets. But he won't leave her to the mercy of brigands, either—and as they race for the coast, he can't help but wonder if her kiss is as passionate as she is.

With nothing in common but their honor, Colyne and Marie face a dangerous journey to safety through the untamed Scottish landscape—and their own reckless hearts . . .

His Captive

With a wastrel brother and a treacherous former fiancé, Lady Nichola Westcott hardly expects the dangerously seductive Scot who kidnaps her to be a man of his word. Though Sir Alexander MacGruder promises not to hurt her, Nichola's only value is as a pawn to be ransomed.

Alexander's goal is to avenge his father's murder, not to become entangled with the enemy. But his desire to keep Nichola with him, in his home—in his bed—unwittingly makes her a target for those who have no qualms about shedding English blood.

Now Nichola is trapped—by her powerful attraction to a man whose touch shakes her to the core. Unwilling and unable to resist each other, can Nichola and Alexander save a love that has enslaved them both?

His Woman

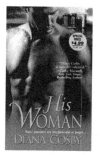

Lady Isabel Adair is the last woman Sir Duncan MacGruder wants to see again, much less be obliged to save. Three years ago, Isabel broke their engagement to become the Earl of Frasyer's mistress, shattering Duncan's heart and hopes in one painful blow. But Duncan's promise to Isabel's dying brother compels him to rescue her from those determined to bring down Scottish rebel Sir William Wallace.

Betraying the man she loved was the only way for Isabel to save her father, but every moment she spends with Duncan reminds her just how much she sacrificed. No one could blame him for despising her, yet Duncan's misgivings cannot withstand a desire that has grown wilder with time. Now, on a perilous journey through Scotland, two wary lovers must confront both the enemies who will stop at nothing to hunt them down, and the secret legacy that threatens their passion and their lives . . .

His Conquest

Linet Dancort will not be sold. But that's essentially what her brother intends to do—to trade her like so much chattel to widen his already vast scope of influence. Linet will seize any opportunity to escape her fate—and opportunity comes in the form of a rebel prisoner locked in her brother's dungeon, predatory and fearsome, and sentenced to hang in the morning.

Seathan MacGruder, Earl of Grey, is not unused to cheating death. But even this legendary Scottish warrior is surprised when a beautiful Englishwoman creeps to his cell and offers him his freedom. What Linet wants in exchange, though—safe passage to the Highlands—is a steep price to pay. For the only thing more dangerous than the journey through embattled Scotland is the desire that smolders between these two fugitives the first time they touch . . .

His Destiny

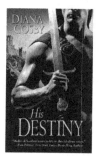

As one of England's most capable mercenaries, Emma Astyn can charm an enemy and brandish a knife with unmatched finesse. Assigned to befriend Dubh Duer, an infamous Scottish rebel, she assumes the guise of innocent damsel Christina Moffat to intercept the writ he's carrying to a traitorous bishop. But as she gains the dark hero's confidence and realizes they share a tattered past, compassion—and passion—distract her from the task at hand . . .

His legendary slaying of English knights has won him the name Dubh Duer, but Sir Patrik Cleary MacGruder is driven by duty and honor, not heroics. Rescuing Christina from the clutches of four such knights is a matter of obligation for the Scot. But there's something alluring about her fiery spirit, even if he has misgivings about her tragic history. Together, they'll endure a perilous journey of love and betrayal, and a harrowing fight for their lives . . .

His Seduction

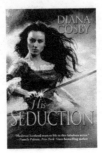

Lady Rois Drummond is fiercely devoted to her widowed father, the respected Scottish Earl of Brom. So when she believes he is about to be exposed as a traitor to England, she must think quickly. Desperate, Rois makes a shocking claim against the suspected accuser, Sir Griffin Westcott. But her impetuous lie leaves her in an outrageous circumstance: hastily married to the enemy. Yet Griffin is far from the man Rois thinks he is—and much closer to the man of her dreams . . .

Griffin may be an Englishman, but in truth he leads a clandestine life as a spy for Scotland. Refusing to endanger any woman, he has endured the loneliness of his mission. But Rois's absurd charge has suddenly changed all that. Now, with his cover in jeopardy, Griffin must find a way to keep his secret while keeping his distance from his spirited and tempting new wife—a task that proves more difficult than he ever imagined . . .

His Enchantment

Lady Catarine MacLaren is a fairy princess, duty-bound to eschew the
human world. But the line between the two realms is beginning to blur.
English knights have launched an assault on the MacLarens, just as the
families of Comyn have captured the Scottish king and queen. Now,
Catarine is torn between loyalty to her people and helping the handsome,
rust-haired Lord Trálin rescue the Scottish king . . .

As guard to King Alexander, Lord Trálin MacGruder will stop at nothing to
defend the Scottish crown against the Comyns. And he finds a sympathetic,
and gorgeous, ally in the enigmatic Princess Catarine. As they plot to rescue
the kidnapped king and queen, Trálin and Catarine will discover a love
made all but impossible by her obligations to the Otherworld. But a passion
this extraordinary may be worth the irreversible sacrifices it demands . . .

Printed in the United States
by Baker & Taylor Publisher Services